HENRY MOSQUERA

ODDITY
MEDIA
LLC

Status Quo

An Oddity Media LLC Book

www.redroom.com/member/henry-mosquera

Cover Design: Merc Designs

www.mercdesigns.com

ISBN: 0991660102

ISBN-13: 978-0991660100

TO MY BROTHER
THE FIRST PERSON WHO EVER
SAW ANY TALENT IN ME

"A satirist is someone who has a very skeptical view of human nature, but who still has the optimism to make some sort of a joke out of it. However brutal that joke might be."

— Stanley Kubrick

ACKNOWLEDGMENTS

I would like to thank my wife, Cecilia, the love of my life, for always being my partner in crime. To my family and friends for their support. To my cat, Meeko, for showing me the true meaning of indomitable spirit. We miss you. To my dog, Shadow, the other love of my life. To Roger Waters The Wall Live for finally dislodging whatever it was in my brain that led me to write this book. And to the Writer's Digest editing and proofreading services.

PROLOGUE

It was an island with ivory sand and calm, sapphire waters. He walked from the shore towards the mainland, feeling the warmth of the ground squeezing through his toes. The sun was kind and his steps were steady, though his eyes suffered from a slight case of glare. It wasn't uncomfortable, just bright enough to endow everything with a soothing halo. Then the first figures came to his attention. Lennon jammed with Marley, joined by Hendrix and accompanied by Harrison and Cobain. Janis sang along with Freddy, as Morrison rested his head on her lap, stealing glances from his poems to watch Bruce playfully sparring with Brandon, while James and Michael showed Elvis a few moves. Kubrick couldn't care less, his eyes intensely trained on the chessboard, while Brando rambled on about the best clams in the Caribbean. Kirby sat away under a palm tree, crafting a universe on his drawing board. Dalí argued with Picasso about the Surrealism of Cubism in front of their easels, unaware of Hitchcock discussing with Kurosawa the best way to shoot this scene. James was absorbed in his sports car while a cigarette dangled from his lips. Hemingway drank and held court with Wells, Philip, Asimov, Agatha, and Sir Arthur, laughing at something Pryor had said, or was it Carlin? Everyone was there. One by one they came into his view, but it wasn't until he saw Chaplin mimicking his walk that he understood each step took him to the center—the primordial core. He wanted to press on so he could bump into van Gogh, Monet, Verne, and Lovecraft. If he ran, he would encounter Mozart, da Vinci, Michelangelo, Shakespeare, Cervantes, but he knew he wasn't supposed to be there. He didn't belong.

He was stuck; his legs felt heavy and gained no purchase. Elation turned into desperation, but nobody noticed. He was a ghost. He didn't register; a speck of sand had more presence than his entire frame. He was sucked violently back into the ocean, as the vacuum around him drowned his screams. The scene melted away like burned celluloid and all that was left was a light as bright as the sun and utterly uncomfortable. In that moment, he knew he'd learned a new meaning of sorrow. He knew he was trapped and began to remember why he hated himself. He was still alive.

Was that the beginning? Maybe it was the end. Perhaps a dream? No, his eyes were fixed calmly beyond the wall in front of him. A hallucination, then? A daydream? It could be a flashback, the light at the end of the tunnel, or the last thing he saw before he was born? Who cares? He didn't. Not now, submerged just below the neck in a bathtub, wishing he could float to complete this surreal sensation.

The blood pouring from his wrists looked like

smoke slowly tainting the water. It merged just above his pelvis, obstructing its transparency. He could feel his life beat away ever so softly. *This must be the end,* he thought.

Then again, a lot of beginnings started with the end. Especially if the end was a failure, then it only became a continuation. His life—the same life he was watching as it colored his surroundings—had been a series of continuations. A chain of failures, which, strung together, could be called an existence. There was an important difference here—life had a purpose. Otherwise it was just an existence, a state of being other than dead. As children, the future held nothing but promises. You could be anything you could imagine, as long as you could imagine it. Creativity was the only limitation. But what happened when creativity was what you imagined to be your future?

His name was Lemat. He wasn't French, Belgian, Canadian, Monacan—or whatever the people from Monaco are called. People traveled and names moved along. Unless you were one of the original humans from Africa, everybody was from somewhere else.

Lemat was on the wrong side of thirty: single, no pets, not even a plant. When asked what he did for a living, he answered, "Breathe. Continuously." As for the question, "What do you do for money?" Lemat would say he prostituted himself in a service occupation, which some would deem creative. Where was he born? "In a hospital," he would say. One that happened to be in Caracas, Venezuela, an obscure country most people can't find on a map—the type of place that if you had a dream, it had better come with a suitcase and you'd better be willing to use it. But enough with geography—let's not forget Lemat bleeding to death here.

So what's this? A frustrated artist at the end of his rope? No, if you were paying attention, you'd notice he's not hanging himself. You could also argue that this is—or was—a desperate cry for help, a quintessential plea for attention. To be frank, this was the kind of idea you had when you ran out of them. The way he saw it, this was either a reset button or an "off" switch. It was a change of perspective either way.

CHAPTER ONE

The neighborhood looked like a pile of dirty dishes—packed, gritty, and uneven. It was hard to imagine how it looked when it was newly built, or even if it ever resembled what the architect saw in his head. Lemat dragged his feet from the bus stop, following a trail of junk and graffiti towards his home. The random tags were the only color in the otherwise gray formation, if you didn't count rust stains. In fact, the only thing not marked was the neighborhood's address.

The one street lamp flickered as if refusing to die quietly. Lemat always thought it would give off the effect of a strobe light to an observer. That's when he saw him, just a silhouette standing under a billboard advertising the lottery, the red dot of a burning cigarette in his mouth. The streetlamp seemed to buzz its last breath, but it kicked back to life. The figure was gone. Lemat did a double take and then hastened his pace. The last thing he needed was to be mugged.

The echo of his steps decreased as the sounds of

dogs, crying babies, and dinners cooking were amplified. Lemat took the shortcut through the alley underneath the balconies and their canopy of drying laundry. The alley was the fastest route to his apartment, but it wasn't without its hazards in the form of cascading mop water, falling cigarette butts, or the occasional toy from an overeager kid. Tonka and Fisher Price were particularly feared for their robustness.

Lemat's place was wedged between two buildings like a bridge to nowhere—a studio, which begged the existence of any construction permits. From the alley side, it was as tall as a second story. From the other side, the "patio" side, the ground was lower, making it as high as third floor. Its only window looked to the alley, because God forbid the tiny place had any endearing features. Music from a lonely cello added to the depressing ambiance.

Lemat stopped to pick up an old sneaker, put a dollar inside, and throw it right into a second floor window. The music ceased and a few moments later, it played a haunting rendition of Black Sabbath's "Iron Man" as Lemat walked away.

"That's pretty neat."

The voice made Lemat look around disconcertedly.

"Up here."

Lemat looked up at the dangling leather boot over his head with its laces undone.

"Hey! Hi," she said from a hammock tied between two balconies. She was skinny, with short, scarlet-dyed hair. "Does he play any Portishead?"

He looked at the window from whence the music came. "Nah, it's all classics. Sometimes Yo-Yo Ma. If you're lucky, he'll do something from 'Hush,' but I suck at the McFerrin parts."

"And Sabbath." The puzzled woman looked at the window.

"He knows what I like, but he doesn't take requests per se. He just plays what he feels, like musical omakase."

"Neat! I'm Ink, by the way. I just moved in."

"I'm Lemat."

"You're the guy from 2B. The one who committed suicide."

"If I was, I wouldn't be talking to you, would I?"

"I'm a big believer in the afterlife."

"What are you doing lying on a hammock between two buildings?" Lemat said as he tried to change the subject.

"There's not enough space in my terrace." She motioned with her head to a balcony that could barely hold two people standing. "So, are you the guy?"

Lemat looked at his hands covered by the oversized gnarly sweater he always wore, his fingers barely peeking from its sleeves. "How do you know?"

"I didn't. I've just been asking everyone I see walk by. So it's you, isn't it? Did it hurt?"

"Why do you want to know?"

"I'm just curious. I'm always researching ways to kill myself, you know? What would be the easiest, fastest, most effective, and least painful way to do it? Well, not painful at all, really."

"Why?"

"Just in case."

"In case of what?"

"In case I ever want to end it all."

"Why would you want to do that?"

"Why did you? I personally think it's a good idea to have an exit plan, you know? Just in case."

"You're asking the wrong guy—I clearly suck at it."

"Good point," Ink pondered. "So, can I see them?"

"See what?"

"The wounds. Are they gross? What kind of suture pattern did they use?"

"Look... Ink? Right?"

"Right."

"Is that your real name?"

"That's what people call me."

"Because you draw?" He pointed to the large drawing pad pressed against her chest.

"Because I'm a tattoo artist."

"Is that what you do for a living?"

"I do a lot of things, but I get paid for that one."

Lemat chuckled. "I have to go."

"Wait, I'm sorry. I didn't mean to freak you out. It's just that you're the only suicidal person I know who... Well, you know, the only one still around. Anyway, I'm just curious, like I said, and I can be a little obnoxious when I'm curious."

"'A little?'"

"I've been working on it."

"Keep at it."

"So can I see them?" she insisted.

"How would you feel if someone asked you to show your breasts?"

"I'd be flattered, if I had any to show." She peeked over the drawing pad down onto her chest. "You want to see them?"

"Sure." He shrugged.

Ink sat up and nonchalantly lifted her shirt. Her breasts were small. They reminded Lemat of a dark, beautiful woman he once saw sunbathing topless on a beach in Europe. The image stuck, as he was sure this one would too.

"No tattoos?"

"Just one," she said.

"An ink-challenged tattoo artist? Isn't that like a toothless dentist?"

"I never liked anything so much to commit to it permanently."

"Except one," Lemat thought out loud. Maybe he should have asked to see her tattoo instead of her boobs.

"Satisfied?" she said.

Lemat nodded.

"Good." Ink covered herself again. "Now hold on for a second—I want to see those puppies up close." She balanced her way perilously towards her balcony and disappeared inside the apartment. A few moments later, she ran downstairs to meet Lemat. She was still carrying her drawing pad with her. He was able to get a better look at her from this vantage. Petite, Ink was almost as tall as Lemat and a darker shade of pale. She bared her midriff under a cutoff Japanese-printed T-shirt which displayed a toned stomach and a tiny, jeweled belly ring. She wore undone overalls for pants, riding low on her hips, showing white and orange underwear.

Lemat sighed. He didn't want to do it, but Ink's showing her tits felt almost legally binding. He rolled up the sleeves of his sweater, unwrapped one of his wrists, and offered it sheepishly to her.

Ink paused. "You saw *two* breasts, didn't you?"

Lemat sighed again and showed her the other wrist.

"Lock-stitch suture, Nice!" she said. "That's going to leave a pretty cool scar." She touched the wound carefully with the tips of her fingers. "Nice work."

"You're into scars?" Lemat asked.

"I love them!"

"What's so cool about them?"

"Each scar is like a photograph, but better. A picture can only show you a moment. A scar has a whole history attached to it."

"I never saw it that way," he said, touched by the idea. "I like that."

"Why did you do it?"

"Is that what you do? You become friends with someone because you think suicide is some morbid validation of how deep and intense you are as an artist?"

"Well, no, my suicidal friends never failed, so I've got no one to ask."

She had a good point, he thought. And "Suicidal Friends" would make a hell of a rock-band name.

"Maybe another day," he said and hurriedly rewrapped his wrist. "I'll see you around."

Lemat almost reached the stairs when he heard her say, "Hey, Lemat. It was really nice meeting you."

Lemat looked back, unsure if he found her attractive or just plain annoying. She was peculiar, all right. But then again, he was always a beacon for odd souls. "OK," he said, breaking eye contact. It was time to go home.

By home, Lemat meant the scarcely furnished studio chock-full of books, movies, comics, video games, and cassette tapes. Lemat didn't like MP3s; he found them cold and impersonal. So he crafted careful lists of songs that he mixed on tapes (making CDs was too easy and not as fun). He had mastered the art of queuing the beginning and end of each song. He did this on an old boom box he'd had since he was fifteen years old, an old companion of many a writing night.

Lemat always dreamt of living in a loft, some old industrial place with brick walls, exposed beams, and large windows, but all Lemat ever had was the whole rundown thing. His apartment looked more like a small storage room, with a pretty decent flat-panel TV and surround sound.

"You're home," Dep said from his usual spot on the left side of the couch. His voice sounded like feet dragging.

Lemat had met Dep late in elementary school. They found each other at the yard waiting for a class, when Lemat pondered about the future of those around him in a decade's time. It wasn't until he turned the same inquiry inward that this forlorn guy stepped into his life. In truth, Dep had always been there, like most of Lemat's inner circle. They kept circling around one another, until they finally reached that fateful day.

"What are you watching?" Lemat asked as he moved for the fridge.

"Nothing, really. I'm just trying not to think at all." He punctuated the phrase by biting down on a cookie, his dark-brown eyes hidden by his greasy hair, dangling over the perennial Band-Aid on his forehead.

"What else is new?" Lemat said. "What's helping you not think?"

"Jockeys."

"You know putting batteries inside the fridge won't recharge them, right?" said Lemat, looking at the row of AAs and the museum of takeout leftovers. Lemat closed the door and rummaged the cupboards.

"Do you know apprentice jockeys are known as 'bug boys'? They're called that because of the asterisk that follows their name in a race program. It looks like a bug." Dep clamped down on another cookie.

"Don't tell me you ate the jar of Nutella."

"The one you hid in the oven? Yeah, sorry."

"How many times have I told you to just let me know so I can buy a new one?"

"I know, I know. It's just that it tastes better that way. You can't beat the flavor of forbidden chocolate. Hey, do you know that jockeys' jobs are so dangerous, their insurance premiums are some of the highest in all professional sports?"

"Anything about them getting buried in manure so they can lose weight?"

"No. But the show just started."

For a split second, Lemat thought about actually doing something like that to trim down his sedentary physique. He peeked out of the kitchen and said, "Are there any more of those cookies?"

"Thish wash the lash one," Dep said with his mouth full.

"Of course." Lemat went to the window and opened it to let the cello's music fill the tiny place. It was something ominous, maybe Wagner. He liked it— it was dramatic and had character. A perfect fit for his return home from the hospital. Lemat ran his hand over the brown, unwieldy mess that was his hair and noted he needed a shower badly.

Dep said, "Do you ever wonder how it would be?"

"To have a cookie?"

"To be a jockey."

"The only thing I ride is the bus," Lemat said as he collapsed by Dep. He picked up a bottle of beer by Dep's feet. "That's all you left me, a half-empty bottle of beer?"

"Half-full."

"That's funny coming from you," Lemat said.

"You shouldn't drink anyway. Alcohol thins out your blood and you have fresh stitches. You could bleed yourself to death… again, but this time not on purpose. Drink orange juice."

"Is there any?"

"Did you buy any?"

"God!" Lemat threw himself back and held his face in frustration. "You're a fucking black hole, you know that?"

"That reminds me, I recorded this show about quantum physics. Did you know—" Lemat's stare cut him short. "Oh, yeah… sorry. Can you go to the store and get donuts?"

"Get them yourself," Lemat said with his face still covered by his hands.

"You know I don't like leaving the house."

"Then learn to bake."

The sound of the TV and cello filled the silence.

"Lemat?"

Lemat exhaled. "What?"

"I'm glad you're back."

"…Thanks."

"Lemat?"

"Uh huh?"

"What are you going to do now? I mean, *do* do."

"I don't know."

"No more writing?"

Lemat inhaled deeply. "I don't think so," he said.

"Really?"

"I think it's about time I moved on with my life… do something different for once."

Dep said, "Well… for what it's worth, I think you should try to do something simpler."

CHAPTER TWO

"What do you mean?" Lemat said.

"Simpler," the client said on the phone. Lemat had just arrived in the office less than an hour ago. He was gone for a couple of weeks and didn't miss the place one bit. The place was a former textile mill turned into a creative boutique, which catered to the rapidly expanding Hispanic market. Lemat had languished there for fifteen years. He loved the building but could care less for the people inside, and the feeling was mutual. The small agency was the only job he could find after college, thanks to a classmate and the fact that he could speak Spanish fluently.

"Simpler?" Lemat repeated, grabbing the printed page with a few business card mockups he had designed. This one, in particular, was a pretty clean design: sans serif font, periods instead of dashes for the phone and fax numbers, the essential information, and a small red rectangle on the lower left corner as the only design feature. "Are we looking at the same page, the one with the five designs I sent you last night?"

"Yes," the man said, annoyed.

"Design 5?"

"Yes."

"OK—what do you mean by, 'simpler'? No red rectangle?"

"No."

"No as in 'No rectangle,' or no as in 'No, that's not the right answer'?"

"I told you in the beginning that I was going to make you work for your money," the client said.

Lemat squeezed his brain trying to find a way to simplify what was already simple. "You know, like I said before, it would be helpful to know what you're looking for."

"And I told you, I'm not going to do your job for you."

"Well, sir, my job is to create something that'll represent your business. Unfortunately, I'm not a psychic; I can't read your mind. I've been designing dozens of business cards for you in the last month with very little input from you. Perhaps if you give me an idea of what you're looking for, what you like or at least dislike, then perhaps we can get somewhere."

"Just make it simpler," the client said and hung up.

Maybe if I write the information as a barcode? he thought.

What Lemat truly wanted to be was an author, a person who writes stories for a living, a challenging dream compounded by the fact that English wasn't his first language. But he took the necessary steps: Lemat left his country, a place bereft of a literary tradition or creative avenues, and applied himself to master his adopted language in a way that confounded the natives. How could someone who spoke with a bit of an untraceable accent have such dominion over their own tongue?

Lemat was a dreamer, but even so, he had a modicum of a pragmatic mind. He knew that before he could make a living as an author, he had to make ends meet. College was not to his liking, but Lemat saw it as a ticket to the United States and a step closer to fulfilling his dream. The only thing that attracted him was art school—majoring in English would have been too much of a struggle for his language skills at the time—and graphic design seemed like a viable profession to make a living in a creative way, while waiting for the whole novelist thing to take off. Sadly, the brilliant plan lost its luster in the long run.

There was a time—right after college—that Lemat liked his work. The fact that someone had given an inexperienced graduate a chance in the "real world" was thrilling. He was grossly underpaid and overworked, his benefits sucked, the commute was horrendous, and he lived in fear that he would be laid off when the company hit hard times. But he had a job after school, doing what he was trained to do, and he wasn't unhappy.

"Living the dream in the real world," as his boss said each time he short-changed him. Sure, most people hated their bosses, especially when they had no skill that involved the actual business. Lemat's boss ran a creative boutique passed down from his father—a saint of a man by all accounts—a graphic artist from the old school, the ones who could work on oils, inks, pastels, and operate an airbrush, the kind of artist who had to measure the picas on a font before laying them out. Sadly for Lemat, the apple had fallen far from the tree and rolled down hill a few miles into the gutter.

"Looking at the paper is not going to solve the problem," said his boss in Spanish with a heavy American accent.

Maximiliano Hauer was the kind of man who would blend seamlessly into a corner office—a former pre-law-frat-boy-turned-business-school-graduate from some semi-decent college, for which he still pined.

"I trust the next batch will be a little bit more elaborate," Max said.

"The client wants it simpler."

"Let me tell you a little secret: the client wants what we tell him he wants. They think they know what they want, but they really have no idea. That's your job. If you need a little help, I'll be happy to show you some ideas later in my office or you can always check in with Luna—she can show you how it's done. Anyway, I just talked to the client for the cosmetics website. He's not happy with the design. He told me he sent you some examples. Did you get them?"

"Yes," Lemat said. "Look at this." He clicked on his computer and showed him the six websites he had bookmarked. Each one of them belonged to a multinational makeup brand. They boasted supermodels in highly artistic photos. The text was short, concise, and evocative.

"So? Just do it like that."

"Are you kidding me? Check this out." Lemat opened the site he designed. It had a handful of amateur pictures of products, accompanied by lengthy rows of text that had to be scrolled down.

"I can see why the client is upset," Max said.

"His 'examples' are the top brands in the business. These people spend millions in creating an image. This man doesn't want to pay for a professional photographer to shoot his products, let alone models. He took these pictures himself. As for the text, he refuses to shorten it into smaller paragraphs because he claims his clients need to know all this information. People don't read, especially online."

"Don't be ridiculous. Lemat, you're a designer. So go ahead and design. All this bellyaching won't make that site look better. You just got back from a vacation. Stop complaining and get to it. Frankly, I don't know why my old man liked you. While you do have flashes of good design here and there, I'm simply too busy to hold your hand every time you run into a wall with a client. You're supposed to be a professional, so act like one." And with that pearl of wisdom, Max was gone.

When Lemat was in college, he enjoyed being in art school. It was a time where he could let his creativity run wild. Now, the only thing running wild were his clients, and the sole creative part of his work was to figure out their minds.

Office life was not a good fit for Lemat either. Its interactions were parallel to high school, and Lemat had already failed at that, abysmally. He wasn't a water-cooler-chatter type either. And his happiness at just being a designer was viewed as lack of drive. In the corporate world, conformism is anathema, and ambition is king; Lemat studied to be a designer, not a manager. All things considered, he felt comfortable doing the work, not telling people what to do. It was truly a corporate sin.

The only reason he wasn't fired was because he was cheap labor with a lot of mileage in the biz. Lemat did the work nobody wanted and didn't cause waves while people were promoted over him, so really, nobody had any reason to go after him. When he was on "vacation" this last time (of course, he didn't tell a soul why he was actually gone), nobody even noticed.

But there he was, in the last cubicle flanked by the janitor's closet and a little-used hallway that led to the emergency exit. Lemat at least appreciated the irony in this.

Lemat needed more coffee if he was going to tackle the day's work. As he walked to the kitchen, he was intercepted by Marcos, always amiable because he always needed help.

"Epa, Lemat!" said Marcos in their native tongue. "Do you think you can check out my billboard for Gypsies? I need to present it to the client at noon and I don't know what to do. It's mostly because of the text." The placard on Marcos' office read, "Creative Director."

"What's wrong with Luna?" Lemat replied.

"Oh, you know her. She can't think under pressure. You're not doing anything important, are you?"

Like Lemat, charismatic Marcos was a South American; he was promoted with astonishing speed despite the fact that he couldn't speak a lick of English. Receiving accolades based on an award he won six years ago, Marcos had the masterful ability of delegating all if his work by using his impeccable social skills.

"Sorry, I'm swamped. And Max already chewed my ass out this morning. Try Amber."

"I don't think she's in today," Marcos said. "Her husband is pretty sick."

"Sorry, can't do." Lemat knew this would be reflected in his performance report as "not a team player."

Just a few paces from Marcos' office sat Amber in her cubicle, close enough to be at Marcos' beck and call, and just far enough away to "hide" their office romance. Amber's cubicle walls were littered with pictures of her wedding, birthdays, vacations, and other events, all of them showing Amber surrounded by coworkers.

"Marcos is looking for you," said Lemat. "He needs help with the cigarette thing."

"Oh, OK. I'll get to it in a moment."

"I heard your husband is sick."

"He has a fever of one hundred and four."

"Jeez! Is he going to be all right?"

She shrugged. "I guess. He's a big boy; he'll be all right." Amber was a company drone who still believed in the preposterous concept of the "corporate family."

Lemat couldn't walk away from her fast enough. When he finally made it to the kitchen, he bumped into Luna, who said, "Max said you needed my help?" She was pouring the last of the coffee into her Mondrian-patterned mug.

"It's OK; it's nothing I can't fix. Don't worry. Thanks." Lemat busied himself with brewing more coffee to avoid looking at her.

"I saw your work for the makeup site. That's a nice little website you've got there—simple. Some people like that."

Luna subscribed to the philosophy that "nothing

comes from nothing," which was basically a euphemism for her ripping off other people's more clever designs.

"Thanks," he said. "I know where to find you if I need help."

"Whatever. I just don't want Max dumping this on me at the last hour like he always does," said Luna as she left the kitchen to go back to her computer to browse for a new job, update her social media, or take care of her jewelry-design business.

One thing was for sure: Lemat didn't stay at the job because of any kind of fervent loyalty to his colleagues. He simply had nowhere to go. The old man may have liked him, but the truth was, Lemat was hired a few months out of college due to a need in personnel for a big emergency project. What was supposed to last three months became six, then a year, and finally turned to a full-time contract with a miserable salary. Lemat had tried to seek work elsewhere many times, but his efforts never even garnered an interview. He knew he was stuck in this job, and lucky to be so. The alternatives were unemployment, a turn in the service industry, or a dreadful existence helping his father run his chain of pharmacies.

Lemat always thought there was a place for him in the world. Otherwise, why would he be born with a vocation for crafting stories? The barren walls of his cubicle were a testament to this. Unlike his coworkers, Lemat refused to allow his personality to decorate his surroundings; not at work. He fought the notion that what he did for a living defined him as a person. This job was not his life; hence, his life wasn't attached to it. Lemat subscribed to the idea that he would find success if he worked hard, made sacrifices, took risks, and went after his writer's dream. There was one element in that philosophy that kept eluding him his whole life: to be in the right place at the right time. Lady Luck never graced him with her presence.

The clock on the wall showed it was ten past ten. Lemat sat back at his desk, set the coffee aside, and French-pressed his brain into coming up with a simpler way to do the client's business cards. He looked at the blinking cursor, hoping a solution would present itself. His mind began to wander.

Within

Thump, thump, thump. The cursor flashed to the rhythm of Lemat's heart. Sweat ran down the side of his face as he typed the last paragraph on a pop-up window on top of his work and texted it away to his contact on a computer far away. The man copied and pasted the paragraph at the end of a chapter of an incomplete novel. The story was nearly finished, but the risk of getting caught was greater with each communication. But, Lemat knew it was too late to turn back. The story needed to come out at any cost. There was still some time left before the window had to be closed for fear of detection.

Lemat quickly wrote a short paragraph. When he was about to send it, he noticed something unusual on the tiny red square adorning the business card design in the background. It seemed to be glowing, faintly. It took less than a second for Lemat to realize the scarlet box was actually flashing an almost negligible alert. Lemat grabbed the monitor's cable and tried to yank it off, but it was too late.

Marcos walked by Lemat's cubicle with his eyes trained on him. Lemat knew he had been caught. He thought about making a run for the emergency exit, but Marcos was already at the threshold of the cubicle. The creative director's legs stopped, but his torso continued walking, as a new pair of legs emerged from within his body, and a complete upper body surfaced from the legs he had left behind. Lemat watched helplessly as the two versions of Marcos grabbed him by his arms and pulled him away from his desk.

Lemat struggled to break free, but his captors' grips were mechanical in their strength. The Marcos twins dragged him into Max's office, where Lemat's coworkers waited around a chair fitted with straps. Lemat was promptly restrained as his office mates watched in silence. Luna stepped forward with a digital tablet and showed Lemat some text. It was the story Lemat had been smuggling out of the office for quite some time. Luna passed page after page with a move of her finger, showing Lemat the almost completed manuscript. He was so close.

"Tsk, tsk, tsk," Luna clicked her tongue disapprovingly and stepped back. Max snapped his fingers and Amber showed Lemat a case of brains, each with its own digital display explaining what they held inside. One was Businessman Lemat, another was Construction Worker Lemat, the next one was Dentist Lemat, and so on. But before more choices could be seen, Amber had already made her decision. She picked up the brain of Pharmacist Lemat and everyone grinned in apparent approval.

Lemat squirmed and screamed as if he had been dipped in a vat of acid, but his bindings wouldn't budge. Max approached him carefully, held each side of his face, and popped Lemat's head open like a shampoo cap. A hurricane of ideas blasted the office. Creations fully formed and partially imagined swallowed everything in their path, including Lemat's restraints.

A distant phone ringing snapped Lemat back to reality. It took him a moment to gather his bearings. He cursed under his breath when he saw the clock on the wall; it was now close to 11:00. He took a gulp of his cold coffee and got back to work.

Lemat finished the day's work around 4:30. Then he killed time by browsing the Internet and looking busy. This was a little trick he picked up from his coworkers some time ago, after he was chastised when his boss found him reading a book. For the next few months, Max made sure he had a surplus of busywork. His coworkers had learned long ago that productivity was nothing compared to appearances. Nowadays, he'd leave the office at 5:20, just to make sure nobody could claim he did the bare minimum.

CHAPTER THREE

After work, Lemat liked to walk. As a writer, he believed it was truly essential to fully experiencing life. Yet, he dreaded when life actually interacted with him. It wasn't because of any antisocial behavior. It was because Lemat had a tendency to attract some peculiar dramatis personae. He preferred to keep to himself, a quiet observer of life.

Lemat usually stopped by the park on his way to his usual bar. There was something about drinking during the daylight that didn't sit well with him. He sat at his usual bench right in front of a human statue, for whom he had deposited a dollar in a worn hat sitting out front. The golden-hued man stood still for long periods of time, only changing positions when he got a leg cramp or something.

The fountain behind him displayed an epic scene of two armies facing each other, dramatically holding muskets, swords, standards, and flags. Two horses rearing back dominated the piece, each with an impassioned rider. Lemat felt lucky to witness this scene. He sat placidly listening to music from his phone, as people walked by, took pictures, and contemplated the statues.

At sunset, police arrived and quietly started to evacuate the fountain. One by one, the statues around the horses came to life, stretching their stiff muscles, lighting a cigarette, and talking to the officers. At last, only the two bronze horses remained. It was time for Lemat to go.

Approaching the dive bar Fausto's, Lemat was always heralded by the raw steel guitar of Fingerless Joe, the partially blind blues player fixed at the corner of the establishment. If you talked to Joe, you would find out that he had been just about everywhere. Nobody ever confirmed if this was true, but the man certainly looked well traveled. He sat on a wooden stool as old and frayed as himself, and his guitar case lay by his sandaled feet awaiting donations. Lemat usually dropped all the change from his pockets into the case before walking in, a toll for the toll man.

Fausto's used to be a mechanic's shop in the '50s. It was turned into a bar in the '60s and had remained untouched since, with the exception of the owner's impressionistic paintings that decorated the walls. The joint was small, the drinks simple, and the clientele was scarce but loyal. They rarely played with the uneven pool table or the broken dartboard—not that it mattered, since the darts had no tips—with the sole exception being the Coin brothers. The bar's true saving grace was the old jukebox stacked with classic-rock tunes.

When Lemat walked in, there were five people in the bar including the owner, and Led Zeppelin's

"Ramble On" played in the background.

"How's it holding up, buddy?" said Fausto with his easy, golden-toothed smile, already pouring Lemat's preferred dark ale. Per usual, he was sharing smokes with Clover at the end of the bar. Fausto was a wire of a man, who looked like something between a gypsy and an aging rocker. "Something to relieve the workday's pain, coming right up," Fausto said and passed the overflowing mug to Clover.

"That would be great. Thanks," Lemat said.

"Here you go, honey," said Clover in that insincere way she had at dispensing pet names. She rested her arms on the bar, which thrust her ample cleavage forward. Clover was attractive in a blue-collar way. Her hair was a little too blonde, her implants a little too big, and her jeans a little too low. Yet she worked those assets and her roguish grin in a way that always got her good tips. "Tough day?" she said.

Lemat emptied his glass in one gulp and said, "Not anymore."

"Take it easy, handsome. The night's still young."

"That's just the opening salvo," said Fausto and served Lemat another beer. "Now my man can relax and enjoy his evening."

Lemat wasn't sure if Clover was part owner of the joint or if she had any history with Fausto or what the deal was. It was the bar's great mystery. Clover was always there and took over the bar when Fausto had to be somewhere else.

Harry "Specs" Chaser, the slouching man a few stools from Lemat, took the unlit cigarette from his mouth and said, "Salud!"

"Salud!" Lemat obliged. "How's work?"

"Shitty, with a side of hopelessness," he said. A forty-something ginger with Zappa facial hair, Specs got his nickname from the unsolicited, speculative screenplays known as "specs," in the industry's lingo, which he pitched constantly.

"That bad, huh?" Lemat said. "Hey, it could be worse, right?"

"I don't see how," Specs said. "God, I miss smoking!" He was told to quit smoking by his doctor, so now he satisfied his addiction by sitting next to smokers. Specs had been an aspiring screenwriter dating back to his late teens. His claim to fame—meaning, he was the only one that had claimed it—was a spec script for *Forrest Gump,* which he said he based on his brother-in-law.

"Cheer up, Specs. If it was easy, everybody would be doing it," said Heads, a big guy lining up a shot at the pool table. Heads tended to be quiet, drank only dark beer, and had an encyclopedic mind for all kinds of useless information. He had a thing for Clover, but he was too shy to act on it.

"Yeah, who knows? One of these days you may hit it big again and ride the white lines once more," said Tails, the oldest and smaller of the Coin siblings and the one who was more gregarious.

"Don't say that," Heads said.

"Why? It's true," his brother said.

"Just play the game."

"Any luck finding a guitar player?" Lemat said.

"Nah, they're all fucking divas," Tails said.

The siblings were musicians. Heads was a bassist and Tails a drummer, but they seemed to spend most of their time putting bands together rather than actually playing in them.

"I told them to get Fingerless Joe out there," Fausto jested.

"A few more weeks of auditions like this and we might consider it," Heads said.

"So, Lemat, back from the dead?" Fausto said. "We haven't seen you in a while. Is everything all right?"

"And what's with the wristbands? Are you playing tennis now?" Clover said.

"I just took some time off," Lemat said.

"Where to?" Fausto said.

"Nowhere in particular. I wanted to get away from everything, that's all."

"A vacation of the mind," Fausto said and slid another beer in front of Lemat. "Welcome back, brother. It's good to see you."

"It's good to be seen."

"How's the writing going?" Specs said.

"It's going nowhere," Lemat said.

"Welcome to my world." Specs raised his glass. "My last script? Turned down by every single studio. I'm telling you, I'll give it one more year. If nothing changes, I'm calling it quits."

"You've been saying that for the last ten years," Fausto said.

"No, I'm telling you. This time is for real," Specs said. "Every meeting I had for my last script was the same bullshit. 'Do it more like *Avatar,*' they say. Shit, a movie grosses over a billion dollars and now they want to make everything into the same damned thing. I had an idea about a comedy involving a road trip with a member of the Tea Party and a guy from Occupy Wall

Street. And I get, 'Yeah, no, that sounds great. Kind of like *Avatar,* right?' How the fuck is that like *Avatar?* Am I going to have blue people fucking in a tree at some point? Seriously. Never mind the fact that fucking *Avatar* is like *Dances with Wolves* or that Tom Cruise flick where he's turning Japanese."

"It's also the story of Pocahontas," Heads said from the pool table.

"Really?" Clover said.

"The real one, not the Disney version," Heads said.

"Oh," she said. "I didn't know that was based on a book."

"Christ, and then what would you do, Specs?" Fausto said.

"I'd be a carpenter," Specs said. "My old man? He used to build all kinds of stuff, you know? I can fall back on the family trade."

"Don't fall back too hard, Specs," Fausto said. "You might break your ass or something. Who are you trying to kid? You're a scriptwriter through and through. It's in your blood."

"Yeah, I know," said Specs. "Creativity is a heavy burden."

"I guess I haven't missed much, then," Lemat said to Fausto.

The bar owner laughed and said, "Oh, you missed tons! It's just more of the same thing."

"Hey, Lemat," Specs said, sliding his way closer to him. "Have you ever contemplated the meaning of birthdays?"

Here we go again! Lemat thought. Specs must have reached the fifth-gin-and-tonic threshold. They called it "Tarantino Time," otherwise known as when

Specs went on some convoluted meant-to-be-clever alternative explanation to some trivial thing.

"Think about it," Specs said. "What do they do when you have a birthday?"

"I don't know—give presents?"

"And what else?"

"Sing 'Happy Birthday'?"

"Candles!" Specs said while bumping sluggishly against Lemat. "You light candles, right? One for every year." He mimed placing candles on a cake. "And then what?"

"You eat the cake," Clover said, egging on the conversation.

"You blow!" Specs said.

"Hey! No need to get nasty, you fat turd," she said.

"No. I mean you blow the candles out, right?" Specs said.

"Right," Lemat said.

"You see?"

"See what?" Fausto said.

"The irony! The meaning!"

"It's a tradition that dates back to the ancient Greeks," Heads said as he leaned against a wall and waited for his brother to finish his turn. "It was a way to pay tribute to the moon goddess, Artemis. That's why you have a round cake symbolizing the moon while the candles stood for the moonlight." Impressed, Clover looked at him. Heads blanched and looked away.

"Hey, Moon Boy. Your turn," Tails said.

"That's not the point," Specs said. "The point is that we blow them out, don't you see? Every year, we extinguish a candle. Every year we add a candle and we put it out. Five years, five candles. Ten, forty, sixty—"

"After a while, some people just use one fucking candle," Fausto said.

"Or those silly ones in the shape of numbers," Clover said.

"You're all missing the point!" Specs said. "What matters is that we put them out, don't you see? They're a reminder of the time gone by. The years you'll never get back. Each light you extinguish brings you closer to death."

"Shit, Specs, you should take that act to children's parties! You'll be a fucking millionaire!" Tails said.

"No, that's interesting," Heads said. "A popular German tradition was to put a candle in the center of a cake to represent life's light. So he's not that far off."

"Great! I'll go to the restroom and drown myself," said Lemat, rising.

"No clogging the toilet!" Fausto said.

The sole restroom doubled as a broom closet. Lemat had to squeeze his way through a mop and a bucket to get to the toilet. He came out after relieving himself, when something caught his attention in the corner of his eye. There was a man sitting by himself in the furthest booth from the bar and nursing a glass of red wine. He was clad in a gray suit and was rolling a cigarette, which he promptly smoked before busying himself with his smartphone. Lemat cast a quick glance, since he didn't notice him when he walked in, and returned to his seat to order another beer.

"So what are you working on now?" Clover said.

"Nothing," Lemat said.

"Out of ideas?"

"Out of steam. Maybe it's time for me to look for something else to do."

"You want to build furniture?" Specs said. "I'll need a partner."

"Come on! What's wrong with you two?" Fausto said. "A little writer's block is nothing to worry about. Give it some time."

That was precisely what Lemat feared. He knew that sooner or later, Talia would come back to his life, full of promises and honey-like whispers. She'd seduce him into another "project," some long-suffering, labor-intensive creative endeavor that would leave him with the taste of ash in his mouth and nothing to show for it. Each time Lemat relapsed, it was harder for him to gather himself and move on. He was getting too old to chase after dreams and ideas would be of no comfort in old age, when even Talia's allure would fall short.

I'd rather jump off a building, he thought, bade everyone good night, and headed home.

CHAPTER FOUR

Lemat looked down at the ground from the roof of his apartment. "I'm not sure I can do it," he said. The sky was overcast as he and Dep played "Kamikaze F-Bombs." The mechanics of the game were simple: Dep would grab a rejection letter and fold it into an airplane, while Lemat would dip a cotton swab in alcohol, place it in the tail of the airplane, light it on fire, and watch it fly away into the empty swimming pool below them.

The idea was to hit the trash floating in the murky puddle by the deep end. Each piece of rubbish had a designation: a soda crate was a supply ship, a broken tricycle was a patrol ship, the "zombie" toy baby was a transport ship, but the mother of them all was a toilet seat. Getting a perfect hit right through the center meant they had hit a submarine. The last strike had fallen short of taking out a destroyer—a straw hat that they knew would be glorious to set on fire if they ever worked out the maneuver.

"What's next?" Lemat said. "Give me something

good."

"Let's see," Dep said, ruffling through the stack of papers. "How about a rejection letter from that agent that represents all those paranormal books? It says your supernatural story 'doesn't fit our agency's profile.'"

"Pilot, you're cleared for takeoff!"

"Copy that!" Dep said, folding the letter.

"So this is where you've been hiding," Lisa said as she climbed the folding ladder from Lemat's apartment and came out through the tiny roof access—another mysterious eccentricity from the architect. "I should have guessed you'd be here crying like a little bitch until your testicles dropped again," she said while placing a six-pack on the roof. Lisa wasn't particularly tall, but she was lean and muscular, a punk devotee (complete with black and green Mohawk) who had the kind of physique forged by a lifetime of struggle.

"No, no crying. He's done," Dep said. "It's time to move on—the question is, where to? I mean, Lemat isn't really good at anything else but coming up with stories. And now he's too old—"

Lisa snapped, "Oy, Morrissey! Why don't you find some place to hang yourself?" She turned to Lemat. "The last time you listened to this fuck-wad, you took a bath in your own blood."

"Can we have one conversation without all the cursing?" Dep said, looking at his feet.

"Fuck, no!" Lisa said.

"Yeah, I know. Sorry," Lemat said and leaned back on the wall.

"No shit!" she said. "You know what's going to happen: you'll hang out with Rain Man here for a couple of months, trying to convince each other of how miserable your lives are, and then—"

"Please don't mention her name," said Dep playing with the rejection letters to avoid eye contact.

"Oh, grow a pair!" Lisa said. "You know she'll be coming crawling back through the door like a hungry stray, that miserable cunt. Just one look at her will give him a hard-on. He can't help it. You know you're pussy-whipped, right?"

"Can we skip this?" Lemat said. He rubbed his eyes tiredly because he felt a migraine coming.

But Lisa was just beginning. "She'll hump your brains out and you'll be back chasing some fucking idea for next few years of your life. Remember the political thriller? Four years researching, writing, editing, and pitching it to every literary agent who represented the genre."

"All two hundred of them," Dep said.

Lisa continued, "And for what? Nobody gave a flying fuck about it."

"I wouldn't count on Talia coming back," Dep said. "Did you just miss what happened? What he needs to do is figure out something else, something pragmatic. No more daydreaming."

"Oh, really? And what do you propose he do? Hint: if you say pharmacy, you'll be the next thing set on fire and landing in that pool."

"I don't know," Dep said. "I'm sure the military will take him—unless he's too old for that as well. Oh, and he's definitely no good at running either… and he can't do pull-ups… or pushups. No, he sucks at those—"

"Shut your face, Sling Blade!" Lisa said and turned to Lemat. "You're creative, that's what you are. That's what you do. At this point in the game, you knew there was no turning back. You're all in, man. You might be outnumbered, outclassed, and outgunned, but this is the fucking Alamo. You don't pussy out and surrender. No fucking way! You grab your knife and take as many fuckers you can to hell with you."

"The Alamo has been overrun, señorita." Dep waved the stack of rejections.

Lisa yanked the letters from his hand, threw them on the floor, pulled her pants down, squatted, and peed on them. Then she doused them in alcohol and set them ablaze. "Fuck 'em!" she said.

Lemat met Lisa during his junior year in college. In that pivotal time when academic safety gave way to the looming realities of the so-called "real world," Lisa was the motor that helped Lemat push forward when the odds seemed insurmountable. Every time a door was slammed in Lemat's face, each time a letter began with "Dear writer," or when a detractor dared to speak up, Lisa was there, middle finger ready and full of piss and vinegar.

Lemat knew he had hurt her when he tried to kill himself. He knew Lisa would have rather taken that razor and sliced open the throats of anyone telling him he wasn't good enough. To her, the word "can't" just meant another challenge to conquer and then shove that success down somebody's throat. But Lemat also knew that Lisa would never abandon him. No, Lisa reserved her anger for anyone who dared stand in the way of Lemat and his dreams.

Lemat drank his beer and watched the rejection papers burn into the wind. Dep contemplated each page, remembering every rejection and wondering what was the use. He had been beaten too many times, time was fleeting, and a storm of anxiety brewed inside him. He saw no possible alternatives other than to steer the ship as it was and hope for the best. Lisa hugged her knees and looked into the horizon. Drinking distractedly, she planned the next wave of attack to help her friend break into the creative field. Lemat had gone through this too many times. He knew Lisa was right: Talia would return at some point; that was a given. Lemat pondered the odds of him turning her away and moving forward with his life. Could it be possible after what he had just gone through?

He finished his beer, left his buddies alone on the roof, and walked a couple of buildings down to what was known in the neighborhood as Nancy's. On the way, his mind was the usual bluster of activity. The cement jungle that was his neighborhood came alive in all sorts of ways: a sci-fi complex where genetically inferior people were forced to live; the former remnants of an ancient culture disguised by modern structures to hide an unspeakable horror; a human ant farm the government used as a test facility on unwitting civilians. He passed an overweight housewife, wearing a Mumu and in hair rolls, who became a cyborg with extendable limbs and multiple head cannons. The thin man donning a dark suit would blink a third eye as Lemat passed by and disappeared through a crack in the wall. Soon, Lemat realized he was in an elevator going to the ninth floor…or was he passing through the throat of some mystical behemoth, on his way to the wizard that lived in its stomach?

Lemat knocked on the door marked "9C"—hence, the clever moniker "Nancy," a useful code for those in the know. Lemat waited a few minutes for the door to open and when it did, there was nobody on the other side, so Lemat turned his head both ways to check who opened it. Finally, Lemat looked down and saw Big Mick standing in front of him with his blond dreadlocks tied in a ponytail and his trademark jumpsuit. He was no more than four feet tall, if anything.

"You know, that shit is getting old. Come in," said Big Mick, rolling his eyes at him and walking away.

The apartment was essentially a large living room with one bedroom, a bathroom and a tiny kitchen. The small balcony had fallen off at some point, leaving a glass sliding door to nowhere, or down, as Big Mick liked to say. A man, who wore a gas mask that was jerry-rigged as a bong, was passed out on a hand-shaped chair parked in front of the balcony.

"I thought you killed yourself," Big Mick said.

"I did."

"And? What happened? You ran out of rope?"

"Turns out I bleed pretty slowly... and the landlord wanted his rent and wouldn't take death for an answer."

"He called 911?"

"He did."

"Hmm. That's mighty decent of him."

"What can I say? The man likes his rent more than his own children."

"Take a load off," Big Mick said.

Lemat sat down on the back seat of a minivan doubling as a couch.

"What can I do you for?"

"I just need something to last throughout the day... you know, the usual."

"I thought you were on the wagon for a while."

"Dude, I just need something to help get through the work day. Especially now, after… you know."

"All right, your life, your dime." Big Mick went to the kitchen, opened the oven, and pulled out a Pez dispenser topped with a big smiley face. He filled it up with pills from a Winnie-the-Pooh cookie jar. "Have a nice day," he said as he set the dispenser down on the legless air-hockey table that served as a coffee table. "You can pay me later. Same price."

Lemat didn't know what the pills were. He had developed an aversion to the knowledge of any drug or medicine due to his negative association with the pharmaceutical industry—his dad's industry. All he knew was the pills worked. The trip home seemed to take longer. The towering buildings, grimy and oppressively crowded, shielded their dwellers from the sun. The people he met along the way looked tired, tortured, and drab. It was nothing like the trip coming over to Big Mick's.

Back in his apartment, Lemat planted himself next to his old boom box and started to compose a set list for a new mixed tape. He opted to go the classic route: Cream, The Who, the Stones, Hendrix, The Doors, nothing past the '70s. Lemat browsed through piles of CDs propped against the wall, searching for the right songs that could fit in a 90-minute cassette. He scribbled the running time of each song on a yellow pad and then proceeded to formulate the arcane algebra that would fit each song perfectly into a 90-minute cassette tape with the right mix. "Teenage Wasteland" would open the A-side to kick everything off with the right energy, followed by "Whole Lotta Love" and then "L.A. Woman," then Lemat would record a slower song—"Piece of My Heart," maybe—to pull things back for minute, before blasting away with "Paint It, Black" or something akin to that to get the blood going again, always making sure there was the right spacing between songs to maintain the perfect mood. The last song of the first side was very important, too. It had to create the impetus to make the listener flip the tape over to the B-side, paying special attention not to any empty air at the end (which was easier said than done). Lemat had to engineer all of this on his boom box, which was so old, he had to spin the CD with his finger first so it could gather enough speed to play. This extra challenge just added to the enjoyment of making the perfect mixed tape that would find a home among the dozens more Lemat kept categorized in shoeboxes under his bed.

It occurred to him that it would be nice if he could move somewhere else. Perhaps now that his mind was grounded (thanks to Big Mick), he could forget about the whole writing business, reinvent himself, and seek out a new goal in life.

CHAPTER FIVE

The next day, Lemat took the bus to work. He found something existential in riding the bus: a group of strangers trapped in a box, looking out large windows to the great world around them. Or more to the point, it was the world watching the menagerie of souls washed with fluorescent light, quietly keeping to their thoughts, and exhausted by the day's work. A crowd of beings heading in the same direction, subjected to the whims of traffic, but with no control of how to navigate their destination. A cab you could direct, and the subway was fast and had the protection of traveling underground. No, a bus had a definite feeling to it.

The commute also offered Lemat a time of physical idleness, where he could engage his imagination. Unfortunately for him and because of Big Mick's pills, all he could think about now was what his life would be like if he had never chosen to obsessively pursue his dream of becoming a real published writer.

The Path Most Traveled

The day was bright and the sky was clear. The house was like all the others in the neighborhood: one storied, red-tiled roof, manicured front lawn, and white picket fence. The smell of coffee, bacon, and eggs wafted over to a clean-cut Lemat wearing a sports jacket, buttoned-down shirt, and jeans. His smiling wife greeted him by the kitchen. The kids—boy and girl—were sitting at the table and eating their cereal. The small TV on the counter showed a morning show. The conversation was routine: don't forget to buy this, remember to pick up that after work, Johnny's game on Saturday and Jenny's recital Friday night, no you can't have a dog (it's a big responsibility), and so on. Everybody said their goodbyes and off they went in their minivan and mid-size sedan.

Lemat fought through traffic to drop the kids off at school. The radio blasted the latest pop wonder, something catchy, shallow, and annoyingly repetitive. But who cared? The kids were not paying attention—they were on their phones or portable games while still managing to annoy each other. Lemat finally dropped them off with kisses (not here, Dad, my friends are watching), be good, do well, and then, peace and quiet.

Lemat scanned through the pre-programmed radio stations. He

couldn't find anything worth his while, so he kept browsing through stations, not realizing he had gone three times around the dial. He settled for a commercial about erectile dysfunction. It was a classic-rock station, so he knew he'd soon listen to something that he enjoyed. "Satisfaction" came to the rescue a few moments later. The commercials kept droning on: hair loss, dating sites, energy drinks. He moved on to the news. Tensions in the Middle East, a celebrity arrested, a shootout in a school, and then the weather: nice today, cold and rainy tomorrow.

Traffic was hell. Lemat waited to move another few inches when a digital billboard caught his attention. It wasn't really the ad that was interesting, but the man tinkering behind it. An idea popped up in his mind: what if someone used those things for some sort of plot, a heist, a hidden communication? Ideas started to swirl in his head. By the time he came back from this little mental exercise, his car had moved almost two miles.

Lemat smiled; there was a familiarity to this. He used to have dozens of these moments a day. Now, they were few and far apart. Lemat made a mental note to write something about it when he got back home. He could use the voice-memo function on his phone, but he hated the sound of his voice and knew he wouldn't be able to stand listening to the notes later on.

By the time Lemat got to work—an ad agency where he worked as an associate art director—he had forgotten about the idea. Lemat was swamped with meetings and half a dozen ad campaigns. Most of his work was not creative; he chose, delegated, and dealt with a good share of drama that wouldn't be out of place in a high school. He wanted to leave at five, but today it was not going to be possible. They had a deadline on some mail-ins for a cell-phone company. He had to call his wife and arrange for the kids to be picked up and their activities shuffled. His wife couldn't do it, so his sister-in-law had to pick up the slack; thank God for Karen...again. Overtime ended up being almost two extra hours. The twenty-somethings that comprised the creative team made plans to meet for drinks and catch the latest hyped flick. Lemat hadn't stepped into a movie theater in four months, but he could definitely use a drink. No time for that.

More traffic. Lemat cursed the fact that two hours after rush hour, he still had to deal with this bullshit. The radio had abandoned him; the news was either depressing or downright stupid (a bear gave birth at the zoo?). He finally hooked up his phone to his car to play some music. It helped. He trailed behind an attractive sports car, the one he always wanted, but good luck with that. When he was younger, there was no way he could afford it. Now that he could, it wasn't practical with the kids or even the groceries. Besides, by now, it would be seen as some sort of mid-life-crisis-penis-compensation stunt, and forget about a motorcycle. Lemat chuckled bitterly. He thought, why could women get away with all kinds of silly possessions: ridiculously expensive and useless jewelry, a gazillion shoes or clothes they'd never wear twice? If men bought something they wanted—vehicles, gadgets, etc.—it was seen as a "toy" for growth-stunted juveniles. The quintessential catch 22. Toys were solely for the kids now.

Lemat sought diversion in reading billboards. This reminded him of the idea he had earlier—what was it? Something about a guy fixing them? He'd probably remember it later—he hoped. Right now, the ad with the stunning lingerie models reminded him of something else. His sex life was virtually non-existent. He loved his wife. Hell, with all those yoga and spinning classes, he still found her incredibly hot, but where was the sex drive? "The mood," whatever that meant, had taken its place next to the Loch Ness Monster. He wasn't finding any excuse to fuck his wife; that was for when they were dating. Then making love became the form, and even that lost its luster. And it went both ways—she was not surprising him with anything provocative or doing those little

naughty things that went a long way.
Sure, it was to be expected, that was
the way relationships went, right?
What you got bombarded with by the
media everyday was a constant wet
dream, a moment of pleasure, a
promise of intense lust with
impossibly beautiful-looking people.
A fantasy as absurd as any action
flick or a musical.

A bell alerted him of a text
message. At least traffic allowed him
to check it without danger. It was one
of his buddies; he was inviting him to
poker night. Yeah, right, there was
no way Lemat could do that. He had
kids and the wife would kill him. Why
couldn't this guy take a hint? He had
already shut him down for a fight
night, a concert, and going surfing.
Lemat would love to have a break, to
talk to someone about something
other than kids, good school districts,
surface streets to work, or travel
plans. He hated that topic, because it
always came down to the "When I
was in college" litany of traveler's
anecdotes. It occurred to Lemat that
perhaps it was he who should take a
hint. Sooner or later, all his single
friends had drifted away and he
couldn't blame them. He hated when
he was the single guy and had to see
his married friends taking a different
route in life. Lemat always thought
that was the right thing to do; if you
had kids, your life became about
them, otherwise, stay childless.

After a monotonous day at work,
Lemat made his way home. His neck

and lower back were killing him, and all he wanted was a glass of something, as long as it had a kick. As soon as he walked through the door, he got assaulted by a number of things: did he pick up his dinner (no); then he'd have to prepare something because everyone had takeout and there was nothing left. Could he help Johnny with homework? Then, Jenny wanted to sing him her song for the recital. He told her that he'd get to it all as soon as he could put his bag down and take off his shoes, but the request went unheard. Meanwhile, his wife was telling him about some sort of leak in the master bathroom. What did she want him to do? He wasn't a plumber or even one of those do-it-yourself guys.

"Call someone," he said.

"You do it," she answered, and that was it.

The TV in the living room was showing the kids' recorded shows and then there was the wife's parade of dance shows, reality shows, competition shows, and so on. That was fine—Lemat didn't watch TV that much, only "the boring channels": history, music, arts, military, Discovery, science, and whatnot. Movies were a neutral ground, but he always got out-voted. That was fine, too. If he could only find refuge in sports, but he never cared about them.

A few hours later, the house was dead quiet. The kids were finally asleep, and so was his wife (wearing flannel PJs with a book in her hands). Lemat took a shower and sat in his home office. A blank Word page sat open in front of him and he was trying to remember that idea he had this morning—something about a billboard. He sighed. He was tired and thought, *Who cares?*

Lemat turned off the computer. He went to the kitchen and prepared a screwdriver. It was the only way he could drink vodka, because he hated cranberry juice and tonic. Now he had to brush his teeth again. He sat at the kitchen table in the dark. He was happy about his life. Lemat loved his wife, a beautiful woman who was smarter and more successful than he was, by far. His kids had good grades, were well-mannered, read voraciously, had hobbies, and were very happy. He got a kick out of teaching them things and guiding them through life. He even enjoyed when his children made fun of him when he showed them movies he loved. "This is lame," they said.

Lemat had a nice house; they traveled once a year. Sure, it was Disney World or the Harry Potter tour when they went to London, but he still got to see some of the world. One day, the kids would go to college and he'd have to start another chapter in his life. Maybe take on a hobby or something.

No, he knew when he took this path that life would no longer be about him. It was about his family. All his dreams and his desires were

now his wife's and children's. All his
efforts were for their sake. Still,
every now and then, Lemat thought
about his younger self, the guy who
was going to set the world ablaze
with his ideas. The guy who could
have gone the distance, but now he'd
never know. Lemat would spend the
rest of his life getting glimpses of the
guy he wanted to be, the guy he
never was, the guy he chose not to
be.

Lemat watched the cars outside his window. He liked to
wonder who these people were: some obviously
wealthy, while others were barely making it (or at least
their cars were). Some were attractive, others sang,
maybe one was a real criminal and the guy behind him,
an undercover cop. Yet everybody was isolated right
next to each other. Maybe it was for the better; Lemat
wasted enough time figuring out his own life.

That's when he saw him—or at least he thought he
did—driving a silver, convertible Mercedes, going
through traffic—the man in gray he saw at Fausto's the
other night. He wasn't sure. The car caught the yellow
light and left the bus behind. Was he the same guy?

CHAPTER SIX

Part of Lemat's plan to refocus his life was to do things differently. Like any addiction, to stop doing something wasn't enough. The hole had to be filled up with something else. That's why Lemat was knocking on Ink's door with pizza in hand. He had resolved to gather some courage and invite Ink over for dinner. No one could refuse pizza. He became nervous when he heard rustling behind the door and saw the shadow of feet under it. The door opened, and Ink looked curiously at the pizza first and then at him. Then she smiled. He thought she was radiant.

"Hey, neighbor! What's up?" she said.

"Ah—not much. Er… how are you?" He wanted to kill himself… again. Now the whole idea seemed completely ludicrous.

"I'm great. Please tell me that you just brought me pizza."

"Kinda."

"Anchovies?"

"Only one half. I—"

"You can have the other half." She winked. "Let's go to your place, though. Mine is an unholy mess. Besides, I want to see that funky little apartment of yours."

"Sure," Lemat said. Ink grabbed her sketchpad and led the way.

It took all of five minutes for Ink to check out Lemat's place. What really caught her attention were all the manuscripts and notebooks filled with ideas crammed around the space. Ink grabbed a draft of a novel at random and started to flip over the pages.

"Sins," she read the title. "What's this about?"

"That was a working title. It's about serial killer who commits murders based on the seven deadly sins."

"You mean like the movie *Seven?"*

"Basically. It even has the same ending," said Lemat, grabbing a pencil from the mess.

"Fanfic?" said Ink, putting it down and picking up another folio.

"Nah, I wrote it some three years before the film came out."

"Really? You should have tried to publish it."

"I did. Nobody wanted it." Lemat twirled the pencil like he did his straws. "I couldn't even land an agent."

"That sucks. And this, one of those paranormal stories?"

"That's a very old one. Back when I wrote it, the whole supernatural thing wasn't that big."

"And you didn't have any luck with this one either?"

"Nope."

Ink put the papers down and dislodged another manuscript from under the clutter. "That's weird— nowadays, it's all about ghost this and psychic that." She started reading the first chapter. "Huh. Sci-fi," Ink muttered. Lemat waited until she was done. "This is great. Do you mind if I take this one home?"

"Why?"

"I want to know what the fuck is up with that naked chick that turned up on Mars all of sudden."

Lemat was beaming. He shrugged and said, "Sure."

"I have to say, this is all pretty amazing."

"Thanks," he said, sitting on the floor in the middle of the living room. Ink joined him, delighted by the pizza's aroma. Lemat said, "Sadly, they don't pay the bills."

"They don't have to," she said.

"It would beat my design job any day."

"Is that what you do for a living?"

"Yeah, I'm a graphic designer—well, a graphic provider, as I like to say."

"So what? You do that to pay the bills and this," she waved the pages in her hand, "to be happy."

"A writer with no readers feels a little masturbatory, don't you think? Anyway, to me, it has never been about having a hobby, but making it a career. Nothing would make me happier than being a novelist 24/7."

"A man with a calling. Nice."

"Or just plain stubborn," Lemat said. To him it felt more like a curse. Other people seemed to be able to put their dreams aside and conform. Not him. "Did you go to college?" He was starting to feel silly about sharing his inner yearnings and changed the subject.

"Yeah, but I dropped out of college in my sophomore year."

"What was your major?"

"Theater with a minor in social studies."

"It didn't pan out?"

"I just thought college was a huge waste of time and money," she said. "Don't get me wrong—it's definitely a must if you're going to be a doctor, a scientist, or an engineer or something, but the liberal arts? I believe in going back to an apprenticeship system. Like the old masters, you know? Learn your craft under someone experienced and talented."

"So what happened? You just dropped out and started to ink people?"

"Not quite. I gave college a shot. It wasn't for me. The whole 'college experience' was the nerdiest thing ever. I mean, if you need to go to college to drink beer and get laid, maybe you should worry about your social skills to begin with."

"And the networking thing?"

Ink shrugged. "Talk to people. Make friends. Frat houses are for the character-challenged. And what's the first thing they tell you when you get your first job?"

"That what you were taught in college is completely useless now that you're in," Lemat put some bass in his voice, "'the real world.'"

"Then why the hell would anyone waste their time there?"

Lemat didn't see many holes in her logic, but he couldn't help but feel attacked. "I went to college," he said. "Art school."

"And what did you learn that you couldn't by reading about and practicing yourself? From what I see, you were on your way as a kid," she motioned towards a pile of old notebooks behind her.

"It got me out of my house and out of a country where I had no future."

"Hmm… OK, that's a good reason to go to college."

"Why tattooing?"

"Oh, high school—" she said.

Lemat shot her a quizzical look.

Ink swallowed her food and elaborated, "These two guys who sat behind me during chemistry … all they talked about was tattooing. So I learned more about inking people than chemistry. I found the concept of people using their bodies as a canvas kind of interesting. I mean, think about it—there's really no room for error there. And until recently, you had no real way to get rid of such a commitment. So when I left college, I dated this guy—well, 'dated.'" She made air quotes with her fingers. "And I started to learn. I like the work, so here I am."

"All I learned from anyone I dated is how fucked up I am and what I needed to fix in order for the relationship to succeed. So what do you want to do in the future, own your own tattoo parlor or something?"

"No. Stay alive, have fun—maybe move to Asia and live on a beach. Who cares? I'll figure it out when I get there."

Lemat sighed. Maybe that was his problem—he had a blue-collar approach to his artistic sensibilities. The concept of the starving artist had never appealed to him.

"So why don't you do what you love to make ends meet?" Ink said while chewing.

"Easier said than done, don't you think?"

"In your case? Maybe. Is that why you tried to kill yourself? I already pegged you for the intense, aloof, brooding type."

"Sort of."

"Are you going to lock up on me again, Mr. Darko?"

Lemat sighed. "Er… no, it's just that right now, it seems extremely stupid."

"But back then it outweighed your life." There was no judgment in her eyes, but the way Ink was holding his stare was so candid and matter-of-fact, it moved something inside him. He felt disarmed. Lemat had no idea what to do or say. His heart warmed up when he saw her smiling sympathetically at him.

"You've been having a rough time lately," Ink said while closing the lid of the pizza box and setting it aside. Lemat just looked away, deflated. She continued, "We like to think we have some sort of control: luck, faith, or our own will. We make all these plans, but in the end, the only plan that matters is Life's. It's really survival of the fittest: adapt and overcome. And truly, sometimes she is just a big, fat bitch."

Once again, Lemat couldn't argue with Ink's logic. He just sat there allowing her words to dawn on him like some sort of truth-lava burning its way through his brain. When Ink stood up, his heart sank. Lemat realized that she was about to leave. He couldn't blame her; he had become a sort of human sinkhole, sucking everything around him into his sad core. But Ink didn't move—she stood there with a cryptic half-smile that intrigued him.

"Do you want to see my tattoo?" she said.

Lemat was confounded.

"My tattoo," she said, with a tone that bordered on the offended, "the one I told you I had when we first met?"

"Sure."

Ink moved closer to him. She undid her jeans and pulled them down, revealing underwear dotted with tiny pink skulls. There it was, suggestively placed on top of her pelvis, the mask of Comedy and Drama. He was aroused, and now, a bit perplexed. He wanted to ask for meaning, but something told him that it could wait.

CHAPTER SEVEN

"I didn't notice you were left-handed," Ink said as she held his penis while cuddling next to him on the living-room floor. Lemat grunted, casting a look down at his penis, wondering what made her say that. "Your dick, it veers to the left," she explained, reading his mind again.

They had sex, finished the pizza, and then did it a couple more times. Now they were too tired and comfortable to move. Ink was pleasantly surprised with Lemat's performance. He was a handy guy to have around. She had found that more often than not—and by reason of trial and error—the quiet omega male (for lack of a better term) was more reverential in bed than the typical lover.

"God, I needed that," Ink breathed.

Lemat couldn't argue. He felt like he was floating.

"So, why *this* tattoo?" Lemat said, caressing it. She allowed his hand to venture slightly lower a few times.

"Whatever we run into in life, ultimately, it's up to me to decide if I want to let it in. The experience can be sad or happy because it's within my power to make it so."

"That's pretty deep for a sexy tattoo," Lemat said, both impressed and tickled by Ink's wit. "So you're responsible for your own happiness?"

"And my sadness, yes."

"So you're happy now?"

"You don't see me crying—or bolting out the door, for that matter." Ink shifted her body so she could face him. "So, you've seen my tits and we did the dirty deed. Are we close enough now to talk about your suicide?"

Lemat was stunned. *Did she just sleep with me because of her scar fetish? Am I really that naïve?* Lemat forced his thoughts to cease abruptly. He just had a great dalliance with an enthusiastic partner. Lemat knew by painful experience that overthinking or (even worse) saying too much was always a mistake.

"I read a book while doing research for a story," Lemat said.

"Are you changing the subject?"

"No, I cut my veins open because I read a book."

"Intense. I never really believed in all that pen-is-mightier-than-sword business. What was the book about?"

"Quantum physics," he said.

Ink sat up, hugged her knees, and said, "OK, you need to explain that."

"Are you familiar with string theory?" he said. Ink pulled a face for an answer, so Lemat explained, "It's the premise about multiple universes, you know? Infinite, parallel universes?"

"So you killed yourself out of sheer boredom," Ink said.

Lemat wasn't amused.

"Sorry. Go on." She mimed locking her lips.

"In essence, the book said that for every decision we make, all the other options are taken in a corresponding dimension. So if you went right, another version of you goes left. If you say 'no,' in another universe you said 'yes,' and so on."

"OK. So every option is explored."

"All of them," Lemat said. "In this universe, I'm an out-of-luck graphic artist struggling to make it as a writer."

"And in another one, you are a ballet dancer."

"Or have succeeded in my attempts and live a great life."

"Hmm, interesting," she mused.

"So the thought of me being the one stuck in the universe in which I am an utter failure depressed me to no end." He shifted to face away from Ink because being so exposed made him feel uncomfortable. Every time he spoke out loud about his wants and dreams, he felt silly. Perhaps it was because he feared that no one would understand them.

"How do you know this isn't the dimension where you're a late bloomer and you'll become a runaway success later in life?" Ink said.

"Because I'm never that optimistic."

"Is this whole writing business really that important to you?"

"Yeah, you want to know why?"

"Sure."

Lemat took out a straw from one of the sodas near them. "What do you see over there?"

"A stack of old magazines," Ink said.

"And what else?"

"A stack of old magazines and a magazine rack."

"Is that it?"

"That's it."

"OK, let me tell you what I see." Lemat suddenly looked taller, the straw in his hand in perpetual motion. "A kid goes to visit his grandfather. He uses the toilet and picks up a magazine at random. They are old, collector's items, maybe. It's a *Popular Mechanics*. It teaches you how to make your own radio. The kid's bored, has no friends, and he's stranded at Grandpa's for the summer. He's no good with tools, but he goes to the garage and builds a ham radio. Every night, he tries to communicate with someone, just out of sheer boredom. He finally reaches someone and they establish a friendship over the airwaves.

"Now, you have your choice from the menu. If you want a thriller, the kid is talking to someone who has been kidnapped by some psycho who uses her as a sexual slave and the kid has to piece together who the girl is and how to find her. If you want a horror story, the kid actually contacts the spirit world, and shit starts to happen at the farm. If you want to go sci-fi, then substitute ghosts for aliens and you have insightful conversations about the absurdity of humanity. But maybe you'd rather see a drama, so the kid talks to this guy—an alcoholic war veteran with no legs and suffering from post-traumatic stress disorder—and through him, the kid learns valuable life lessons. It's your classic coming-of-age story where this kid learns how to be a man. Should I continue?"

"That's pretty impressive," Ink said.

"And that's just one story. What if a person picks

up a magazine and something falls from it, something that sends the protagonist on some sort of quest? It could be a note from his wife's lover, or the combination of an old locker. What if this person is deeply depressed, has low self-esteem, and suddenly gets an epiphany from reading some bullshit magazine like *Cosmo?* He takes one of those crappy quizzes that sets him on a path of self-discovery. Then the next article gives you something like '20 Different Ways to Be Better,' or something like that. So this character uses this magazine like a bible on how he's going to live his life. There's your comedy right there."

"OK, you should definitely be writing something."

"That's all I ever do," Lemat said matter-of-factly, yet she could tell he was mired in frustration. "Ever since I can remember, I come up with stories, characters, worlds—you know how some people have an aptitude for music, math, sports? Well, I can't do much else, but I can create. Why not make a living out of what you love doing the most? I mean, every day, you wake up and go to work. You spend a good chunk of your time there and you do so day in and day out for many, many years. It's one of the most pivotal activities in the human experience. Why not do something that's important and reflects who you really are? If you're going to spend your days doing something, then do what you're passionate about, right?"

"You're preaching to the choir," Ink said. "But you understand that what you are saying, to be successful as a writer, it's quite the challenge. It's like winning the lottery."

"I didn't say I wanted to be a millionaire. Sure, that would be nice, but all I want is to make a decent living out of it, you know? Pay my bills doing what I love. That's all."

"That seems like an attainable goal."

"Is it? I wouldn't know."

Ink stretched herself out. "Well, all I know is, that next time you try to kill yourself because of a book, at least make sure you wrote it, you know? I mean, bleed for what you believe in, not for what someone else tells you." She plopped back down on the floor, wrapped her legs around him, and sighed heavily. After several minutes, she was fast asleep with a peaceful grin on her lovely face.

She spoke the truth and Lemat suddenly felt fortunate that he was alive to realize it. Why *not* make the best of it? Why not focus all his energies on the work he was already doing and try to make the best out of a bad situation? Lemat could start climbing the corporate ladder—he could wear better suits, earn more money, and go on an actual vacation. He could pay his bills in that way and find satisfaction for his creative urges doing something else. Self-publishing could be an option. He could write his stories and put them out there cheaply or even for free. Who knows?

Nobody could ever say that he didn't try to make it as a writer. On the contrary, he gave it his best shot every single time. Lemat never held back. That's why each time he failed it was so painful. And that was his problem—it was getting harder and harder each time to get up off the mat afterwards. Lemat felt he was at a crossroads. There were so many questions in his mind, but he was getting a migraine, so he pushed all thoughts aside, found comfort in Ink's warmth, and fell asleep.

CHAPTER EIGHT

When Lemat rose the next day he was alone and naked, with the damned pizza box crammed under his ass. "Uck, cheese," he mumbled, as he pulled a string off one of his butt cheeks. Then he noticed something taped to his TV. It was a drawing of him asleep, signed by Ink. The caption read:

"Sleep, for when you are not it's when you dream,
and it's those dreams you bring to life.
A life spent for those who dream. Sleep."

Lemat took the drawing and retaped it to the wall that greeted him when he got home. He then jumped into the shower and got ready for work with a newish spring in his step.

On the bus ride over, he convinced himself that perhaps the answer wasn't getting a new job, but enjoying his old one. *If you can't be with the one you love, love the one you're with,* Lemat thought.

A client wanted a large chunk of text to be displayed on their website? *Can do, sir! With pleasure.* Lemat didn't concern himself with whether folks read the text or not; that wasn't his job after all. And when they didn't like the design of a page? No problem! Lemat would rip off their competitor's website. Branding? Sure! Lemat would look for the most cliché, trendy style he could find and dish it out with gusto. Time flew by and Lemat couldn't believe how much more he got done in a single workday. He didn't even feel stressed out or tired; he was elated.

He left the office and chose to stop at a café instead of his usual pilgrimage to Fausto's. Lemat was determined to change *all* his habits. So he wandered into Maya's Place, a classic example of modern-rustic. It had polished wood with round edges and leather sofas, tied together by tame ambiance music, and a dozen ways to drink castrated coffee from as many Third-World nations. While Lemat waited for his triple espresso, he realized how quiet the place was. There were at least ten to fifteen patrons and at least four employees, yet things were pretty hushed. A quarter of the clientele sat by themselves typing away on their laptops. Others focused on their phones or read a book. The few people talking seemed to be outside.

Lemat got his drink and found an inviting chair to sit in. He didn't know what to do. Play with his phone maybe? He couldn't imagine himself working in this place. There was no privacy, no real comfort. He thought that perhaps these people had no Internet connection at home and that's why they flocked here. Maybe he could download a book and read the whole thing while ordering cup after cup of coffee, like everyone around him was doing. Well, he could read here, but then again, his sofa at home was so much more comfortable, plus the lamp by it didn't give off such a glare, like the café fluorescents did. *So much for trying new places, huh?* And with that, he was out the door.

Lemat found a lonely bus stop and sat down to wait. He sipped his to-go cup of joe and browsed the news on his smartphone to pass the time, which inevitably led him to entertainment news.

He let out an audible sigh. Everything was a reboot, a remake, a rehash, a retelling, or a sequel. Lemat didn't have a problem with that. His only regret was that there seemed to be no room for anything else, and if that was the case, there was no room for him. Lemat caught himself digressing and immediately forced his mind to think on other, more pleasant things, like Ink's tattoo maybe.

Lemat made his usual bus transfer, when he recognized a familiar face in the last row. It was Mr. Freeman, the cellist. He was an ancient black man with reading glasses and wearing—with an air of quiet dignity—an equally ancient brown suit. Lemat walked towards him.

"Mr. Freeman?" he said. The old man looked up, annoyed, not only because his reading was interrupted, but also because someone had dared to break the invisible privacy barrier of public transportation. It took Mr. Freeman a few seconds to realize who was addressing him.

"Hello, young man. How are you doing?"

"Good. How are you?"

"I can't complain. Please, have a seat." The old

man pointed to the spot next to him with his book, a well-read paperback copy of *The Grapes of Wrath*.

"I don't want to bother you." Lemat understood quite well the need to be alone in a crowd.

"No, son. It's no bother at all." Mr. Freeman moved his weathered briefcase. The next best thing to an empty seat was one occupied by someone familiar.

"Coming back from work?"

"Yeah," Lemat said. "You?"

"Me, too. My car broke down and money is tight, so I guess I'll be riding the bus from now on."

"Not many concertos?"

Mr. Freeman chuckled and said, "Is that what you think I do for a living?"

Lemat nodded, and Mr. Freeman laughed louder this time. Lemat liked his laugh; it was boisterous but comforting.

"I'm an insurance salesman. Been doing it for forty years. The cello is just my hobby. Been playing since I was eleven."

"You never played professionally?" Lemat was incredulous. He was no expert, but the old man could play on recordings, he was *that* good.

Mr. Freeman was amused at the surprise on his young companion's mien. "No. There is no money in playing the cello—well, there is, I just couldn't find any. I tried, though. I went to music school and everything. But, after a few years, nothing happened. But the bills still needed to be paid."

"I'm sorry," said Lemat, thinking out loud.

"Why? I still play; you know that. Everyday."

For a moment, Lemat thought he had unwittingly insulted Mr. Freeman.

The musician continued, "Music is a big part of my life. It always has and it always will. We all need something to soothe our souls, wouldn't you agree?"

"Absolutely," said Lemat and grinned in spite of himself.

"Uh, I saw the ambulance that week by your apartment. Are you OK?" the older man asked.

Lemat wasn't sure if Mr. Freeman knew about his stunt in the bathtub, but the look on the old man's eyes made it clear that news—especially that of morbid nature—traveled very fast in the complex. Lemat stuttered a candid yet vague answer without capitulating to any gossip the cellist could have heard. The old man listened patiently, but the scrutiny of his expression appeared to cut through Lemat's efforts.

"I just want you to know that if you ever need to talk to someone, my door is always open," Mr. Freeman said. "If you ever feel like dropping by and having a couple of beers, I'd be happy to play you a few pieces without the need of throwing an old shoe."

Lemat simply smiled and nodded.

The bus arrived at the duo's stop. They walked in silence for what felt like a long time, until the older man wished him a good night and climbed the stairs to his home.

"Hey, Mr. Freeman! Maybe some Metallica when I come by with those beers?" Lemat called after him.

The old man didn't turn around but just laughed his characteristic laugh as he walked through his apartment door and disappeared.

As Lemat climbed up the stairs to his own place, he wondered if he should stop in on Ink, but the sight at the top of the stairs made him instantly freeze. There

she was, looking beautiful, sensual, and alluring—
everything Lemat had ever desired. Her gaze gave him
that familiar jolt. But there was a lingering feeling of
awkwardness. He looked at her feet, in fear of making
eye contact, because he knew Talia could see deep into
his soul. Lemat took a deep breath and proceeded up
the steps slowly.

He had met Talia a long time ago, as far back as he
could remember. It started out as one of those great
childhood friendships—no baggage, no awkwardness,
just immediate best friends. They had spent all their
time together. Talia brought out something special from
Lemat. If they played *Star Wars,* Talia would guide him
in creating his own smuggler, his own bounty hunter or
Jedi, instead of playing one of the known characters
like all the other kids. If they drew comic-book
characters, Talia would encourage him to create his
own member of the X-Men. In time, Lemat would have
his own unique team and his own comic book all
together. With Talia around, Lemat always did his own
thing. By the time he was in the fourth grade, Lemat
had created a veritable cast of original characters with
their own stories and their own realities. He and Talia
lived happily in their creative world.

As they grew up, so did the vastness and reach of
Lemat's dreams. At fifteen, he reached a landmark
moment in his life. At some point during the
monotonous school day, an idea dawned on him: he
wanted to write for a living. Of course, such an idea
seemed far-fetched for someone living in his country,
but that wasn't going to stop Lemat. It was at that point
when his relationship with Talia turned serious.

Lemat didn't care that people thought he was

wasting his time. Later in life, he would feel sorry that he never had a mentor but had to do everything alone with his own drive feeding his ambition. His friends—or what passed as such back then—were of no use. They were too busy projecting their insecurities and shortcomings on him. Lemat never had supporters, but detractors he could give away for free.

When Lemat moved to the United States to attend college, Talia followed, happy that they were one step closer to achieving his dreams. From then on, everything had a purpose, each new project had to have a definite goal in the real world. No more creating for its own sake. If it couldn't be pitched, then it was useless.

Lemat lost something in those years, that spontaneous naïveté of the imagination. He would come to regret that later in his life, because he never got it back. Lemat's relationship with Talia had been great up until then, but everything began to change after graduating college. That's when all the drama started.

Lemat always thought he was going to be a college dropout, something quite in vogue during the '90s. In his mind, he would break out big time, rendering college irrelevant. That didn't happen, of course. And life after college was nothing like he expected. There was no one out there waiting for him. Nobody cared how creative he thought he was—there were millions of people like him out there vying for the same thing—and there were far better writers. Lemat started to get into fights with Talia; he spent more time with Dep and relied more on Lisa to stay focused. And fifteen years later, there they were, awkwardly in each other's presence with nothing to say.

"Hey," Talia said.

"Hey." Lemat was ill at ease. He knew this moment would come sooner than later. There was nothing he could do to avoid it.

"How are you?"

"Alive." Lemat wasn't sure if deadpan was the way he wanted to play this meeting. She smiled sadly at his comment.

"We haven't seen each other since—then." Talia began to play with a lock of her hair, looking to comfort herself, and said, "I—I just wanted to say that I'm sorry. You know, I never even dreamed of anything bad happening to you—and I know—I know this time was different. We've been at this for so long, you and me. Time hasn't been kind to us. There're too many scars, too much pain and disappointment. I know it hasn't been easy living with me." She let her words linger, as if waiting for his reaction. Lemat just looked at his shoes. He couldn't bring himself to look at her or otherwise he would erupt in anger. "I know you're mad at me. I can't blame you."

"I have nothing else for you," he said, jaws clenched. "If you came to apologize, that's fine; apology accepted. Thank you and goodbye."

"Please—"

"Please, nothing!" He checked the level of his voice. "I'm too old for this shit—do you understand that? I can't spend the rest of my life chasing after some childish dream, OK? We tried and tried and tried some more, and nothing happened. It's not meant to be. I don't know about you, but I'm tired of the apathy, the slammed doors, and hitting my head against the same fucking wall. I'm done! We're done! So if you came here with intentions other than to say you're sorry, I have news for you—I don't give a shit. I'm taking my pathetic life and I'm trying to make something out of it—anything! I don't care! Anything is better than the big nothing I've been living until now. So please do me a favor and quit trying to seek me out. Just let me be…"

Talia took a long time before she moved a muscle. When she did, she just stood up and walked down the stairs. Lemat never looked at her. He moved out of her way far enough so there was no chance of physical contact. Talia stopped just beside him, but she sensed him pulling away from her with borderline violence. She cast her eyes down and just kept walking.

CHAPTER NINE

"Just like that?" Lisa said in disbelief from the kitchen service window. She sliced through an empty soda can with a kitchen knife. As they were gathered around the kitchen, Lemat's laptop played The Cure in the living room while he washed dishes. He had told them about his encounter with Talia the day before. Dep sat with his head hanging over a glass of milk, where he was dipping his Oreos.

"I can't believe it," Dep said. "Do you really think she's gone for good?" He watched as a drop of milk formed under the cookie in his hand and dropped back into the glass. "It's not going to last, you know? She'll be back sooner or later."

"Just chew your fucking cookies, OK?" Lisa said, pointing at him with the knife. "So OK, you told the bitch to go to hell. Now what?"

"I don't know," Lemat said, looking into a beer bottle like a fortune-teller. Sadly, the bottle had no answers for him.

"You need to know, man," Lisa said. "If not, the bitch is going to burrow through your skull again like a flesh-eating virus. So what's the plan?"

"I don't think he's strong enough to keep her away," Dep said. "You'll see, she'll be back in no time, and then he'll be fucked."

Lemat said, "I won't be fucked."

Lisa said, "Totally fucked."

Dep said, "That's fucking great."

"No one is fucking anyone!" Lemat said, slamming his beer against the narrow counter. "OK, so I'll just focus on work and save up some money."

"What for?" Lisa said.

Lemat searched for an answer. "For… a trip, a class… some gadget. Take your pick."

"No, you tell me," Lisa said.

"I don't know what to tell you," Lemat said. "So what are my options here? Maybe I should join a religion, or get married and have a couple of kids, spend all my money on them, then save for my retirement so I could travel to Europe inside a bus or take a fucking Caribbean cruise."

Dep said, "I don't know—what about pirates?"

Lemat ignored him and said, "Then I can find comfort in my kids going to college and getting on with their lives, and by the time I lay on my deathbed, I can say I lived a full life."

"That's the biggest pile of shit I've ever heard in my life!" Lisa said as she stuck the knife on the counter and stood up. "Fuck, man, if you ever say that again, I swear Talia will not be the only bitch walking away. I thought you sliced your wrists, not your balls! I mean, who the fuck are you? Really? You want to get rid of

Talia? Fine! Get rid of her, but you don't have to bend over and sell out everything you stand for."

Dep shook his head nervously and repeated, "This is not good. What the hell is going to happen? This is not good at all… not good—"

"And what do you want me to do?" Lemat said. "What choices do I have? Go back to school? Join the military? Get a service job?"

"You already have a service job! Remember?" Lisa said.

"Oooh, right below the waist," Dep mumbled.

Lisa wasn't done by a long shot. "Look, you knew what you wanted to do was not easy. Your chances were close to zero. How many people have the courage to put everything on the line and just go for what they love? Everybody says they would, but they sure as fuck don't put their money where their mouth is. All you need is to catch a break."

"And when is that going to happen, when I'm fifty?" Lemat said. "Because that's a wonderful age to start a career. And then what? Die by the time I barely have a body of work? Who the fuck wants to work with a middle-aged rookie?"

"He has a point," Dep said. "By then, he's not going to have the energy or the edge to do anything worthwhile. Don't get me wrong—he can still do great things, but it's basically a second life. Let's face it—he made the wrong decision."

Lisa said, "Says who?"

Dep said, "Him!"

"Yeah, that's great, you fucking Prozac-guzzling motherfucker. That's all he needs to hear," said Lisa. "The only reason he almost offed himself is because he listened to you in the first place."

"Have you ever thought for a moment that maybe, just maybe, he tried to kill himself because you drove him too hard?" said Dep, playing nervously with the two halves of his cookie. "You and your psychotic do-or-die attitude hasn't been exactly helpful, has it?"

"You're so full of shit!" Lisa said. "I'm the only reason he gets out of bed every morning. Me! Not you! If it was up to you, he'd be filling prescriptions by day and taking them by night, so he could deal with his fucking miserable life."

Dep said something, but neither Lisa nor Lemat could make it out. "What did you say? Speak up!" Lisa said.

"I said that Talia was the reason he gets out of bed," Dep said. "Not you."

Lemat tensed up; he was sure Lisa was about to stab Dep. Just her glare made Dep flinch.

"Oh, yeah? And where is she, huh?" Lisa said. "Where's Dream Girl? She's the reason for all of this shit, but I don't see her around. Do you?"

Dep whispered, "He kicked her out—"

"Oh! He kicked her out! Well, isn't that fucking wonderful?" Lisa said. "And where is her divine inspiration now, huh? He sure can use some of it now to figure out a way to move on with his life, right? Well, where the fuck is she?"

Dep said, "She—"

"She's not here, that's where," Lisa said. "The fair-weather cunt. All she's ever good for is to fill his head with ideas, but none of them have ever panned out, have they?" She looked at Lemat.

Lemat said, "No."

"No!" Lisa said. "Face it. At the end of the day, it always falls back to you and me," Lisa said. "And frankly, I'd rather you jump off a bridge for all the help you are."

Lemat finished his beer in one gulp and turned the music off.

"Where are you going?" Lisa said.

"Nowhere, it seems," said Lemat as he walked to his room.

"Wait, what are you going to do now?" Dep said.

"I don't know," Lemat said. "Conform?" He shrugged. "There has to be more to life than seeking out self-fulfillment."

"Yeah, like what?" Lisa said.

Lemat closed the door behind him, leaving Lisa and Dep to their fight.

CHAPTER TEN

Lemat did a few searches in his laptop for ideas. He couldn't decide what to do, so he made a list of activities to do throughout the week, in hopes one of them tickled his fancy. The criteria was simply to do something different, something he wouldn't normally do. The working logic there was that if he did things outside his comfort zone, he'd get a different result, a different experience from what he was used to.

On Monday, Lemat popped two pills from Mr. Happy, the name he gave to Big Mick's handy Pez dispenser, and got ready for work. It had never occurred to him until now how long and boring his commute was. Usually, he could barely remember what he did between getting up and sitting at his desk in the office. Now, each minute stretched out, feeling instead like ten; every block seemed three times longer. Traffic exasperated him to the point he felt like getting out of the bus and just running to work. The endless urban landscape seemed to repeat itself like the background of an old cartoon. All Lemat could do was bury his head in a book and drown out the noise while listening to his iTunes.

Once at his desk, Lemat kept his nose to the grindstone. He had to work on yet another website. This time around he had to cram the myriad of links the client wanted to see on the oversaturated navigation bar, user-friendliness be damned. Lemat didn't care; he was happy to oblige. This was the same project that Luna had tried to get him in trouble for by telling the boss the mockups were all wrong because Lemat didn't organize the horoscope signs in proper alphabetical order. It made sense to Max but not anyone who had actually ever read a horoscope page. To add insult to injury, Lemat got an email from Max that morning saying that the client wasn't happy with the way the page was turning out.

"It looks like any other page out there," Max derided. *Of course*, Lemat thought, *Damned you if you do, and damned you if you don't.* He thought about a solution for a while. He stared around, hoping for some sort of inspiration that never came. Lemat browsed a few design books—nothing. He couldn't come up with anything, so he simply Googled a few more sites and ripped them off. Then, after work, it was time for him to try a new hobby from his list.

Monday: Cooking class, Fun with Sushi. It was a pretty decent-sized class, about twenty people or so. There were friends and couples, and the rest quickly made friends with each other. Lemat stood in the back row, by the corner. It seemed that nothing had changed from high school.

Lemat's sushi was an unmitigated disaster. Too

much vinegar on the rice, and he either packed it too tight or way too loose. His fish cuts were too thick and rather asymmetric. Lemat hid the worst pieces in his pockets, which he dumped twenty minutes later in a trash can a few blocks away. Nobody sat next to him on the bus on the way home, and a couple of cats stalked him when he crossed an alley.

Tuesday: Two more pills. Lemat tried to make the bus ride more enjoyable by paying attention to the kind of business he passed on the way to work. The closer he was to home, the more fast-food joints, strip clubs, liquor stores, gun shops, bail bonds, mini-malls, and ethnic foods from the developing world there were. The closer he got to work, there were more health stores, yoga studios, shopping centers, kids' shops, gyms, specialty stores, and European restaurants. Gas stations were evenly distributed—they just got cleaner the farther he traveled.

At work, Lemat had to solve the issue of wedging a few dozen pictures into a website. The old him would have suggested keeping the images to a couple of the most significant shots, establishing a nice balance between images and nuggets of text. Instead, he found himself trying to stick the photos into an ocean of text. There was also a memo from the boss, reminding people that blue jeans weren't allowed in the office: *The creative boutique is a professional business and everybody has to dress business causal.* At the end of the day, Lemat left work hoping no one noticed his Levi's and wishing this next activity would brighten his day.

Muay Thai, or Thai Boxing, seemed straightforward enough. Also referred to as the "The

Art (or Science) of Eight Limbs," it had thirty basic moves and used almost every surface in the body to strike. Lemat thought this would be a good way to get in shape and learn some useful self-defense techniques. The idea started to fade away as soon as he got to the gym. The first thing he noticed was that people largely kept to themselves, unless they already knew each other, and every guy was sizing him up. It wasn't the most welcoming of environments to say the least.

When the class began, Lemat immediately learned a few things: (1) He wasn't very limber, (2) he had the physical constitution of an eighty-year-old smoker, and (3) coordination wasn't his forte. Halfway through the class, the instructor asked students to pair up and run some drills. Lemat turned around, looking for partner, but everybody seemed to be avoiding him. When Lemat managed to ask a couple of people if they were free, he was immediately met with, "I already have a partner." Lemat found himself without a partner again. He spent the rest of the class working on the heavy bag.

Wednesday: Another boost from Mr. Happy. Lemat watched *Taxi Driver* on his phone to drown out the commute. Work started with a surprise when Max told Lemat that he was assigning Amber to do the actual navigation on the site he was working on, because, "Let's face it—you're not the most technical guy, and we can't afford to fuck this up." The old Lemat would have hated this. But, the new and improved Lemat just swallowed that hate and smiled. *Less work for me,* Lemat told himself. He just went with the flow. Flow would come in handy for his next after-work class.

Salsa dancing was the last thing Lemat would ever

want to do or have interest in, so it made the perfect choice in his quest to radically change his life and broaden his horizons. When the teacher asked where his accent was from, Lemat said he was from Spain. Cultural racism aside, he wanted to avoid the shame of being seen as the only South American who couldn't artfully wiggle his ass. Lemat had two left feet and neither of them had any rhythm. He also displayed a sort of dancing dyslexia and spent more time trying not to bump into his classmates than dancing. When the instructor said, "All right, pair up," there were no surprises. Lemat ended up with a broom. The women in the class decided it was better to dance together than work with him, though there were only two other men in the class.

Thursday (although to Lemat it felt more like a Tuesday): More Mr. Happy. He played Angry Birds on the bus to lessen the commute. He started the day with a meeting where he sat at his usual station, at the furthest corner of the room, and hoped to remain unnoticed until they adjourned. No dice today.

"The client is very unhappy with her website," Max said. "I mean, look at this." He started to point out everything that the client had specifically asked him to accommodate: too many pictures and too much text, and then everything that Luna had done with the navigation. Max highlighted the lack of design cohesiveness, or, as he put it, "The elements of poor design." Lemat tried to explain himself, but his boss cut him short.

"Who's the designer on this project?" Max said. Lemat didn't answer; the question seemed rhetorical. "You only have one job to do, and frankly, I wonder if you put in any work on this at all." It occurred to Lemat that what he called his best effort was just seen as mediocre, while his lackluster efforts were always seen for what they were.

Max gave the project to Luna, so she could "save it," and told Lemat he would find something else for him to do. He spent the rest of the day sitting by his computer with nothing to do. The new project never came. Lemat dragged himself to the afternoon's activity. It turned out to be rather fortuitous.

Wine appreciation was fun. It started out like all the other classes—nobody engaged him, and the impressions he shared with his classmates of the first tastings were received with open apathy and even disdain. But by the second half of the class, Lemat was chatty, charming, and engaged everyone with eloquent wit. Maybe it had to do with the fact that he didn't spit the wine out, as was customary. By the end of the night, he didn't quite remember what he said, but he was asked not to return and was given his money back. At least he slept like an angel.

Friday morning was a little frantic. Lemat overslept due to a massive hangover. He had to take a cold shower, swallow his daily pills along with something for his punishing headache, and run out the door. His socks didn't match and his shirt was unevenly buttoned, but he didn't care. He missed his bus and the next one was ten minutes late. The trip to the office felt like it was done through a river of molasses on the back of a snail. When he finally got to work, twenty minutes late, the receptionist told him that the boss wanted to talk to him as soon as he arrived.

"You wanted to see me?" said Lemat, walking into

Max's office.

Max took note of Lemat's appearance before saying anything. In fact, he seemed to want to make a comment but changed his mind and invited Lemat to take a seat. The office was a shrine to Max's achievements, however few they were: diplomas from school and small courses, awards that went back as far as high school.

"How are you doing?" Max said, trying to start the conversation with some nice, obligatory small talk.

"Fine...fine... So, what's up?"

Max waited a few beats before talking. "I'll tell you what's up. You've been with us for a long time, haven't you? Twelve years?"

"Fifteen."

Max was impressed. "Wow. That's a long time." He made a pregnant pause. "Are you happy? I mean, here, with us?"

"...Yeah... I'm happy. Why?"

Another pause by Max. "There's no easy way to do this—"

Oh-my-God, Lemat thought. Time slowed down, like when you watch a car accident right in front of you and you're frozen in place. "I'm sorry, Lemat, but I'm afraid we have to let you go." He might as well have shot Lemat in the face.

"...Wh...why?"

"We both know your designs haven't been up to par. Our clients haven't been happy. Frankly, at your age in this business, I would have liked to see you in a managerial position. But you made it clear that you didn't want that, so here we are. Now I'm stuck in this situation, and I'm afraid there's no other way out. I'm sorry."

He wasn't, but nobody ever wanted to be the bad guy, especially the bad guys. When he asked Lemat to say something, nothing came. He just stood up and left the office, never looking back.

That night's activity was supposed to be Acting, but Lemat thought he had enough drama for the day.

CHAPTER ELEVEN

Ink's tattoo shop sat on top of a medical marijuana store; a metal staircase in an alley led to the former nail salon where the parlor did business. The place was small, basically a hallway with a back room. It was called "Tagged." Ink shared the place with two other artists: Ruz—short for Walrus—a bear of a man with ear gauges and tribal piercings; and Vinci, a slender guy with two-tone hair and a pinstripe, three-piece suit with no sleeves.

Vinci worked on a client, while Ruz parked his massive frame in front of a tiny black-and-white TV with rabbit ears showing an episode of *I Love Lucy.* He was drinking Cherry Coke from a flower vase. Ink busied herself by painting stencils onto an old couch with some white paint. Her red T-shirt had a picture of Mao and the caption *Don't Punish the Job Creators.*

"Hey!" Ink said.

"Hey," Lemat said. "So this is where you work?"

"Yep," she said.

"You want to grab dinner?"

"As long as it's noodles."

"Cool."

"Bring me some rice, will 'ya?" Ruz said.

"Second dinner?" Ink said.

"Evening snack."

"Wouldn't want'chu to starve on us, now, would we?" she said.

"Just bring me the goddamned rice."

"There'd better be a 'please' in all that shitty attitude."

"Please. Sorry. Thank you." Ruz stretched the words out like a petulant child.

"Right, I'm off, boys," Ink said.

Ink took Lemat to Juan Chow's, a Chino-Latino restaurant just around the corner from her work. They sat at a tiny table by the window. Lemat ordered a kung pao mofongo with salsa verde, and Ink ate a moo shu chimichanga with moros y cristianos. He washed his food down with tamarind juice. She drank green tea.

"A disease?" Ink said, chewing.

"A psychological problem," Lemat said. "I read this article about a study from the *Journal of Psychiatric Research* that linked creativity to mental illness."

"What kind of illness?"

"Bipolar disorder, for one. It said that writers in particular were more likely to be diagnosed with schizophrenia, depression, anxiety, and substance abuse. No shit, right? It also said that writers were something like fifty percent more likely to commit suicide than the general population."

"No arguments there, but a disease? I don't buy it,"

Ink said. "Besides, why are you so thrilled? It's like you were just told you had cancer and you're happy about all the weight you're going to lose."

"I always suspected there had to be something wrong with me, and now I have scientific proof."

"No, what you have is mental diarrhea. So let's say the article is right and you do have a mental problem, what do you do with that information?"

"I can finally get rid of this... thing. It's been driving me crazy all my life," Lemat said.

Ink just stared at him incredulously. "Well, I can definitely say you are one sandwich short of a snack tray," she said. "Everyone can be creative."

"Everyone can have creative thoughts, but pursue a creative career? Most creative people are drunks, drug addicts, manic-depressives, or damn-right depressed— they suffer from anxiety attacks and all kinds of other mental disorders."

"We are fragile creatures."

"Exactly! Yet, we put ourselves out there—our thoughts and ideas—for everyone else to see and criticize."

"Sure, but a disease? I don't know. I think you're reading too much into it. What would be the treatment?"

"A full frontal lobotomy."

"Harsh."

"No, I really think it would be a mixture of rehab and some antipsychotic pills."

"And then off to a job at the assembly line, nine to five, dressed in a uniform and looking forward to a weekend parked in front of the TV rooting for some sports team—classic. And I'm sure there would be hymns that we could sing before our work day."

"You're not taking me seriously," Lemat said.

"Oh, I am. Trust me. I'm not sweating because of the spicy pork. The question is, why would you want to do that? You have a gift most people would kill for."

"I could also have the gift of flight, but who cares if I never use it."

"But you do," Ink said. "I think you have a very romanticized idea of how your life would be. Even if you were a professional author, every job has its ups and downs."

"Those downs would beat the ups of a nine-to-five job any day."

"You have a point."

"By the way," Lemat said while poking his food with his chopsticks. "They fired me."

"What? When did that happen?"

"Last week."

"And you wait until now to tell me? What happened?"

"The inevitable, I suppose. They said they weren't happy with my work, so they let me go. I guess the feeling finally became mutual."

"Are you OK? I mean, money-wise?"

"For a little while. 'Little' being the key word."

"And why keep it a secret?"

"I just didn't care about talking about it. I hated that place."

"So what are you going to do?"

"Become a day trader, hit the international lecture circuit… Look for another job—what else?"

"What I meant was, what are you going to do with your free time now that you're not chained to the oar of the corporate ship? Why don't you take advantage of this and write something? At least before you go back to the Gulag, no?"

"I don't know. I think I'm done with writing. I've got to think about my future and how the hell I'm going to pay the bills."

Ink had a sudden clear picture of herself pushing a boulder uphill—at least that was how the conversation felt to her. They both tried to busy themselves with their food for a while. Ink took a long time before she spoke again. "So what now? You're going to undergo a lobotomy? Is this like your last supper or something?"

"I don't know what I'm talking about. It seems all I can do lately is bitch about everything."

"Maybe you should start a blog, 'Life's a Bitch.' Who knows? You might make some money with it if you get the traffic," she said while Lemat chuckled. "I'm worried about you."

"I thought you were fascinated by suicidal people."

"Now you're just being stupid. Is that why you came to have dinner with me, to pick a fight? Because I can tell you right now, I'm not interested. I'm not your punching bag."

"I know—I'm sorry. It's just that lately," said Lemat, sighing, "I don't know. I just wish I could put aside this whole writing thing and get on with my life."

"Can you?"

Life's a fucking mess! he thought. Perhaps he was right after all—maybe checking out of this world was the most viable thing to do for him. If there was something painfully clear to Lemat since childhood, it was that he was ill equipped to navigate *this* life.

The conversation stalled. Lemat asked Ink about

her day and forced himself to talk about his own week and his attempt at a new hobby. They finished their food and Lemat couldn't say good night fast enough. Ink was grateful to wrap things up, too. She was sure tomorrow would be a new day and Lemat would see things with a clearer head.

Lemat walked to the nearest bus stop. The thought of being cooped up in his apartment listening to Dep and Lisa argue, or combing through the few job offerings that he could find, was unbearable. So Lemat decided to pay Fausto's a visit.

When Lemat arrived at the bar, Fingerless Joe had already called it a night. Fausto was at the bar smoking and talking to Clover as usual. The Coin brothers were playing darts by straightening the damaged tips of the few workable ones. Tails ranted that his brother's lead was due to the malfunction of the old, electronic bullseye. Heads just laughed and patiently waited for his turn, sipping on his stout ale. The bet was always the same, a dollar. The same bank bill had passed between the siblings every night from a time neither men could remember. Sitting at the bar, Specs looked particularly happy that evening while chatting with Caesar Durango, a cab driver with a tropical slant to him who always ended his shift at the bar.

Everybody knew Caesar was an expert on something new every time he walked through the door. According to him, he had been a political activist, a professional musician, a metaphysician, and a photographer. Tonight he was arguing with the Coin brothers about which language was going to be more important in the future, English or Chinese. Durango weighed in from his stool, due to his claimed expertise in linguistics.

"Hey, love, where have you been?" Clover said.

"Oh, you know, work," Lemat said, sitting down.

"Well, we are celebrating tonight," Fausto said as he overfilled a beer mug and placed it in front of him.

"What are we celebrating?" Lemat said.

"I just sold a script on spec," Specs said.

"Really? That's great," Lemat patted his back. "Which one?"

"A new one," Specs said, glowing in his success. *"Emma and the Vampire."*

"You've got to be fucking kidding me," Lemat said.

"I'm not fucking kidding you."

Lemat looked stunned. "You wrote a script based on a Jane Austen—"

"With a vampire in it," Specs completed.

"And they didn't throw you out of the office when you pitched that?" Lemat said.

"Nope, they gave me a contract," Specs said. "It's not that it hasn't been done before. There are a pair of her books with fucking monsters already wedged in them. So I said, 'I can do something like that,' and I did."

"Unbelievable, right?" Fausto said.

"I admit, I was in a really low point in my writing," Specs said. "I was considering quitting altogether, but then I went, 'What the hell? Let me do something completely radical. The worst thing that could happen is that they say no.' And here I am."

Lemat couldn't shake off his amazement. Although, it wasn't the first time that Specs found success and then came crawling back to Fausto's after messing things up. When on the upswing, Specs liked to hang out with the fast-living cocaine crowd.

"Well, bottoms up," Fausto said while raising a glass of his own.

"You know, honey," Clover said, "if you ever need an actor, let me know. I studied method acting when I was in New York. I even auditioned for the Actor's Studio."

"Sure, babe," Specs said. "But you know Hollywood. Let's see where this whole thing leads first."

Lemat sat at the bar, ordered a beer, and listened to the conversations around him. He accepted a hit from a joint when Fausto offered it some time later. Other than that, his glass never stayed empty for long. As time went by, the bar started to empty out until it was only Clover and Lemat. At some point, she said something about stepping out for a second before closing for the night, or something. Lemat was too drunk to really care. He just sat there, contemplating the last quarter of his beer.

Just one fucking chance, Lemat thought. That's all he ever wanted. One chance to show what he could really do—that's all he asked for. Lemat had tried so hard to be unique so he could get a break, to no avail. It had occurred to him lately that perhaps the path to success lay in simply conforming. Maybe that was the one lesson he refused to learn.

"Long day?" the man said, interrupting Lemat's thoughts.

Lemat just grumbled an answer, avoiding eye contact.

"Care for a smoke?" The interloper offered an open

silver case with hand-rolled cigarettes in it; there were two missing.

Lemat shook his head. The man lit up. The flame from the match made him look more sinister and the tobacco stench was strong and bitter.

"Do you have the time?"

Lemat pulled his sleeve up, revealing his lack of timepiece; he was getting antsy. That's all he needed, one of the hordes of crazies he tended to attract whenever he roamed the streets.

"Not much of a conversationalist," the man said. "It's all right. I'm Guy, by the way."

Lemat volunteered a half-hearted "Hey." He wanted to get up and go home, but now he wasn't sure if Clover told him to wait for her. He also wasn't sure he'd make it to the door. Something else dawned on him as well: busses stopped running at 11:00 and it was almost 2:30. *Shit!* he thought. *Now I'm going to have to hail a cab.* And that wasn't going to be cheap.

Guy said, "Are you OK? You look lost."

"No, I'm just tired. That's all."

"I bet. And what do you do for a living?"

"Breathe." Lemat laughed. "No… I'm graphic designer. Or at least I was until I got my ass fired."

"An artist."

"A designer."

"A pragmatist."

"A realist. Anyway, it's a living." Lemat shrugged.

"No, it's just an existence, isn't it?"

The comment made Lemat suddenly take stock of his companion. It took him a few seconds to realize that the man he was talking to was familiar. He dressed sharply in a gray suit with a black and white tie.

"Do I know you?" Lemat said.

"We've seen each other around every now and then."

"So it was you, the guy I've seen around?"

"That's right."

"Have you been following me?"

"I think it's just the other way around. You've been looking for me—well, someone like me. I guess it's time for us to talk."

Lemat wasn't about to take cryptic answers from a shifty stranger, like some kind of mystery story. "I think you need to explain yourself."

"I've been watching you closely for some time now. I'm always scouting for new talent, but the reason I didn't approach you before was because you weren't ready to hear what I have to say."

"And now I am?"

"I believe so."

"Why?"

"Because you've hit rock bottom. Your projects have gone nowhere, you were fired from your work, and frankly, you have no idea what to do with your life."

"And how can you possibly help me?"

"I guess you can say I'm like those people who search antique stores for an undiscovered Picasso or whatnot."

Here comes the pitch, Lemat thought. All those nice platitudes could only herald some kind of petition. Lemat braced himself and said, "Any luck?" He was trying to find out what was this guy's angle was.

"All the time. You like sports? Of course you don't, but bear with me for a second. Scouts always go to the big colleges, right? That's where everybody knows most of the great talent is. Not me—I like to go to the little towns, the ones no one gives a damn about, and find that one diamond in the rough that otherwise would never be discovered."

"Yeah, yeah. The forgotten Picasso thing. I get it."

"It's been a long fight, hasn't it? I can tell by looking into your eyes. You look like a soul that's tired of struggling. You rarely get to see that. It's easier when you check your brain out and let others do the thinking for you. That's why they do it, you know? Religion, society—they've laid out all of these little landmarks for you. It makes life, as uncertain as it is, more bearable. It gives people an illusion of control in an otherwise unpredictable world. At a certain point, you should work, get married, have children, retire, etc. Going with the flow is so much easier. It warms my heart to know there are people like you still out there."

"Deadbeats?" Lemat said.

"Dreamers. The world might not like you, respect you, or even care about what you do, but it so sorely needs you. Not everybody was meant to be a doctor or a businessman. And how many workers does the world really need? I think it can afford a few unlucky fellows to carry the burden of looking in from the outside and holding a mirror to the crowd. Or at the very least make the rest forget their problems for a while."

"Unlucky sounds right," Lemat said as he finished off his beer. "Anyway, it's not like I can do anything else."

"And why would you need to? More importantly, can you? Would you? You don't seem like the office type to me."

"Well, my former boss certainly seems to agree with that statement."

"You're stronger than you think. At your age, most people have quit on their dreams and settled into a pedestrian existence, letting society write their lives for them. But I can tell you're at that point, aren't you? You're about to hang the gloves and call it a life, aren't you? Let me guess—you're now trying to find a way to justify falling in line with the rest, hoping you'll find some sort of satisfaction…"

Lemat stared at Guy, trying not to appear too drunk. The conversation was getting a little too bizarre for his taste, and that was saying a lot coming from someone like him.

"But you know, it's not too late," said Guy, sitting up straight.

"All right, that's all great, but if you'll excuse me," Lemat said, getting up. "I've drunk a little too much and I want to go home now—"

"Can you? You've sailed too far from terra firma and now there's no turning back. Not for you."

Lemat fell back on his stool. "OK, what's this all about?" He clumsily felt his way towards the cocktail straws behind the bar and picked one, leaving a mess behind. Lemat started twirling away, seeking comfort.

"Have you been listening? Because I'm definitely not talking to myself here. This is about you. You've got talent, and more importantly, you've got drive and foresight. That's rare among you creative types. It's usually the same story: all the talent in the world but no discipline, no plan, no goal. The problem with you is, you just don't have the slightest clue on how to get there. And that's where I come in."

Lemat let out a chuckle, sending a little spittle out. He wiped his lip self-consciously. "Really? And why would you do that?"

"Because that's what I do." He handed Lemat a napkin. "The question is, how badly do you want to make it?"

"What kind of question is that?" said Lemat.

"The most important. Are you willing to do whatever is necessary to finally make your dreams come true?"

Lemat laughed awkwardly and said, "Wait, who are you, again?"

"I'm the guy who can help you get where you want to go. Here's my card." He handed him a black business card with white letters. It simply stated *Guy. Talent Manager.*

Lemat was impressed—the printing of the card was flawless. *Simple*, he thought and laughed inwardly. Lemat didn't know what to make of his encounter with this... Guy. "OK... all right. Let's say I—" He changed his mind. Lemat had a weird feeling he should choose his words carefully. "OK, how can you help me? I mean, if we work together. What can you do for me?"

Guy reached over the bar and worked the tab to get a refill for both of them. "I don't like drinking by myself," he said. "You don't have to drink it, just nurse it until I'm done with mine." That wasn't going to happen. Lemat's nerves compelled him to take sips absentmindedly. Guy continued, "Simply stated, I can place you in the right time and in the right place. You see, a lot of people think that success is all about hard work, sacrifice, taking risks, and being focused like a laser beam. That or nepotism."

"And it's not?"

"That's just part of it. Think about it—if that were true, there would be far more successful people in this world, don't you think? Now, don't get me wrong. You do need all those other things. Let me put it this way: those are the parts of a car—the engine, the wheels, etc. But even the best engineered vehicle needs that little spark to start the engine and make the whole thing run."

"And what's that?"

"Luck—pure and simple dumb luck. You can break your back all you want, but if you don't have luck, you'll be going nowhere fast. Think of all the successful people you know. They all had that one— sometimes more—moment in time that allowed them to push forward and reach their goals. Whether they want to admit it or not—and the smart ones do—luck has played and will always play a pivotal role in success. Luck is just an opportunity, but you have to be ready when the opportunity shows up."

"If it shows up," Lemat said.

"Now you're listening. That's where I come in—I create those moments."

"And how do you do that?"

"I'm a student of human nature. It fascinates me— always has. And when you understand the nature of something, it is easy to crack its code. I can see this might be a little too esoteric for you," said Guy, looking at the vapid expression on Lemat's face. "Tell you what, Sport—let's meet tomorrow, when your brain cells are not having a party."

Lemat brandished Guy's card. "And how do you propose we do that?"

"Don't worry. I'll contact you."

CHAPTER TWELVE

His head was pounding. Lemat crawled out of bed and made it to the bathroom as if he was walking on needles. He searched for some pills for his headache, making a mess, and then forced himself to take a shower. He needed to drink a lot of water and reminded himself to get some potassium, too. So when he got to the kitchen, he ate some banana bread that had gone a bit too hard while he waited for his coffee to brew. It was better than nothing.

As he went through hangover control, Lemat tried to remember how he got home. He didn't remember anything aside from his conversation with Guy. *What a strange night,* he thought. Lemat couldn't recall if Clover came back to close the bar, or his cab ride home. He obviously took one—there was some cash missing from his wallet. Lemat saw his phone on the floor. He had missed the kitchen counter when he took it out of his pocket last night. Everything could wait for a moment; he needed some coffee first. Once he had his oversized cup of java in hand, he took care of his cell. He had a message that read: *Meet me at the playground. Guy.*

The playground? Lemat thought. That place made a demilitarized zone look like a picnic. Lemat wasn't convinced this Guy guy could actually do anything for him. The only thing he had going for him was that Lemat was out of ideas. He didn't know what else to do with his life. So in the interest of searching new horizons, Lemat thought it harmless to listen to what Guy had to say. Even a bad idea was better than no idea. He donned his sweater—his trusty armor against the world—grabbed his coffee, picked a straw from a mug shaped like a brain, and left the house.

Rain loomed in the horizon and that was fine with Lemat. The last thing he wanted was to be blasted by the sun post-inebriation. The playground was at the edge of the building complex. It looked like the place where childhood dreams came to die, all muddy and rusty. Guy was waiting for Lemat, leaning against a jagged slide, his sleek, gray suit in stark contrast with his surroundings.

"Ah, you made it," Guy said.

"I thought I'd see you at home or something."

"Or something is right. The world is my office." Guy raised his hands in a dramatic manner. "You can't be creative trapped inside four walls. Think outside the box." He winked and scratched a match on the slide to light up his smoke. "Besides, your place is kind of crowded as it is. I'd rather talk somewhere quiet, just the two of us."

"OK. So, here I am. What now? How does this work?"

Guy sat on the only safe spot on the merry-go-round, which made Lemat wonder if he cared about getting dirty at all. Guy said, "It's simple—you create and I make sure you sell."

"That's your master plan?"

"With a little proviso, of course."

"Of course."

"You want to make your dream come true, am I right?"

"Right."

"Right. So all you need to do is do what I say and I guarantee I'll get you there."

Lemat cackled. "Well, excuse me. I didn't think it was going to be that simple." He walked around what used to be the swings and held on to their bare chains. "And where were you in all the years I've been busting my ass trying to become a professional writer? I could have used the help, oh, some fifteen years ago or so."

"I told you—it would have been a waste of time."

"Says who?"

"You. Tell me something—would you have been open to hearing what I have to say back then?"

"I don't know what you're about to say."

"No, but when you do, you'll understand why talking to me then would have been useless."

"OK, so here we are. Go ahead."

"The reason that you haven't been able to have a career as an author is simple: you're not speaking the language, and therefore, you're not reaching your target audience."

"And what language is that?"

"Money. You see, every time you sit in front of someone who can give you a break, you go on about 'doing things differently,' 'having your own voice,' or 'pushing the genre.' Right?"

"I don't sound like that."

"Don't go off on a tangent now. The problem is, the people you're talking to—the agents, publishers, producers, etc.—they don't care about that. What they're looking for is demographics, profitability, market shares, and all of those things you don't give a shit about. But they do."

"So instead of spending all of those years creating, I should have been getting an MBA."

"It wouldn't have hurt, but that's not my point. J.K. Rowling was told that children don't read. The all-knowing industry people told her what she was doing was, in so many words, a waste of time. Look at her now. She turned the whole thing on its head and singlehandedly kick-started a whole new wave of young readers. Who cares if her new novel becomes a bestseller or not?"

"You know that you're truly successful when you can afford to fail," said Lemat.

Guy stood up and started to pace. "Did you know a group of scientists in England have come up with a way to mathematically predict a hit song? They analyze tempo, duration, beat variation, and a host of other variables. Their success ratio is 60%. Do you want to get an Academy Award? Get the lead in a biopic about someone mentally challenged. Chances are, you'll get your golden man."

"Is there a point to all of this?"

"All right, smart ass. If this is all so obvious, what's the point I'm trying to make?"

"Money is king," Lemat said. "Do I get a prize

now?"

"So why are you unemployed and whining about never getting a break, then?"

"OK, so what's my problem?"

"The stuff you've done so far is—well, you haven't set the world ablaze, have you? That rejection pile of yours is the size of a phone book. And the self-published stuff has drowned in the ocean of other hopefuls. Too much white noise, too many works clamoring for attention, is that correct?"

"Yeah."

"So we need a fresh start."

"I got nothing."

"That's a first," Guy said, surprised. "The problem is, you're thinking along the same old lines you've always worked with: themes, layers, and symbolism. Those are all great; don't get me wrong. But who cares, a handful of people? Nah, we need to talk to the masses. Think commercial. You see, one of the reasons you haven't succeeded is because, as good as a storyteller you are, you always fail to communicate. Like I said, you can't go to an agent or an editor and tell them you want to articulate a creative thought. No, that's some kind of hippie crap in their minds. But if you speak dollars and cents—if you can put it in their heads that there's money to be had with your idea—then we're off to the races."

"So you want me to write trendy shit. That's your master plan?"

"And get handsomely paid for doing so," said Guy, squatting in front of him. "You want to keep doing it your way? Go ahead. Me, I'm offering you the one piece you've been missing all your life."

Lemat was confused. "Wait a minute—that's it? You invite me here, lay down some Chinese fortune cookie wisdom on me, and I'm off to have a writing career? As simple as that."

"Who said it had to be complicated? And besides, I'm not saying this is fait accompli. What I'm offering you is the greatest chance you'll ever have at getting a break, not a career, but finally getting your foot in the door. That's all I can do. The rest is on you."

"What's the catch?"

"None, but there's a price."

"Of course," Lemat said.

Guy lit up another cigarette and said, "That's one of the inescapable truths in life, my friend. Nothing is free. For some people, it's their family, time, their career and opportunity, youth—it can be anything as long as it's of any value to you. That's the first rule I want you to remember."

"Oh, we have rules now. I guess there are going to be three, right? That's usually how it goes."

Guy stood up and said, "Are you done? May I please continue?"

"Sorry," Lemat said. "You want me to write something with commercial appeal, and there are some rules. Go on."

Guy started pacing again. "New doesn't sell; it rarely has. Think of all the things that are successful right now—are they really new? No. What you need to focus on is packaging. Grab a pig and put some lipstick on it."

"OK."

"Rule number two." Guy wheeled around. "Name your price now, before your judgment becomes clouded with whatever may come."

"Why?"

"If your dream exceeds the price you set now, you'll know when to call it quits. You want to live your dream, not turn your life into a nightmare."

"I'm willing to do anything," said Lemat, rising to his feet.

Guy stared at him for a moment and said, "All right."

"So what am I writing about?"

"That's your job. But in the immortal words of George Bernard Shaw, 'The secret to success is to offend the greatest number of people.'"

"Something commercial and shocking," Lemat said.

Guy clicked his tongue and mimed a gun at Lemat, "Nothing sells better than outrage—look at Madonna."

Lemat didn't know what to make of all of this. What Guy was saying made sense, logically speaking— or at least that's what Lemat thought—but was it worthy?

"I don't know if I can do this," Lemat said, walking around. "Maybe I'm not the right guy to do this, you know?"

"Maybe. It's a very common story. Everyone has dreams, but very few are willing to do what it takes to make them happen. It's not easy, not if you're not lucky. You see? That's why I had to wait for the right time to approach you. But here we are and you've decided it's not for you. That's all right. No harm, no foul. Have a good life." There was no hint of sarcasm in Guy's parting words as he walked away.

"Wait!" Lemat said. "Can you really do it? Can

you help me get crack at my dream?"

"Kid, I'm the last shot you'll ever have." Guy flicked his cigarette butt away.

"And what if you're wrong? What if you fail?"

"Me? It's all on you, buddy. I'm just here to guide you. And if *you* fail... Well, does it really matter? What do you have to lose? The real question is, what if you *succeed?"*

CHAPTER THIRTEEN

When Lemat got home, he was actually quite surprised when he saw Talia standing at the top of the stairs. She was as beautiful and evocative as ever. Probably the biggest question in his mind was, why was she there? It was mainly because Lemat had no clue why she would be involved in what he was about to do. Surely if Lemat were to indulge more time thinking about it, her presence would be seen as a negative thing. She was definitely the last face he thought he would see at this particular point. *What does it matter?* Lemat thought. At least hers was a familiar face, and in the end, he was probably going to need her. No words were exchanged between them. He grabbed her by the hand and disappeared inside his apartment.

For the next few days, Lemat returned home to a litany of trite concepts waiting for him to sort out in a viable commercial vehicle for his stories. He was sure this would allow him to create a beachhead in the entertainment world, from where he could then unleash his creative mind. Each night was something different.

On the first one, Lemat had to shotgun his way through a flood of zombies. He hated the living dead and thought that fast zombies were cheating. The throes of animated corpses inched their way around him, reaching for his flesh with filthy, broken nails and decaying teeth. Lemat, Lisa, and Dep pushed the apartment's door closed, leaving the dead to wander outside while Talia just sat on the couch impassively filing her nails. There wasn't much Lemat could do with zombies that everybody and their grandmother hadn't already done.

Next came the vampires, some sexy, others hideous. Lemat crossed the courtyard towards his place deploying all kinds of weapons. The undead hissed and crawled around in shadows, trying to find their way to his neck. Even a few werewolves tried to bite into the action, chasing Lemat unnervingly close to his heels, but their fate was no better than that of their fanged peers. They all knew as well as Lemat that their reliable position as folkloric mirrors to humanity's terrors and desires, as well as their iconic representation of what lurks in the dark, was played out—at least until they rose again from their eternal slumber.

Lemat let loose a few more cross-shaped, holy-water-soaked, silver-tipped, oak arrows from his crossbow, right before Dep and Lisa nailed the window shut with the dinning room table. Talia ate popcorn as she channel-surfed. Lemat would unrepentantly wake up the next morning surrounded by three beautiful vampires, after a meaningless night of unbridled debauchery. They had sucked his essence all right, but they faded away with the sun, along with any hopes of finding immortality in a new story.

No more monsters, Lemat thought. The following night, the path to Lemat's home was littered with orphans. The adorable but aptly pathetic children clamored for his attention.

"Would you help a poor boy, kind sir?" they said in cockney accents for some reason. But to Lemat, these children needed no aid. They were the offspring of mythological characters, superheroes, ancient sorceresses, and all sorts of special legacies. Each and every one of them was waiting for an opportunity to find their true self, learn important life lessons, and fulfill their destinies by defeating some inevitable evil.

"Care to help me, me lord?" said a girl dressed in period clothing with tentacles flailing behind her.

"Piss off!" Lemat said before kicking the door closed behind him. *No orphans.*

Lemat was losing interest fast. The following day, the courtyard was filled with symbols, masterworks, old books, and a multitude of paraphernalia and clues leading to some ancient discovery, hidden by convoluted conspiracies and mired in a series of riddles. Sinister antagonists peeked from tucked-away corners, watching Lemat's every move.

"Here," a strange man said, approaching Lemat from a doorway. "The lost puzzle box of the Knights Hospitallers." The old man handed him the box with utmost care.

Lemat never stopped walking. He took the wooden object, shook it next to his ear, and threw it over his shoulder.

"The forgotten book of the library of Alexandria," said a blind woman, handing him the tome.

Lemat ripped it apart and cast the pages over his head.

A hunchback limped towards him. "The secret key of the—"

Lemat slapped it off his hand. He shut the door behind him, drowning another claim of a mysterious object.

Talia looked at Lemat through the apartment's window with evident disappointment. It pained her to see him wasting his time in these pointless efforts. And at the same time, she was amused by Lemat's eagerness to delude himself. It was like watching an Olympic sprinter trying to compete in synchronized swimming.

"Nothing works," Dep said the following evening while doodling absentmindedly on the back of a notebook. He, Lisa, Talia, and Lemat sat on the roof surrounding a wastebasket almost filled to the brim with discarded ideas.

"You know the rules, Edgar Allan—what you got?" said Lisa, clicking her pen anxiously.

"Zombie strippers from outer space?" Dep said.

"That's retarded," she said.

"I thought we agreed not to be judgmental… or offensive," Dep said.

"I'm saying the idea is retarded. You, on the other hand, are a shithead," Lisa said.

"Come on, guys, let's not lose focus here," said Lemat, laying on his stomach, illuminated by his laptop's screen, the perennial straw twirling nervously in his fingers.

"Chuck it," said Lisa, giving it a thumbs down.

"Yeah, I don't know about that—" Lemat said. "The name has a ring to it, though."

"No zombies, remember?" Lisa said.

"Fine. Chuck it," Lemat said.

Dep crossed it out, ripped the page out, balled it up, and threw it towards the trash can. It bounced off the rim and fell among a few others. Lisa voiced her disapproval sardonically.

"All right," Dep said. "What do you have? You don't even write anything down. All you do is play with that stupid pen."

"What the fuck? I thought you said 'no judging'?" she said.

"Sorry," Dep said.

"What about you?" Lemat said.

Lisa checked the notes she had scribbled on her arms and hands. It was hard to read them among all her tattoos. She finally found it near an elbow. "Kid gets possessed by the spirit of a vigilante while playing with a Ouija board and starts offing bad guys in the projects."

"You have all of that written by your elbow?" said Dep, pointing at her with his pen.

"In shorthand," she spat back. "I don't need to take notes like a fucking nerd."

"Chuck it," Lemat said.

"What? No way, it has action, some supernatural shit, and appeals to the urban crowd," Lisa said. "It's fucking genius!"

"How about if he starts to get the attention of the cute neighbor that never paid attention to him before?" Dep said.

"Weak," Lisa said. "Maybe if she's bi-curious."

"Chuck it," Lemat said.

"Well, you come up with something better, then,"

Lisa said.

"You need to chuck it," Dep said.

Lisa gave him an incredulous look, but Dep just stared at her, waiting. Lisa rolled her eyes and threw her gum inside the wastebasket. Then she looked at him to see if he was satisfied. Dep returned to his notebook.

Talia had been watching the whole exchange with a bemused expression. She lay on her elbows on a pillow, resting her head on her hands and curling her legs up. "I like the idea of going sci-fi for this project. How about a secret mission to the dark side of the moon, where these astronauts find alien structures in which they discover the real origins of life on earth?" Nobody spoke for a moment.

"Where are your notes?" Dep said.

"I don't take notes, sweetie," Talia said.

"Of course not," said Lisa, doing a jerking-off motion in the air.

"That's too good," Lemat said.

Lisa said, "Chuck it!"

Dep said, "I actually like it. It sounds pretty interesting, no?"

"That's exactly why we have to chuck it," Lisa said.

Talia said, "Why are you doing this, seriously? This is nothing but a waste of your time and your talent. I mean, look at you. We're sitting up here trying to come up with mediocre, uninspired ideas in some half-cooked, desperate attempt to change your fortune. Is this how you want to go about this?"

"We talked about this, remember?" Lemat said. "If you want to stay, you have to help me with this. So no deconstruction of the genre, or any of the other shit that no one could give two fucks about. What I need now is some rehashed crap with a few bells and whistles." He would never have guessed how hard it was coming up with a crappy idea that could sell.

Talia flashed that charming smile of hers. "Oh, I'll help you with anything, love. You know that. All I'm saying is that you can do *way* better than this."

"We're not looking for way better—we're looking for universal appeal," Dep said.

Lemat nodded approvingly, then said, "OK, how about this? Self-help guru is really a serial killer, using his books to find his victims."

"Self-help guru?" Lisa said.

"No, something else. Come on," Lemat said.

"How about if a guy helps a celebrity ghostwrite a book and he kills the celebrity?" Talia said.

"Ooh! That's good," Lemat said, typing it down.

Dep said, "You think? Maybe it can be about a real celebrity. Well, that might get us in trouble. Maybe we can do a character that is pretty close to someone famous in real life." He scratched his head. "That could be troublesome, too, no? I don't know. Maybe it's a stupid idea."

"You think everything is a bad idea," Lisa said. "But, as much as I hate to admit it, I like her idea."

Lemat looked at the computer screen. "Hmm."

"What?" Talia said.

"This is a good start, but I think we're still missing something," Lemat said.

"Like?" Dep said.

"Well—I think we need a 'wow' factor," Lemat said.

"What do you mean?" Lisa said.

"Like a hook or something that grabs the reader right away," Lemat said.

"Perhaps you can start the story from the end and work your way backwards to the beginning," Talia said.

"That sounds cool," Dep said.

"I don't know, Charlie Brown," Lisa said. "That sounds dangerously too creative for our shitty enterprise."

"You're right," Dep said.

"We need something shocking," Talia said.

Lemat contemplated throwing the computer off the rooftop for a second. Every time he thought he was close to a fitting story, something came up, threatening to derail the whole endeavor. More than creative sabotage, what crippled Lemat's efforts was the impending sense of doubt. After all, he was treading on unknown territory.

"Hello?" Ink's voice came from the apartment below.

Lemat peeked his head through the access to the roof.

"Hey," she said. "I thought I heard you talking to someone."

"I was just thinking out loud," Lemat said.

"I brought Chinese," Ink said as she lifted up the takeout bags. She seemed to just have come home from work. "You working up there?"

"Trying to."

"Cool, I'll go up. Here." She passed him the bags and climbed to the roof. "It's a perfect night for a rooftop picnic. What are you working on?" Ink surveyed the rooftop littered with papers, various junk food wrappers, and soda cans. She couldn't believe one man could make such a mess.

Lemat shook his hair wearily. "My next novel."

"That's great. I'm glad you've decided to go back to writing. Listen, I'm sorry about how things went down the last time saw each other. You've been under a lot of pressure, losing your job and everything—I guess I could have been more understanding."

"It's OK. Don't worry about it."

"Good. Let's chow down, then."

Ink asked him about his new book while they had dinner. Lemat explained his frustration and even ran some of his ideas by her. Ink was candid without being brutal or blunt. In the end, she shot down all of his ideas, even though she liked the title "Zombie Strippers from Outer Space."

"I still don't get why you want to go through this," Ink said. "You want to break in by selling out?"

"There's no such thing. Everyone compromises in way or another."

"Then why are you struggling so much?"

Lemat had no immediate answer. "I guess… I guess I'm having writer's block."

"I thought you told me you never had writer's block."

He didn't know what to say.

"Have you ever stopped to consider, what if you actually succeed?" Ink said. "What if you finally break in doing something you actually *don't* care about?"

"Who cares? As long as I make it, then I can do whatever the hell I want."

"And what about your freshman offering? You'll be attached to it for the rest of your life."

The statement made Lemat uncomfortable. He

knew Ink was right, or at least Lemat intuited she was by the wretched feeling he experienced inside him. But then again, everybody needed to pay their dues, he reassured himself.

"I would be offset by the body of work that would follow," Lemat said.

"I don't know. Careful what you wish for."

For Ink, there was nothing else to be said on the topic. She just wished Lemat found what he kept looking for so he could be happy someday. But tonight, she was tired from work, tired of the conversation, and in need of serious unwinding. Ink turned around, kissed him, and began to take off his clothes.

Sex that night felt different. Without saying a word to each other, it was slow, tender, and silent. No dirty talk, no instructions, just the muted sounds of two people who thoroughly enjoyed pleasuring each other. The biggest difference, unbeknownst to both of them, was eye contact. It wasn't furious or lustful, but it was as if they saw each other for the first time. For Lemat, there was a great desire to drive Ink into an orgasm. Tonight, he did so the first time very slowly. It started out almost like a thin mist, at constant risk of dissolving by so much as a whisper. But like an artist uncovering a masterpiece with each stroke, Lemat guided Ink to a climax that shook her very being.

"Oh, God," she said, shivering. "Christ, you're going to kill me!"

And then it hit him. There it was, the answer to his problem.

CHAPTER FOURTEEN

"Are you out of your mind?" said Dep when Lemat told him his idea the next day over breakfast, if you could call breakfast a teeming bowl of Cocoa Pebbles without milk.

Lemat was so excited by the idea, he could barely sleep the night before. It was only by Ink's repeated ministrations that he finally got some rest out of sheer exhaustion. Now he stood up by the kitchen, too excited to sit as he told everyone about his moment of brilliance. Talia hugged the back of a chair in the living room, while Lisa sat on the small kitchen counter, melting a plastic bottle with a lighter. Dep sat on the couch, stunned by what he had just heard.

"Killing Jesus," Lemat told them the title of the book through a mouth full of cereal. "It's brilliant!"

"I like it," Lisa said. "And they say sex makes men dumb. I can't wait to read the thing—tearing religion a second asshole and getting paid for it? You're my new hero, man."

"Not to mention all the free advertising you'll get from offended religious groups," Talia said. She walked towards Lemat and hugged him from behind.

"I don't think this is a good idea," said Dep, standing up and walking to the center of the living room. "Religion is a very sensitive subject. People are bound to get mad."

"Who cares?" Lisa said. "That's exactly the point, Zoloft."

"Guy is right," Lemat said. "People live in apathy. They'd rather pay five bucks for coffee than shell out ninety-nine cents for a book that took the author enough work to grow his own coffee."

"Still, I don't think this is a good idea," Dep said.

Talia whispered into Lemat's ear, "You know what would be great? If your protagonist actually assumes the role of Christ."

"No, no, no," said Lemat, squirming away from her grasp. "He's just going to kill him in the most prosaic way. End of the story."

Talia smiled in that intoxicating way of hers. "But since he's already going to kill him, maybe he can stumble into his role and gain a greater understanding of what the Christian faith means, from a mortal's point of view."

"No nuance."

"Think about it." She slid a finger down his neck, making the hairs on his back stand. "It would be like revisiting the whole faith from a modern perspective, so it can make sense to us in the 21st century."

"Or, he could fight the living dead, demons, and Roman soldiers, like in *Gladiator*." Lemat scratched his neck and moved on.

He got to work right after breakfast. He banged away on his laptop until he had completed a forty-thousand-word first draft. The novel seemed to be writing itself, not because of his particular skill or creativity, but because the story was as straightforward as they came. Lemat seemed possessed by his newfound goal. He slept only four hours, had no breaks, and seemed to subsist on coffee and takeout meals. When Ink came by to ask him to have dinner with her, he turned the invitation down in lieu of his writing. She understood. In fact, Ink was glad that Lemat seemed to have shaken off the funk.

Talia was always sitting behind Lemat with her arms around him, trying to convince him which direction he should be taking in the book. Lemat would listen to her and then do the total opposite. Her breathy suggestions acted as a red flag. He quickly found this the best way of flowing with his work. Lisa and Dep sat behind them, each on one corner of the couch.

Dep sipped from a can of condensed milk. He looked rather ashen and hallow-eyed, all due to mounting bouts of anxiety. He continued to passive-aggressively voice his discomfort with Lemat's project, until Lisa would get fed up and promptly shut him up.

For her part, Lisa smoked and played with her cheap lighter in a way that could make anyone seeing her uncomfortable about her intentions. She loved the idea of the novel and pushed Lemat to complete it. Her only contribution was to tell Lemat that the end of the book should reflect the utopia the world would be without Christianity. But Lemat wasn't about to get into a socio-theological discourse with his manuscript. He could care less about having a sort of message. This was sensationalism for sensationalism's sake.

The second draft turned into a third and a week turned to four. Dep grew even more disquiet with each passing day. Yet Lemat used his doubts and fears as fodder for his novel. If Dep thought something wasn't a good idea, that's exactly what Lemat would write. Every day, it was getting easier and easier to work on the thing. Lisa was just impatient. She paced around and made a mess of the apartment. Her input was the most valuable. If Lisa liked it, Lemat would type it down. As for Talia, she was just happy to be back home. Lemat loved the company, the warmth and joy she brought inside him. He had no idea what he was doing or if it was working. But one thing was for sure— it was completely different than anything he'd ever done.

Ink kept checking on Lemat every evening after work. She would knock on his door, and Lemat would open it and tell her he was in the middle of something important in his writing. Each time he opened the door, he looked thinner, paler, and his beard grew longer. One day, she went by his apartment, knocked on door, and Lemat slid a note from under the door that read: *Sorry, too busy with writing. Almost done with the final draft. Dinner is on me next time. Lemat.* The note had a clipping of an old rug, acting as a beard. Ink laughed. She thought about giving him a few days before inviting him again for dinner, but something told her it would be a good idea to check on Lemat periodically. She had to admit she was curious about Lemat's idea, but she wasn't sure if she wanted to see its execution.

Lemat finished his final draft after six weeks. He spent the next month sending queries to every literary agent who worked on his book's genre. The task was easier said than done. Every agent wanted a personalized letter—preferably showing that the hopeful author had done some research about the agent and their agency. They wanted intro letters, what market the novel would appeal to, examples of similar books, a synopsis of the work, a bio of the author, and why the author thought the work should be published— all of this with impeccable grammar and spelling. Lemat had to be careful, because some of these agents would not consider any submission that was sent to another agent at the same time, or what he called "multiple submissions." It was considered unjust to the agent and of very poor form. *No problem,* Lemat thought. He would wait for them to give him an answer, but there was a catch—most agents stated on their websites that they might not reply to authors. If you didn't hear from them in about three months, you could consider yourself rejected. Lemat wasn't about to sit on his hands and wait for a probable rebuff. So he just submitted to those agents that had no issue with multiple queries, which amounted to about two hundred between the US, the UK, and Canada. It took a month for Lemat to complete his submissions.

I haven't seen Ink in a while, he thought late one night.

Lemat needed out of the house anyway, so he went to her apartment. With a little bit of luck, she would be up for an early dinner at some 24-hour joint. Lemat climbed up the stairs to the second floor of her building, when her door opened.

What a coincidence, he said to himself, glad that she was up and about.

His happiness vaporized when a guy came out of Ink's door. His fashion sense screamed "musician."

"Hey," the guy said as he walked past Lemat, who replied in kind.

The guy took off down the stairs, leaving Lemat stuck in between going back home or knocking on Ink's door. His mind weighed all kinds of possibilities— maybe he was just a friend, maybe he was helping her with something. Lemat decided he'd rather live with certainty than hope for ambiguity. Or perhaps those were just famous last words? He knocked on her door.

"You know, it would be nice if one time you'd stay for breakfast," Ink said from the other side. Welcome to certainty; population, you.

She opened the door just wearing a baseball T-shirt and bunched up socks. Her hair was sweaty. Lemat's heart froze. She looked amazing, but she didn't look like that for him. "Oh! Hey!" she said. "I thought you were—"

"What did you just say? I'm sorry, I couldn't understand you through the door."

"Oh, nothing. I thought you were someone else."

Lemat's line was meant to protect himself, not to excuse her. Sure, Lemat didn't hear her through the door. And yes, he probably was a second too late to see the other guy leave. Ignorance is bliss. Don't worry; be happy.

"What's up?" Ink said.

"I just wanted to see if you were up for some early bird breakfast."

"I would, but I'm exhausted. Sorry."

Please, God, if you really exist, kill me now, Lemat thought.

"It's OK," he said. "It was a stab in the dark anyway. Things are easing up for me, so if you want to catch up—"

"OK. Great. I'll catch you later," Ink said and waved from her door as he departed.

Lemat walked to his apartment dragging his soul. He closed the door behind him and leaned against it. Lemat looked up, unequivocally convinced that God didn't exist; if he had, he would have pulled the trigger by now.

Meanwhile, three agonizing months passed and the rejection letters started to trickle in, or at least those from the agents who were kind enough to acknowledge Lemat's queries. By and large, they were all standardized emails that were addressed to "Dear author." A few managed to write in Lemat's name. There was no advice for him, either. The large number of missives meant those days were long gone. Only one independent agent managed to write a personal letter explaining the state of the current publishing industry. In a nutshell, it said that nonfiction, especially self-help and celebrity-related, was king, and fiction was relegated to the fringes. Essentially, only established authors managed to get work through. Lemat was very grateful for the advice. That was the exception to the rule. There were other replies that stood out; some had misspellings and grammatical errors. One of them was addressed to some other unlucky author, and another one was a mailed photocopy of a standardized rejection letter, signature and all.

In regards to the Ink situation, Lemat just avoided her. She would come around; Lemat would open the door and tell her that he was busy. He always promised her they would hang out soon, but the timing never seemed to be right. Ink took it all in stride. She was interested in what Lemat was doing and she was always making sure he was all right. Lemat was touched, but he couldn't erase what he witnessed that night. Maybe time would put enough distance between his memory and his pain for them to have a friendship. But time went by.

"So much for talking dollars and cents," Lemat said, sitting by the edge of the building's abandoned swimming pool. He had the printouts of every rejection letter in his hand. Guy stood behind him, looking at the sky as if waiting for divine inspiration.

"That's not a problem," said Guy, taking a cigarette from his silver case. "We'll fall back on Plan B."

"And what's that?" said Lemat, turning around.

"Self-publishing." Guy inhaled the first mouthful of smoke, creating a dramatic pause.

"Great. Now I have to become a publisher. Need I remind you that I'm dangerously close to running out of money and that I need to look for a job? Besides, the work is no good. Nobody wants to represent it."

"Yeah, of course. As if the agents and publishers know anything about quality. Have you ever walked into a bookstore? Well, nowadays it would be kind of hard to find one of those, but still. You have a few hardcovers that they push, the ones by the entrance, and what about the rest? It's filler, that's what that is. Even the quality of their bestsellers are not really that great, so don't worry."

"Why would I? I have no job, no money, and I spent the last five months creating a piece of shit that nobody wants. Nah, I'm cool."

"Trust me. We're going to self-publish *Killing Jesus,* and start a grassroots digital movement to spread the word. Make it 'trend,' in digital parlance. And then we're going to sit back and watch the irate, the trend-followers, and the curious work their magic on our sales. Soon enough, the literary sharks will smell the cash in the water and will come circling around."

"For a self-published novel?"

"Please, they have the principles of a prostitute: they'll go to bed with anyone as long as the money is good."

Lemat couldn't believe his ears. *"Jesus,* that's the worst thing I've ever written. A monkey could have done that."

"And that monkey is about to become a very successful author. You have to understand something: success and quality are not mutually exclusive, and the latter can forgive anything else. You don't need to be good at anything, just popular. That's the beauty of this century. If you say something enough times and loud enough, it becomes the truth. So, go back home, try not to spend a lot of money—a cup of noodles once a day for a month or so won't kill you—and start using those graphic design skills to publish your novel."

"And what if it doesn't work out? What if people don't care or they have the wrong reaction?"

Guy lit up a cigarette. "For our purposes, the worst reaction is always the best reaction."

CHAPTER FIFTEEN

It was another night of lust and abandon. No one could meld with Lemat as well as Talia could. Nothing could satisfy him more than her touch. They didn't talk—not that they needed to—but they consumed each other with famished hunger. It lasted the whole night. In the morning, Lemat sat on the edge of his bed working on his laptop. Talia slept soundly behind him.

He was dealing with the promotion of his novel through social media. It wasn't an easy task. Setting them up was, but reaching an audience was a different story. Everybody has heard words like "sharing," "viral," and "trending," but as for what strange impulse makes people tell their friends about something online, Lemat had no idea. Everybody had something they were selling—an opinion, a service, a novel—the list was endless. How did you stand out from the billions of people all around the world clamoring for attention? In publishing alone, the numbers of (traditional and self-) published books in a given year was estimated to be between six hundred thousand and one million, and that was just statistics in the US.

Compounding the problem was the fickleness of the average Web-surfer. Clips about children and animals were incredibly popular, and so were the ones about people doing dumb or humiliating things. There seemed to be a difficulty-to-popularity ratio: the more work and skill something required, the less popular it was.

Lemat looked at the computer screen while he stretched his neck. He could use a hot shower, some painkillers, and a good night's sleep. His eyes were tired, so he got up to go to the restroom and wash his face. A smell caught Lemat's attention. He sniffed the air a few times and realized it was his torn "Han Shot First" T-shirt. He took it off, threw it in the hamper by the sink, and wrapped himself in his bathrobe. Lemat headed to the kitchen. Even the light of the refrigerator stung his eyes as he searched for a snack. There was a knock on his door.

"Yes?" he said, standing behind it.

"It's me," Ink said.

Lemat opened the door. "Hey! Hi."

"I'm glad to see you're still alive. I haven't seen you in, like, a month. Are we OK?"

Lemat's reaction was a few beats too slow. "Yeah."

"I came by the other day, but I heard you talking with someone."

"I was probably just talking to myself. What's up?"

"I just finished reading your novel and wanted to come by to talk about it."

"Great." Lemat wasn't too convinced he wanted to

hear the opinion of someone he respected talking about something he really didn't care for in the least bit. He knew what the score was, and someone like Ink would not look favorably on the kind of commercially driven gimmick he wrote this time.

"How's the promotion going?"

"It's going."

"Good. Hey, you want to have breakfast? I'm starving."

"Wait, what time is it?"

"It's almost six."

"Damn!" He scratched his head, confirming the time by looking at the microwave's clock. "The sun is going to come out any minute. What are you doing at this time on a Thursday?"

"It's Saturday. And since when am I ever on a schedule?"

"True. Where are we going?"

"I know this café that's open all night. We can take my bike," Ink said.

"Sounds good. You want to talk about the book while I get ready?"

"Breakfast first. Actually, shower first. I'm not sitting in front of you to eat if you're smelling like a gym bag."

After Lemat got ready, they rode all the way to a small diner, "Odds," a café built inside a former firehouse. The décor seemed to come straight out of a garage sale, or stuff left abandoned by the curb. Lemat could see why Ink liked the joint. The bar was made out of surfboards and the tables, out of shipping pallets. No chair was the same; there were folding chairs, office chairs, La-Z-Boys, garden chairs. The only thing they had in common was uniqueness and, surprisingly, comfort.

Ink ordered the corned-beef hash with some French-pressed coffee, while Lemat debated between the huevos rancheros and the steak and eggs. He chose the latter with a triple-shot of cappuccino; he was starving. Lemat decided to wait for their food before they started talking about more serious matters. He was mostly quiet; Lemat wanted to hear anything Ink wanted to say. He was tired of listening to himself talk. Ink somehow felt this, so she played along. She talked about work, about this new design for a tattoo she was working on for no specific client. Ink also wanted to show him some paintings she had been doing, a whole series of café drawings depicting people as Ink imagined they truly were, instead of what they pretended to be. It was all done in red pastels, which she called her "red period," or as Ink liked to put it, "Very vagina-centric, if you think about it." The breakfast with Ink was good for Lemat—it lifted his spirits, and he smiled for the first time in a long time.

"So, what do you think about the story?" Lemat said halfway through their meal. The silence was getting unbearable and he decided it was better to cut his losses and move on.

"I don't know what to tell you. Well, I do. But I don't know how to say it nicely."

"Just say it—I don't care. You know what I'm writing it for."

"Yeah, I know. But, is *this* what you want to be *known* for?"

"I see it as sacrifice in order to achieve what I really want. It's like paying my dues in a way. There's nothing wrong with that."

"No, I understand. But—" Ink tried to find the right words. "I think you've just lost your mind. This is not even—this is not you, at all."

"Well, *me* was going nowhere. This might be my best chance."

"I can see this pissing off a lot of people. And religious nuts are not the most forgiving kind of people." Ink turned her gaze to the computer and read the premise, "'A man travels in time to kill Jesus.' I mean, what the hell are you thinking?"

"I didn't peg you as the religious type."

"Don't be reductive—you know what I mean. I don't mind a good allegory that shows the trappings and flaws of religion, but your novel? I mean, the thing reads like a summer blockbuster."

"Cool! I'm thinking Michael Bay for the film adaptation. What do you think?"

"I think you're nuts. And how the hell did you manage to slip explosions into biblical times?"

"Greek fire."

"What's that? Forget it, I don't want to know. My point is, your other stuff is far better than this, and less…controversial. You can't be serious about this."

"I'm dead serious. Look at it from a purely commercial perspective—it has action."

"Yeah, you treat the Twelve Apostles like *The Dirty Dozen.*"

"It has sex."

"Sure, Mary Magdalene knows the Kama Sutra by heart. Who's going to play her in the movie version?"

"I like the girl from *Zero Dark Thirty.*"

"Nice. And all the demonic possessions and

zombies?"

"For the horror fans," Lemat said.

"Did you at least read the Bible for research?"

"You're missing the point—it's fiction."

"It's a travesty." Ink let her fork fall on her plate. "Forget about the religious angle. Like I said, I have no problem with religious commentary in art—on the contrary. But this? This, it's just crass and asinine. What the fuck has gotten into you?"

"I'm trying to do something new. Attack the problem from a different angle."

"I think the problem attacked you and beat all the common sense from your brain."

"I knew you wouldn't like it." This made Lemat happy.

"What gave you the first clue? Are you seriously going to devote your time and money to this?"

"It's worth a try. And we both know there are worse things being published out there. All I've done is try to maximize my chances of getting noticed, but at the end of the day, this might just fail like everything else I've done. So why worry?"

"You are a better writer than this. Don't pin your hopes on this sad, desperate gimmick."

"Then I can start writing what I really want to write about."

"Really? How can you be so sure? You know you'll be stigmatized as, 'Oh, *that* guy.'"

"You have to get there in the first place to find that out," said Lemat, drinking his coffee as if to put an end to the conversation.

"Fine. It's your work. Do what you want. But if you ask me—which you did—I think you're making a terrible mistake. You have so much more to give than this garbage. You are thoughtful, smart, and well-read."

"And broke and insignificant, without any future prospects."

"You know what I really think?" she said. "I think you're burned out after all these years of trying. Artists go through low periods like that. You just have to hold on tight and weather the storm. It will pass and you will go on to create great things. Don't sell yourself short."

"And when will that be? When I'm fifty?"

"Or eighty. Who cares? Nothing can change the fact that you are a storyteller. Even if you never write another word in your life, you are who you are."

Lemat was a touched. Ink was the only person in his life that treated him like an artist. Throughout his life, Lemat was seen as odd, awkward, clumsy, spacy, even slow, but never artistic.

"This is something I have to do," he said. "I'm tired of failing. If succeeding means that I have to crawl through the mud to do it, so be it. I can't just live the rest of my life wondering if this could have worked out and I just wasted my only chance to make it."

This last statement worried Ink. Lemat had already attempted suicide. His failure as a writer consumed him. Ink quickly realized that this attempt, as crazy and cheap as she thought it was, was better than the alternative. She took a deep breath and looked Lemat in the eye.

"Fine," she said. "Go ahead. Maybe I'm the one that's wrong."

"Then you think it's worth a shot?" said Lemat, relieved that Ink was finally getting on board.

Ink placed her hand on top of his and said, "I don't

support it, but I'll support you."

CHAPTER SIXTEEN

The reaction to *Killing Jesus* started small. And like an avalanche, it careened to an uncontrollable force. After having breakfast with Ink, Lemat continued to work on his book's promotion. He made it a point to come up with at least one idea a day to advertise it, even if it was getting into a forum and shamelessly plugging it.

Lemat sent his novel to be reviewed by anyone that would have it, from bloggers to established reviewers that provided clients with an "indie" service. They were "clients," because you had to pay for the critiques, unlike what common wisdom would dictate. Lemat found out that sometimes he was paying for people to trash his novel. The independent award circuit wasn't kind to *Killing Jesus,* as it was completely ignored. Lemat paid no mind to the bad reviews or the lack of recognition. Every time something like that happened, he just remembered what Guy said and soldiered on.

The first signs of life came from the "comments" section of the diverse web pages. It started out with the obligatory trolls and then a few outraged readers deciding to vent. Like any talk about politics and religion, the opposite side soon made its presence felt. Everything would have been contained within the confines of a few people with a lot of free time insulting each other, until someone decided to carry out their own little crusade.

A small ministry in the heartland caught wind of the novel. Its unequivocal title and iconic cover, with a splash of blood in the silhouette of a cross, made it perfect for Sunday Show and Tell. The firebrand pastor used it to rile up his faithful flock. His followers were understandably appalled and some of them decided to take matters into their own hands, venting their anger on the Web. After a week of pouring out their indignation, a local TV reporter decided to stir the pot and cover the story. The young journalist thought it would be a good way to get some exposure, as self-publishing had been gaining attention in last few years. Perhaps she had stumbled upon a semi-relevant story. The girl's instincts proved to be dead-on. The local coverage went statewide during a slow news day. People started to check out what all the hard blowing was about. They did this by the thousands.

Soon, the sales of the book skyrocketed. Other news outlets began to pick up the story, first online, then in print, and finally by the all-powerful television. Guy's equation of *outrage + curiosity = sales* proved to be quite accurate. Critics' reactions ranged from "daring" and "thought-provoking," to "not worth the paper it's printed on."

Lemat was both shocked and delighted. He and Ink sat in his apartment watching as the sales position of the book on Amazon came closer and closer to the top ten. Ink started to read the reviews and comments for fun; the worse they were, the longer they laughed. She would create a character based on the critique and read it as such. It was a great way to deflect negativity. What wasn't funny was the cash rolling in.

At the beginning, having a few hundred dollars a week was kind of nice. But within a month, Lemat was able to pay his rent and most of his bills. A few weeks after that, he had made enough money that he could finally start adding to his flimsy savings account. And it didn't stop there.

Throughout this time, Lemat saw a lot of Dep and Lisa. Dep was on the verge of a nervous breakdown. All the negative attention was making him jumpy and very paranoid. Lisa seemed happy, vindicated. She loved the attention, wallowing in the good comments and reveling in the bad ones. As for Talia, she just sat around the apartment quite taciturn and melancholy, preferring to watch in silent introspection as everything was developing around her. Lemat couldn't tell if she was sad, shocked, or disappointed at the fact that his dream was finally happening and it had nothing to do with her. As for Guy, well, he had delivered. The chain reaction he had helped unleash was just beginning.

The phone started ringing a couple of times a day and emails were piling up. They were mostly from angry people, but soon the media started calling, and Lemat started to feel uncomfortable. He wasn't used to the attention. Lemat disconnected the phone, deleted emails without reading them, and stopped checking out the comment boards about his book. He spent most of his time at Ink's, as if fearing his place was going to burst with all the complaints and inquiries. He was glad he didn't add his picture to the book.

The first sign of trouble came in the form of a couple of news vans parked in front of the apartment complex. The sight wasn't that rare—reporters often came out to report on the latest drug bust, shootout, or occasional sex offender. Only this time, they were looking for Lemat.

Lemat was just coming back from buying groceries. A few months of coffee, ninety-nine-cent tacos, and ramen noodles had left him with an incredible desire to stock his fridge with all kinds of goodies. This was the first time he could go to the supermarket and basically afford whatever he wanted, although he was limited to the amount he could carry. He stood there dumfounded, holding two massive bags brimming with food. Lemat didn't know what to do. He entertained the notion that maybe the bags could obscure his face enough for him to slip by the reporters. But right on cue, a neighbor walked by and was accosted by the cameras. The woman had to run away from them. Lemat took off in a different direction, trying not to run too fast as to attract attention. He quickly thought of alternative paths to his apartment. They were only two alternatives—the regular way or the back alley he always used—poor odds to avoid being spotted. So Lemat hid in the doorway of a nearby building.

"Hey, if it isn't the man of the hour." The voice spooked Lemat. It took him a few seconds to recognize Mr. Freeman, his cello-playing neighbor. "What are you doing crouching in there?"

"Mr. Freeman, you almost gave me a heart attack."

"Are you all right? Congratulations about the book, by the way."

"Thank you."

"What's going on? Is everything OK?" Mr. Freeman saw the reporters. "Is that for you?"

Lemat nodded.

"Feeling a little media shy?"

"You could say so."

"Oh, it's all right. They're not going to bite. Just go talk to them. That's part of the deal now, you know?"

The fact that Mr. Freeman said "deal" struck Lemat as curious. He tried not to think about what Guy had told him about "paying the price."

"I'd rather not," Lemat said.

"All right, I got your back. Don't worry," the old man said.

Lemat watched as Mr. Freeman walked straight to the reporters, who immediately jumped on him with questions. Mr. Freeman told them that he knew Lemat, that they had been neighbors for many years. He also said he was aware of his newfound success. When he was asked about his whereabouts, Mr. Freeman simply said that Lemat had just moved two days ago. "Wouldn't you?" he said, pointing at the apartment complex with his chin. "That's the first thing I'd do if I ever came to some money."

Frustrated, the reporters asked him a few more questions. No, he didn't know to where Lemat had moved. He just saw him moving his stuff and yes, he was a quiet and very nice guy who kept mostly to himself. After a few more minutes, the reporters let Mr. Freeman go. The reporters refused to believe they were wasting their time, so they hung around for another hour. Fortunately for Lemat, the rest of the people the news team encountered had no idea who he was. So they finally left.

But the media attention on *Killing Jesus* was just beginning.

###

"I think it's a disgrace what this man has done," said a cardinal in the news. "This book should be burnt along with the author. Jesus died for our sins! This man has made a mockery of something every Catholic holds sacred."

And on a religious channel on cable: "That's why we are organizing a book burning this Sunday after service," the pastor said. "So bring all your copies of this filthy work of Satan for our 'Rally For Jesus' book pyre. We of the Christian faith will not stand for this abomination!"

Even the morning talk shows: "So the hot topic everybody is talking about this week is a book titled *Killing Jesus,*" the male presenter said.

"Oh, I thought it was *Killing Jesús,*" said his female counterpart, "like some spicy, Latino romance novel. Muy caliente!" The audience laughed.

"Oh, no! It's *Killing Jesus.*"

"Yikes!"

"And the title says it all. There has been a wave of protests in front of churches around the country. Even the Jewish and Islamic communities have weighed in on the issue."

And of course, the late-night talk shows: "Have you heard about that new book that's causing all that controversy among some religious groups in the country?" the political satirist said during his monologue. "The book is called *Killing Jesus.*" The audience had mixed reactions. "Yeah. I know, I know," the host said. "Spoiler alert! It was science!"

CHAPTER SEVENTEEN

"What are you going to do?" Ink said two weeks later in her apartment.

Lemat peeked out of the window, searching for more reporters. "I need to get out of here."

"And go where?"

"I don't know—away? I need to hide somewhere until this thing blows over."

"That could take a while."

"Not really," he said, sitting on a beanbag meant to look like a hacky sack. "I just need to wait for the next catastrophe, celebrity faux pas, or flare-up in the Middle East."

"Way to see the silver lining of things," Ink said, picking up Lemat's laptop from her makeshift coffee table, an old wooden door. She used the keyhole as an incense holder. "You still not checking your emails?"

"I stopped weeks ago."

"Well, you probably should."

"Why?"

"Here," she said, opening his laptop.

"No, don't!"

"I don't care about your porn."

"That's not what I mean. It's going to take forever to download all that crap from the server."

But Ink just moved away from him. "It's just like getting your shots when you're a kid," she said. "It's painful, but you have to do it. You never know." She watched as the messages started to pile up in the browser.

"Never know what? I don't want to ever know."

"Don't be a child," she said, scanning for anything interesting as the emails kept downloading into the triple digits. The better subjects read, *Shame On You!* The worse ones had headings like, *I hope you die!* and *BURN IN HELL!* And yet, Ink found a few promising emails mixed in the shuffle. "Here we go," she said, clicking them open. She turned the computer around so Lemat could see it. "Voila!"

They were from literary agents and a few from publishers themselves. Lemat's first impression was that this was either a joke or an attempt at cleverness by haters to make him read their venomous rants and death threats.

Ink's lips moved as she read the first one. Silence turned to a murmur that turned louder as she read, "… 'We would like to discuss representing your novel. Please contact us at your earliest convenience.' They want to publish your book!"

"Really?"

"No, they want you to drop dead. Look!" She showed him the email. There were at least forty offers. Lemat couldn't believe his eyes.

"He was right!" he said.

"Who was right?"

"Forget it."

"So?"

"I don't know. I mean, what do I need them for now? I've done all the work and I'm keeping 70% of my profits. If I go with them, I'll only get 10% or less, and for what, exactly? Promotion? I've done better than they have with their top titles, and cheaper, too."

"Maybe they can help you with all this madness," she said, pointing at the emails. "You know, some PR, a little buffer between you and the media."

"Maybe. But right now, I have to find a place to hide while I think of what to do."

"Any friends you can crash with?"

"I don't have those kinds of friends."

"How about staying at the tattoo shop? We open late and nobody is going to look for you there."

Lemat didn't like the concept of living in a tattoo parlor, but Ink had just given him an idea. "No, but I can stay at Fausto's."

"Who?"

"This little bar I used to go to when I was working at my old job. They have a small room in the back I could use."

"Nice. You can hide and drown your woes all at the same time. You think the owner will let you stay there?"

"I've known him for years. I'm sure he won't have a problem with me crashing there for a while."

###

"For how long?"

"A while," Lemat said. They were sitting by the bar, facing each other.

Fausto thought about Lemat's proposition for a moment. "Define 'a while.'"

"I don't know—a few days? I just need a place to hide while I get an agent to help me deal with this madness. After that, I'll be out of your hair, as soon as I can. I promise. You wouldn't even know that I'm here. You know what? I can do something to repay you, give you some cash, help you with the bar—"

Fausto wasn't impressed. He took a long drag from his cigarette, pondering. Lemat had come to him during the day when Fausto was restocking the bar. Lemat looked funny, wearing a hat under a hoodie and sunglasses.

"I don't know, man," Fausto said. "All this heat around you? Why not go to a hotel? You certainly have the money now."

"I can't do that. I'll have to give them my name, a credit card; somebody is bound to find me there."

Fausto kept smoking, contemplating what to do. "No, I'm sorry. I can't let this affect my business. I hope you understand."

Utterly deflated, Lemat opened his mouth as if to say something, but he couldn't. Nothing came out. What was he going to say?

"Nah, I'm fucking with you!" said Fausto, laughing. "Of course you can stay here. Are you sure you're going to be all right?"

Lemat started laughing to release his stress. "You

asshole!"

"I got you good, huh?" Fausto punched him on the shoulder playfully. "You should have seen your face." He mimicked Lemat's expression and kept on laughing. "The room is small, though. You know that. Do you need anything?"

"No, it'll be fine. Thank you. Let's just keep this between us."

"You're among friends. Don't worry. I'll give you a copy of the key to the storage room. That way, you can come and go from the back, so nobody can see you."

"Thanks, man," Lemat said. "Hey, maybe now I can finally buy one of your paintings."

"Let me think about it. If I can find one I'm willing to part with, I'll let you know."

Lemat went to the room. The place was no bigger than a large closet, but it had a bed, a nightstand, and an ancient TV set on top of an equally old VCR. There was a guitar case and a cardboard box full of VHS tapes. A string tied between two walls acted as a hanger, where Lemat hung the clothes from his backpack. No window. It was perfect. He had to run an extension cord from the storage room so he could charge his phone and laptop. As for Internet service, Lemat stole the Wi-Fi signal from a nearby café, just as Fausto did. There was no shower, but Fausto showed him a way he could clean up by using a hose in the back alley. Lemat would have to use the dumpster as a screen. The bathroom was the bar's, no way around that. Although Lemat decided it was better for him to use the one from the café when he went there for breakfast. *This will have to do,* he said to himself. He called Ink to let her know he was going to be staying at the bar.

"Yeah?" A male voice picked up the phone.

Lemat was confused. He checked the screen on his mobile to make sure he had dialed Ink's cell phone. He had.

"Can I speak to Ink?"

"Who is this?"

"Who are *you*?" Lemat pushed back.

Lemat heard some hasty mumbling in the background.

"Hey!" Ink said on the line. "What's up?"

"Who was that?"

"Oh, it was just my friend Grit being stupid. Cut it out!" she said away from the phone.

Lemat felt as if he was falling down a dark chasm. "Grit?"

"He plays guitar in a local band. You should come by one night to catch his show. They're pretty cool."

"…I'm sure."

"So what's up?"

"Fausto was cool with me staying here until things calm down."

"Great!"

"Yeah… so, do you want to grab some dinner?"

"Oh, I can't tonight. Grit is playing at the Pit and then I'm crashing at his place. Let's meet tomorrow."

Lemat found it hard to breathe, let alone speak. He wanted to come up with some sort of excuse not to meet the next day, but he guessed nothing he could say would sound convincing. She knew his day-to-day life too well these days. "Ah… yeah. Let's talk tomorrow and see—"

"All right. Talk to you then."

It took Lemat a few seconds to take the phone off his ear. He was dizzy, deflated. Even when things seemed to go his way, they didn't. Was this Grit the same guy he saw coming out of Ink's apartment that night? *Probably*, Lemat thought. *Maybe they're just friends. Yeah, right! After all, Ink was quite the free spirit. What, did you think you were special? Idiot!*

Lemat busied himself by going through every email from literary agents and publishers. He also deleted the throng of messages wishing for his slow, painful demise.

"At least you got to fuck her a few times," Lisa said, doing the opening break of a pool game with Dep. She had a bottle of tequila and a shot glass next to her.

"Can we not talk about this?" Lemat said.

"Sure." She shrugged. "You're the one whining about exclusivity. If you ask me—"

"I didn't."

"Who cares?" said Talia, walking up to him and wrapping her arms around his neck. "She's just one silly girl. Right now, a whole new world is opening up for you filled with endless possibilities. The last thing you'll ever need to worry about," her hand reached down between his legs, "is this. You'll see."

"OK. Reality check. He's a writer, not a rock star," said Dep, leaning against the wall and holding a beer. Lisa's dagger stare made him recheck himself. "What I meant was, it's not like he'll be The Beatles or anything."

"The book is just the beginning of his creative empire," said Talia. "He's famous now. Girls are the least of his problems."

"Princess Lust-A-Lot has a point," Lisa said. "Forget about Ink. That chick is old news."

"I like her," Dep said as he served Guy a beer. "She's nice and cool and fun."

"Yeah. I'm sure she's having a lot of fun with Dongs N' Poses right now," Lisa said. "What? Oh, 'cause I'm sure they're just working on her singing voice." She imitated a blowjob. Lemat was not amused.

"Don't let it get to you, kid," Guy said from the bar while sipping twelve-year-old single-malt scotch. His jacket was off and his tie and vest were undone. "You have bigger fish to fry. Your career is about to take off. The last thing you want is to be chained down by some flaky broad. Keep her around as long as she's useful. Then—" Guy aped blowing something off from the palm of his hand. "Your writing comes first."

"Seriously, can we talk about something else?" Lemat said.

"Fine. So you're going to sell out all the way with this publisher thing, aren't you?" Talia said. She sat in a booth while nursing a glass of red.

"It doesn't hurt to look at my options," Lemat said.

"I don't see how selling out to some asshole, who didn't care about you when you didn't have two cents to rub together, is a viable option," Lisa said while chalking her cue stick.

"It would free him from all the tired menial work, so he can focus on being creative," Guy said.

"Sure. He does all the work so some opportunistic dickhead can swoop in and take a huge piece of the pie for doing absolutely nothing," Lisa said.

"Language, please. He's a writer, not a bean-counter," Talia said lazily.

"You are absolutely right, doll," said Guy, lighting up one of his smokes. "Getting an agent and a book deal is his safest bet. That way, you do what you do best and let someone else figure out the details."

"Are you kidding me?" Dep said. "Am I the only one who's actually worried about what's going on?" He scratched his forehead right next to his ever-present Band-Aid.

"Probably," Talia said.

"Look at the mess he's in now. We can't even go home," Dep said. "I said, 'This isn't a good idea,' but did anybody listen? Nooooo! Nobody ever does."

"And yet, you keep flapping your pie hole," Lisa said.

"Dep does have a point," Lemat said.

"No, he doesn't," Guy said. "Relax! This is just a small price to pay when you hit the big time."

"Let's just hope the big time doesn't hit him right back on the nose," Dep said.

"I say, fuck 'em," Lisa said as she missed her shot. "Your turn, Tears for Fears."

"You always say that, honey," Talia replied.

"And I'm always right," Lisa said. "You have a good thing going now. Don't let The Man come in a take a dump on all of it."

Dep missed his shot, almost scratching the table. "Look where we're squatting now. Does this look like fun to you? We're basically fugitives."

"Well, boohoo! Stop bitching already," Lisa said.

"I say you find some gofer to take care of the minutiae and focus on your next project," Talia said. "You need to wash off the taste of that insipid novel."

"We'll see," Lemat said. "What's the harm in

checking these offers out?"

All he was planning to do was to sit in front of these agents and publishers and listen to what they had to offer. He could probably play some hardball since the interest in him was so high. So, he thought he was in a great position to make the best of the situation. He started making a list of all the folks who had already reached out to him.

CHAPTER EIGHTEEN

The hours went by, but Lemat didn't notice. He was too busy with more of his promotion work and enjoying the feeling that he was safe from media scrutiny, at least for now. When Fausto came back, Lemat thought he had forgotten something.

"It's 5:30," said Fausto, amused. "Time to let the patrons crawl in."

Clover showed up fifteen minutes later, and then one by one, the rest of the usual characters, with the exception of Specs, settled into the joint.

"Well, but if it isn't the country's favorite heretic!" Tails said.

"What did I tell you? Lemat is no Specs," Fausto said. "Fame and fortune don't change a true artist."

"Congratulations, Lemat. I read your book. Pretty ballsy," Heads said. "I laughed out loud on a few occasions."

"Thanks," Lemat said.

"Yeah, I'm not much of a reader myself, but I'm

sure it's great," Tails said.

"What are you drinking? It's on the house," Fausto said with gold tooth shining.

"Well, now I can actually afford it," said Lemat.

"And that's why I can afford to give you a freebie," Fausto said as he winked.

"The usual," Lemat said.

"Ah! Nice and cheap—my kind of giveaway!" Fausto poured a beer.

"Don't be cheap," Clover said. "This isn't the kind of thing that happens everyday. Let's have a round of shots on the house."

Fausto served tequila shots—the cheap kind—to everyone, in honor of Lemat's success. "To Lemat, another artistic luminary that has graced this humble establishment."

"You should put a plaque on the wall," Durango said as he raised his glass.

"Here's to you, honey," Clover said.

After the shots were downed, Lemat held court over a few pints as he answered questions about the novel, his overnight success, and the crazy emails he was getting. The others regaled him with their stories of when they heard about the book.

Fausto had read all about it in the newspaper one morning. "And it was a good thing," he said. "Because otherwise, I would have shit myself." Yet, he confessed that he didn't read the novel.

Heads found out while browsing the Internet one night. "I was searching for a new book to read, when a site about you popped up. It wasn't flattering."

"Tell the truth—you were looking for porn," Tails said.

"You're the one always jerking off," Heads said, concerned about what Clover would think of him.

"Whatever. You were looking for 'naughty priests,' and bumped into *Killing Jesus,*" Tails said.

"Fuck off," Heads said.

"Hey, hey! Don't make me bring out the hose on you two," Fausto said.

Durango heard about Lemat's newfound fame on the radio; some AM program was weighing in on the controversy surrounding the book. Durango spent the rest of the day telling his passengers that he knew the author and lectured them about the history of the Catholic Church while expounding on theology in general, even to a priest he took to the airport.

Durango claimed he had written a novel a long time ago, which nobody could ever find—Heads had hunted for it on the Internet. It was allegedly about a romance between a Contra and a Sandinista in the Nicaragua of the 1980s, a kind of Romeo and Juliet with political overtones, "And prose that could make Gabriel García Márquez weep," Durango asserted. So tonight Durango wore the hat of the Shakespearean scholar and harangued Lemat on how the written word should be the highest form of art; this, despite his confession that he didn't read Lemat's book either.

"I don't read fiction," Durango said. "What you need to do for your next novel is to start working on the first paragraph until you get it down perfect and then move to the next, and so on. You do that and you'll never have to worry about rewrites. That's for amateurs."

Lemat just nodded and smiled at every piece of ill-conceived advice; he was just too happy tonight.

Clover found out about Lemat's novel through a magazine. It was a small article dealing with the popularity of self-publishing and the few indie authors who had managed to find success. Lemat was mentioned as the most recent example. Clover went online, downloaded a copy to her digital tablet, and read the entire work in one sitting.

"I loved it," she said. "It totally spoke to me because I'm a spiritual person, but I don't care for organized religion either. In fact, I don't think Jesus ever existed. I think he's more like Sherlock Holmes or Robin Hood, you know? A make-believe character to teach people something. He's too perfect. And all those powers? It's a little bit like a comic book, don't you think?"

Lemat hated his book, but he had to admit it was incredibly refreshing to find someone interested in his work. He rarely had a chance to talk about it, especially with a person so clearly taken by it. He was enjoying the adulation.

"I bought a paperback copy of your book for you to sign," Clover said. "Do you mind?"

"I would love to," Lemat said.

"Oh, great! Don't let me forget to bring it out when the rest of these characters head out."

This was a happy moment indeed. Lemat didn't have to think or worry about anything; he just had to be himself.

The night was rather enjoyable, but like anything entertaining, it passed way too fast. Everyone laughed and got drunk. And one by one, just as they had arrived, the regulars at Fausto's began to leave. Fausto asked Clover if she could close for the night. She didn't mind.

It occurred to Lemat that Fausto must have told Clover that he was sleeping in the bar for a few nights.

"Shall we call it a night?" Clover said.

"I think my brain checked out a few hours ago," Lemat said as he gulped the last of his beer.

He helped Clover put away the dirty mugs and glasses, locked the front gate, and turned the outside lights off.

"Remember to give me the book so I can sign it," Lemat said.

"I didn't forget. It's in the back. Come with me."

They walked in the cramped back storeroom, where Clover always kept her purse, a cheap leather knockoff of some famous designer. She produced Lemat's novel, a chewed-up pen, and handed it over, all the while beaming up at him like some adoring fan. Lemat hunched over a case of beer and signed the copy.

"Here you go," he said as he turned around, only to bump foreheads with Clover, who had leaned in close to witness his signature. She groaned ever so gently and then suddenly assaulted his lips.

This wasn't a friendly peck but a downright meeting of tongues. Lemat held her close, but he didn't know how far to go. Clover decided for him when she pushed him away and threw off her top to reveal her breasts. She undid his pants, hastily pulled them down, and said, "I've never been with a true artist before. You're just brilliant." And with that, she proceeded to give him the best blowjob of his life. Lemat had to push her off before she brought him too close to orgasm. Clover took the action as a clue that it was time to get busy. She and Lemat fumbled into position and he took her from behind against some boxes of Jack Daniels.

Her tramp stamp—a heart with wings—gained a whole new meaning from this perspective.

"Pull my hair!" she said while moaning approvingly as he obliged. It was the kind of frantic sex born out of reckless impulse, lust finally finding a way out. It was cramped, noisy, sweaty, and exquisitely shameless.

She came loud, almost knocking the boxes of whiskey off the shelf. Clover turned around and kissed him with such aggression, she almost made his lips bleed. She kicked off her boots and freed herself form her lowered jeans.

"Come here!" She ripped his T-shirt off and pulled him close with her legs.

Lemat entered her again. She demanded he go harder. A pile of boxes descended upon them, breaking some bottles, but that didn't halt the action. Lemat enjoyed Clover's tits as she held his face against them.

"I'm gonna come!" she said. "Don't stop! Don't stop!"

Lemat struggled to keep up the frantic pace for what seemed an eternity, and when he felt he couldn't go on anymore, a couple more boxes tumbled over them and then they were spent. After a few moments, they looked at each other.

"Maybe you can help me close the bar again sometime," she purred, satisfied with the encounter and hungrily kissing Lemat.

They both got dressed and said their good nights. It was too late for Lemat to go outside to the back alley and shower with a garden hose. He lay down on the bed, looked up at the ceiling, and said aloud, "Shit!" The statement was either a celebration or an indictment of what just happened. Lemat wasn't sure. Part of him was excited by the liaison; the other part felt guilty because of his feelings about Ink.

Get real! She's getting busy with that asshole tonight and you know it! he told himself. *But what if she was telling the truth and they were just friends?* Lemat didn't buy it. He wanted to, but if he did, what would that make him now?

"I'm a fucking idiot," he said.

"No, you're not," said Talia, lying next to him in the small bed while caressing his chest. She grinned with satisfaction. "Did you enjoy that, my love?"

"Oh, yeah."

"Well, congratulations—you just had your first groupie." She kissed his cheek and parted the hair from his face. "And this is just the beginning, baby. Everybody is about to find out just how wonderful you are."

Lemat didn't feel so wonderful.

CHAPTER NINETEEN

"—You are wonderful. Absolutely brilliant," said Silvio Kneeler, owner of the Kneeler Agency. "Everybody here thinks so."

Lemat tried not to focus too closely on the man's hair plugs. Everything in his office seemed to be compensating for his small stature, even his nose.

"Your novel is like lightning in a bottle; the kind of manuscript that comes around once in a lifetime. It's pure genius. And under the right management, we can make this one of the biggest bestsellers in the world. This isn't just a book, it's an event, a pop-culture touchstone."

The Kneeler Agency had rejected his novel not two months ago. Everyone had. Same book, same author, but now Lemat was a "genius" and his novel an "opus." He had been flown to New York on the agency's dime. Since the publishing business was based in the city, Lemat was going to spend the entire week there going to meetings, twice a day. Once again, Guy had nailed it on the head.

"I'm afraid you're a little too late," said Ink.

Lemat had asked her to come along with him to meet agents. He was too nervous to do it himself and he wasn't fond of planes. As it turned out, Ink had a knack for negotiation. They had never talked about what happened that evening—Lemat didn't want to know if Grit was her lover, nor did he want her to know that he had gotten gritty with Clover. They met the following day as if nothing had happened and moved on with whatever their relationship was.

"The novel is doing well," Ink said. "Lemat gets 70% of his profits, owns all the rights, and has the freedom to do what he wants. I don't see how you can make him a better offer."

Lemat was pleasantly surprised that Ink had done her homework and could "walk the walk."

"Exposure," Kneeler said. "We can reach a wider market share and give the novel the kind of exposure it needs. I mean talk shows, book readings, book signings, conventions, major publications, and top reviewers. That's the kind of access we're talking about."

"But he already got offers for all of that," she said. "If it's just a matter of exposure, then all he really needs is a press agent."

Kneeler smiled condescendingly and said, "It's not that easy. You need someone who understands the ins and outs of the publishing industry and the market. We've been doing this for a very long time. Rights, especially international rights, are tricky negotiations. You may think you're making all this money by cutting the middleman out of the equation, but the truth is, you'll be losing more money by doing a bad deal; same thing with movie or TV rights. Those guys are stone-cold cutthroats. You need to be smart about these things."

"So what's your offer?" Ink said.

"We can talk numbers later, but I can assure you no one will be able to beat it. We want Lemat to go back to what he does best—writing amazing books. Let us worry about all the boring details. You're an artist," he said to Lemat. "You don't want to deal directly with a publisher."

"Why?" Lemat said.

"They're just going to take advantage of you. They're in the business of making money by selling books, not looking out for authors. That's our business."

"To sell authors?" Ink said.

The agent laughed. "To look after them. That's how we make our money, by making you money."

"All right," Lemat said. "Well, thank you for your time, Mr. Kneeler. We have other offers we want to explore before making a decision."

"Let me save you some time," said Kneeler. "I think it's wise for you to weigh your options, so go ahead. But I guarantee you, no one is going to get you a better deal or be in your corner like we will."

"OK," Lemat said. "Thank you."

They left the meeting to visit the Museum of Modern Art. Lemat was glad that Ink decided to come with him to New York. The people paying the bills didn't seem to care about Lemat bringing a plus-one. And that was great for him; New York could be an intimidating city with its crowds and hectic energy. At least when they were done meeting agents, Lemat and

Ink could enjoy the sights. They particularly liked finding stores or restaurants that were open at odd hours of the night. It wasn't out of a sense of urgency that they visited these places—it was just because they could. The following day, it was back to listening to more sweet promises from agents dying to get a piece of *Killing Jesus.*

That morning, they met an owner of another major literary agency, Victoria Gutenberg, a peroxide blonde with a classy boob job and a Botox obsession. She was dressed all in black, very NYC. The problem was that Lemat and Ink associated the meeting with a fancy funeral. Lemat wore his only sports jacket (over his faithful ragged sweater), jeans, and high-top Converse. Ink looked rather cute in a little black dress and Doc Martens. It was their meeting "uniform."

"You've done great for a self-pubbed author. There's no doubt about that," Ms. Gutenberg said. "But let's be realistic for a moment: do you want to write and reap the benefits of your property? Or would you rather deal with distributors, chase after people for payment, design book covers, and the like?"

It seemed that everybody was reading from the same script. Victoria's language was peppered with terms like "property," "market share," "profit margins," and "franchise." The MBA diploma from a highly regarded university (hanging next to her equally impressive one for her English B.A.) explained a lot. Victoria didn't realize it, but she and Lemat had met a few years before, during a book convention. At the time, she was working as an acquisition editor for one of the five major publishing houses in the country. Lemat had approached her about a crime novel he had written. The exchange went something like this:

Her: "Do you have an agent?"

Him: "No."

Her: "I assume you have a copy of the manuscript with you?"

Him: "Yeah."

Her, rolling her eyes: "You're one of those. Let me save you a lot of walking. No one is going to talk to you unless you have an agent."

End of exchange.

"Your novel is doing well now by self-publishing standards," Ms. Gutenberg said, "but we recognize the great potential your work has."

"Actually, my book has been doing better than any mid-level author's," Lemat said, referring to any professional writer who wasn't a household name. "And every day, it's exponentially growing. LitBuzz predicted that I'll be competing with the likes of Grisham at this rate."

"It could, but we are the ones who can actually get you there," Ms. Gutenberg said. "Vanity press is good and nice to satisfy a literary itch, but nobody really wants to be a self-published author. If you are serious about becoming a writer, you have to play with the pros."

"He's already a writer," Ink said. "What we're discussing here is the possibility of you representing his wildly successful vanity project—one that your agency had already turned down, I'd like to point out."

"Really? How embarrassing. I can guarantee you it wasn't from me. Well, you have to understand that we deal with thousands of submissions every month; mistakes are bound to happen. We're only human, after all. And we're not talking about your older work. Obviously, all that effort has molded you into a better writer, wouldn't you agree?"

They were better books, Lemat thought bitterly. Everything he had pitched before was far superior to the shameful cry for attention he had created. "I'm the same guy," he said. "Same writer, same creativity. Nothing really has changed."

"That may be, but now you have a big hit on your hands," Ms. Gutenberg said. "We're talking about VIP treatment. Any publishing house would throw its support 100% behind your work. You also need to think about your future, your career as a writer. What about your next project? You need someone who can help you navigate the publishing world successfully. Let us do that for you."

The meeting was over. The rest of them were similar as the feeding frenzy around *Killing Jesus* grew more harried. Literary agents tried to outdo each other. Publishers were locked in a bidding war for the rights to publish the book. Offers were coming from overseas as well. Even Hollywood made haste to secure the movie rights. All of this worked in Lemat's favor, but he was overwhelmed and he knew he had to make a choice soon.

His trip to New York went from five scheduled days to ten. The answer finally came in the form of Don "The Don" Maxfield, anglophile überagent from the eponymous Maxfield Literary Agency. He could be described in two words: classic elegance. His office was a perfect example of nouveau chic.

The Don was both reviled and revered within publishing circles. He was a legend; a man that the *New*

York Times had once called "a literary alchemist" because of his ability to turn paper into gold. He was behind the success of Pulitzer Prize winners and Nobel laureates, as well as a myriad of international bestsellers. His one regret in life was not being born in the 1920s, as he was convinced he would have represented Ernest Hemingway, the F. Scott Fitzgeralds, H.G. Wells, and T.S. Eliot, among others.

"Your novel is literary drivel," said The Don. "But it's the kind of compost that yields oodles of revenue. It can fetch you six figures at the very least. That's not counting the fated offer from the chaps in Tinseltown. Points and hard cash are usually their spiel. Alas, the latter might come as a bit of a disappointment in the amount it will produce." He puffed on his pipe rapidly, trying to match the speed of his thoughts. "Be that as it may, there's a heap of trouble regarding your public standing and no easy answers about how it shall be swayed."

Lemat was sure The Don was speaking English, but felt like he needed subtitles. He already liked two things: (1) the man recognized bad writing and wasn't afraid to say it, and (2) he was concerned with the blowback from the novel's controversy. It was a great way to start the meeting.

"Can I borrow a pen?" Lemat said.

"A writer without a pen?" The Don said. "A worshiper of the keyboard, am I to infer?"

"It's not for writing."

The answer intrigued The Don. He took the fountain pen from the base on top of his desk and handed it to him. Lemat started to twirl it away. Ink cringed but made no movement and held her tongue.

She wouldn't have if she knew it was a Montblanc Patron of Art Series Louis XIV Limited Edition that fetched about five grand.

The Don said, "Insolent sign or character peculiarity?"

"Artist eccentricity," Ink said.

"Charming," The Don said. "Please forgive my frankness, but I'd like to state my case. I want to represent you, not your novel. I can certainly grant you excellent returns and iron out the wrinkles of your media presence. I can do this and other things, because that's what I do, and I do it better than most. But if I do this, it's for the long haul. I don't waste my time with one-hit wonders, no matter how catchy the hit. I'll take you for no less than three manuscripts to be rendered in a predisposed timeframe."

"Three novels?" Lemat said.

"No less. Your work—crass as it may be—has tremendous commercial appeal. Finding a publisher that wants to profit from your future offerings will be simple. It's a small price to have me in your corner, carefully crafting your career and nurturing an adoring readership."

Why not? Lemat thought. He certainly had the body of work to fulfill that demand ten times over. And as far as his research showed, he couldn't do better than having Don Maxfield. When everything was said and done, he would have a name and a following. Lemat could then decide what he wanted to do with his career. At least by then, he would have one.

"I think we can work together," Lemat said.

"In that case, welcome to the world of publishing, old chap," The Don said, shaking his hand.

A contract was signed. Ink had the unshakable feeling she was witnessing a momentous occasion, and she was happy Lemat had brought her along to see it. As much as Ink was thrilled that Lemat was getting ahead financially, her biggest wish for him was simply to be happy. There would be plenty of time later for both of them to dwell on the coming events. Right now, it was time for celebrating.

Ink made a call to a friend when they left the building. She hailed a cab and took Lemat to the Village. When he asked what was happening, she said, "It's a surprise." Whatever it was, it lay inside a tiny piercing-and-tattoo parlor in a street-access basement. The guy who owned it knew Ink from her days as a struggling actress in New York. This came as news to Lemat. She had asked him if she could please use his shop to do a special tattoo.

"Wait a minute. You're not serious," said Lemat.

"This is important," she said. "Come on, don't be a pussy."

"Nooo, thank you. I'm not into tattoos. No offense," he said to the owner.

The guy didn't care.

"This is not just some tattoo," she said. "It's special. We have to commemorate the occasion."

"Then take a picture."

"Trust me."

Fucking hell! Lemat thought. The sincerity in her eyes was hard to resist. How couldn't he trust her? And then again, they weren't even an item. It was a moot point—relationship or not, Ink had become Lemat's best friend.

"Fine," said Lemat as he sat down. "Couldn't you

have waited until I was really drunk?"

"Alcohol thins the blood down. I don't want to make a mess."

"Blood?"

"Really? Coming from you? Just stay seated."

Ink worked on Lemat's left wrist for about an hour. The needle from the tattooing machine seemed to burn rather than sting. Lemat thought it painful, but he tried not to show it. There was some blood, but it was minimal. Ink kept wiping it off, so it would not interfere with her work. When she was done, Lemat had a small tattoo of a snake eating its own tail, below to the scar on his wrist. The tattoo was very intricate for its size. Lemat didn't know this, but it had required a good deal of skill from the artist. The fact that the owner of the parlor was impressed gave Lemat a clue about Ink's craftsmanship.

"It's an ouroboros," she said, "an ancient symbol that represents the cycle of nature, life and death and rebirth." Ink put a large patch on top of it, gave him the usual instructions to take care of it, and they took off.

They decided to walk from the Village all the way to Times Square, hitting every bar on the way for a tequila shot. They laughed and gabbed and imagined what would happen next with Lemat. Their journey ended at a small and inconspicuous Japanese restaurant in the basement of a building. The place had no signs to advertise its presence, but it had no shortage of patrons. Most of them were chefs themselves, looking for a good meal and a quiet place to unwind at a late hour after a long day of work. Ink had heard of it from a friend who used to work in a restaurant in the city. This wasn't a sushi joint, but a place that served treats such as octopus meatballs and grilled squid.

By the time they were through, Lemat and Ink were too drunk, too wired, and too happy to go back to the hotel. So they found a music club near the restaurant, another business in a basement, which seemed to be the night's theme. Tonight's band played a strange medley of classic-rock songs in funk rhythm. They would Frankenstein a line from a David Bowie song, with a solo from Jimmy Hendrix, and then transition to something from the Stones. Lemat challenged Ink to see who could name the songs that made up the set first. The winner would pay for the drinks. She kicked his ass.

Sometime after three in the morning they stumbled into their hotel room, shushing each other, but that just made them laugh more. Lemat started to take Ink's clothes off.

"What do you think you're doing?" she said.

"I don't know about you, but I'm having sex tonight."

"Really? You think you can rise to the challenge, drunkie?"

"Already there, sister."

"Well, let me take care of you, Mr. Author. I'm not sure how well this is going to end for me with you under the influence."

"Aye, aye, captain."

She pushed him over to the bed and straddled him. The soft warmth inside her felt heavenly.

"Somebody was ready, too," he said.

"Right when we got in the cab," she said, riding him.

Ink may have been a skilled artist, but as far as sex

was concerned, she was a master. She knew how to enjoy herself and make it joyous for her partner. No intricate gymnastics, just the classics. This had been the greatest day of Lemat's life.

"You alive there?" Ink said when they were nuzzling afterwards.

"Barely. You know, I didn't ask you. What is this Chumbawamba supposed to mean?"

"Ouroboros."

"Yeah. Why did you choose it?"

Ink took his wrist and rubbed his scar with her thumb. "I was thinking of giving you something special. Depending on how things went with the meetings, of course. I didn't really know what to do, but I wanted to do something symbolic. This just came to me right at that moment."

"So are you trying to say I should get my head out of my ass?"

"It's a reminder," Ink said, laughing. "For every beginning, there's an end, and for each end, a new beginning."

CHAPTER TWENTY

Don Maxfield made a hefty six-figure deal with Billhook Book Company, one of the top publishing houses in the country. Lemat's self-published version had to stop being offered to the public posthaste. An editor was assigned to shape up the manuscript and a professional graphic artist was hired to design the book. Lemat didn't care about the editor; he'd just go along with everything she'd say. A polished turd was still just a shiny piece of shit.

But the hiring of the "professional graphic designer" really hurt him. The way he saw it, the original design was done by a professional—him. It was a slap in the face, particularly because what the other person did looked just like every other book out there. The worst part was that Lemat had no say in any of these things. The publisher sent him the final art as a courtesy. When Lemat called them about it, they said, "Don't worry about it. We know what we're doing." Lemat told himself to forget it.

Why do you care? he thought. *Later on, you'll have enough clout to do your own thing.*

On the positive side, Lemat was elated when he received a hardcover copy of his novel. Even in the digital era, Lemat thought every author should see his work in hardcover. There was something about it that seemed to announce to the world that he was an author, even though the premise was preposterous.

The money Lemat received was put to good use. He moved to a new building in a better neighborhood and a larger apartment with much nicer things inside: two bedrooms, two bathrooms, a large kitchen, and an ample living room. It wasn't a loft, but it was spacious. Lemat designated one room as his home office. Ink helped him decorate the place by going to garage sales, antique stores, and everywhere else that had furniture that wasn't mass-produced, or required instructions to assemble.

The move was bittersweet. Lemat never thought leaving his apartment would be an emotional affair. He had been living there for a long time. There would be no more nights on the rooftop, no more kamikaze F-bombs, no more cello music when he walked back from work, and no more Ink as a neighbor. *Change is always hard,* Lemat reminded himself, closing the door behind him. He said goodbye to Mr. Freeman, who was very happy for Lemat's success. What he would never tell Lemat was that as a devout Christian, Mr. Freeman found his novel abhorrent and offensive. But he believed that everything, including things he frowned upon, were all part of God's greater plan, and that forgiveness was one of the strongest foundations of his faith. Mr. Freeman played "When You Wish upon a

Star" as Lemat walked away from his place for the last time.

Meanwhile, the news about the acquisition of *Killing Jesus* and its lucrative deal hit the media like a brick through a store window. The outrage had just gone all the way up to eleven. Now even politicians from the conservative right weighed in on the issue, looking to "activate their base" and gain favor with like-minded swing voters. There was nothing better than a good crusade against some asinine paper dragon. It was easier than addressing real problems.

The liberal left stood on the sidelines, emasculated as usual. Too afraid to make a stand for freedom of speech because, God forbid, some voters would run away from them to the other side. When asked by the press about the novel and its implications, their answers were neither here nor there, if not altogether nonexistent. As far as Lemat was concerned, the threat level had also gone up a few notches. It ranged from angry Internet rants to the occasional interview gaffe.

Newscaster: "Congressman, what do you think about the novel *Killing Jesus* getting a six-figure deal from a major publishing house?"

Texan congressman: "I think somebody should drag the writer outside and put him out of his misery."

The congressman would later issue an apology, saying that he was taken out of context. He was joking, and he was sure that no person in his right mind would think he was really endorsing violence. But all of these comments were taken very seriously, as Lemat was about to find out.

The doorbell to his new apartment rang. Lemat was alone, putting some books away. He couldn't believe how much crap he had accumulated in his tiny apartment until he moved. At least now he had plenty of space to organize them properly. Lemat went to the door, thinking it was Ink, since nobody buzzed the intercom. But then again, she had a copy of the key, so why would she be ringing the bell? The answer was a six-foot-six African-American man with a shaved head and a linebacker build. He was dressed in a black suit, no tie, and dark shades. But the one thing that caught Lemat's attention was the silver crucifix hanging from the man's massive neck.

"Are you Lemat?"

Lemat's blood drained from his face. It was obviously a rhetorical question; the man knew perfectly well who was standing in front of him.

"… Can I help you?" Lemat entertained the thought of slamming the door on the man's face for a second.

"My name is Roderick Mason III, but you can call me T-Rex."

"OK."

"I was hired by Mr. Maxfield out of New York. It seems there's some crazy heat on you, and he wants me to provide some peace of mind."

"You're a bodyguard?"

"Personal protection specialist."

"Right. Er… listen, I'm fine. My mind is at peace and everything, so—"

"That's not really up to you. Mr. Maxfield would feel better if I hung around while you go on your book's promotional tour. Do you mind if I check out the premises?"

"No… I mean, come on in."

T-Rex started to assess the apartment's security risks as he spoke. "I was an army MP with two tours in Iraq. I worked for LAPD for ten years in the Metro division. I was in the bomb squad and SWAT. I also have a third degree black belt in Brazilian Jujitsu. I've been working in the private sector for five years with a flawless record. Anybody gives you as much as the evil eye, and they'll need a proctologist to remove my foot from their ass."

"That's good—"

"Is it only you living here? Anybody else have access to this place?"

"My friend, Ink, comes over sometimes."

"Don't worry, you can have as many 'friends' as you like. I know how it is. Trust me. I've worked for some major celebrities and I've seen just about everything. You get to see a lot of things in this line of work. Don't worry, everything will be confidential."

"Sure."

"Everything seems fine here. Nice pad."

"Thanks."

"I'm going to need a copy of your personal schedule, places you like to frequent, people you're regularly in contact with, and who else is allowed on the premises. Mr. Maxfield will be sending me your promotional tour schedule when ready. Basically, I go where you go. I'll drive you around, fly with you, keep people away, and I'll stay on the sidelines when you're doing interviews and such. Let me be the bad guy; that's what I get paid for. You don't want to sign an autograph or talk to someone? I'll handle it. You want some honey to get up close and personal? You let me know. If I tell you to do anything, don't give me no lip, just do it. I see things and situations you won't. That's what I do. You just have to trust me. Are we clear?"

"Uh-huh."

"Good! Any questions?"

"Are you sleeping here, too?"

"No. I don't do that unless the situation calls for it. You're all right, though. Don't worry about a thing. That's what I'm here for."

T-Rex left just as abruptly as he had arrived. A dumbfounded Lemat called Don Maxfield to get an explanation. The Don was glad that T-Rex came by to check out his place. He said it was just a safety measure due to all the negative blowback the novel was generating around the country. "Good for business, bad for health," Don said. He just wanted to make sure no religious wacko got any ideas regarding Lemat's physical or mental integrity.

When Lemat told Ink about T-Rex that night, she was understandably worried.

"Why would they think it's necessary?" she said.

"It's just insurance," Lemat said. "I actually feel better knowing he'll be around as I travel the country plugging my book."

Lemat was in contact with Don a lot during the weeks leading to the promotional tour. The agent advised him to get a new wardrobe. "We want nihilistic-formal," Don said. "Intellectual, but creative; artistic, yet chic. Get that firecracker of a girlfriend of yours to give you a hand with that."

Ink didn't need the agent's blessing or prompting. She was already taking Lemat to vintage stores to upgrade his look, and having a ball with it. It took them about a week to get used to the ubiquitous presence of

T-Rex. The bodyguard knew his business all right. He was largely unobtrusive, aside from a few suggestions of seating arrangements at restaurants, and keeping some privacy while at a store. It was a strange sight to see two unassuming people accompanied by a hulking, sharply dressed guard. He seemed to hit it off with Ink better than Lemat. They started bonding when she asked T-Rex for his opinion about Lemat's threads.

"Nah, man. You look like you're asking for change down at the pier," T-Rex said about one of Lemat's choices. "Listen to your lady."

Changes aside, Lemat and Ink were having a lot of fun together building Lemat's new life. Yet some things remained the same. On most afternoons, they still sat in Lemat's living room eating takeout, watching reruns of their favorite shows, and talking about their day. The other cause for happiness was Lemat's celebration at Fausto's, shortly after his return from New York.

Fausto closed the bar for the night. "Private party," he proudly said to anyone who cared to ask. Everybody was there: Mr. Freeman, Big Mick, the Coin brothers (Tails had brought a date with him), Caesar Durango (who that night was an investment management expert), and Clover. The only one missing was Specs, who was still off somewhere in la-la land. T-Rex acted as the doorman for the evening. Fingerless Joe was hired as the night's entertainment. Lemat paid for everything.

Everyone was having a good time. At one point, Lemat sat back and contemplated the scene. A lot of things had changed, fast. And Lemat couldn't help but wonder what else was in store for him.

CHAPTER TWENTY-ONE

Don Maxfield was planning to play Lemat's exposure for all it was worth and hit as many markets as possible. Lemat wasn't thrilled with having his mug plastered everywhere, but he reasoned that this was now part of his job. Even though he thought his book, not him, should be the center of attention.

Because he liked to travel light, Lemat had packed a carry-on suitcase and took only the essentials. Everything seemed to be ready to go, except he still had one last thing to do, just one phone call to make.

"¿Aló?"

"Aló. ¿Mamá?"

"¡Hijo! ¡Que alegría!" Lemat's mother said.

"How are you? We haven't spoken in a while."

After exchanging pleasantries with his mother, Lemat finally broke the news. "Well, guess what? Your boy finally made it, Ma. I got one of my books published."

"Really? Oh my God, I can't believe it! I always

knew you would make it!"

"I know."

"My goodness! You have no idea how happy this makes me. I'm so proud of you!"

"Thanks, Mom."

"Did you call your father already? I'm sure he's going to go through the roof when you tell him the news."

"Er… no. I haven't talked to him in a while."

"When was the last time you spoke to your father?"

"Oooh, ahhh… his birthday?"

"Lemat! That was almost eight months ago. You should be ashamed of yourself, not calling your father more frequently."

"But you know how it is, Ma, a five-minute conversation about the weather, unless he goes off on his usual spiel."

"That's no excuse."

"I don't know why you care so much about him. You guys have been divorced for almost thirty years. And after everything he put you through when you were together? I mean, I just don't get it."

"He's your father."

"I'm almost forty."

"That doesn't matter."

"Obviously." This wasn't the way Lemat pictured this conversation going. Even in absence, his father managed to trump his victory.

"Lemat, you should call your father. He loves you. He's going to be so happy when he hears that his son is a published author."

"Yeah… I'm sure he will. OK, Mom. I'll ring him up."

"When?"

"Soon."

"Lemat."

"Soon. I promise."

"OK, I'm going to take your word for it. Now, tell me about the book."

Lemat was delighted to recount the recent events of his life to his mother. What he thought would be a fifteen-minute phone call turned into an hour. When he hung up, Lemat was thrilled about how happy she was about the news.

Lemat took a straw from the brain-shaped mug and began to twirl it. He walked to the living room and turned on the TV to the History channel and then went to the large window. He loved the feeling of the soft, plush rug between his toes as he looked out at the view. It faced a park and allowed for plenty of light.

The talk with his mother left Lemat thinking about how his life would have turned out had he accepted his father's numerous offers to work with him.

Safety in Numbness

"Sir?" a voice said in Spanish.

The image in the mirror blinked.

"Sir?"

The reflection looked in the direction of the voice. It was his assistant manager at the pharmacy, the pharmacy he was running to "learn the family business from the bottom up," as his father liked to say. Lemat had been staring at his reflection in the two-way mirror in his spartan office for so long, he actually had no idea how long the assistant manager had been standing there.

"Sir, are you OK?"

"Yes... what's going on?"

"We are running low on suppositories."

"OK."

"We need to place an order."

"Fine." Lemat looked at the papers piled in front of him. There was a notebook opened to its last pages, where Lemat had been doodling and writing down ideas for stories. He looked from under his eyebrows at his assistant, who was waiting for an answer. Lemat felt silently judged by him, so he closed the notebook. "Ah, go ahead, order more."

"How many?"

"How many did we order before?"

"I'll order the same amount. There's also a customer who needs to make a return."

"OK."

Lemat forced himself off his chair and walked down one of the aisles. He could swear that they grew longer each day and the shelves got busier with items; it was like an intricate maze that kept shifting all around him. Lemat found his way to the customer-service desk and tended to the elderly woman in need of an exchange. She wanted her money back. He might as well have told a wall to be a little softer before he crashed into it head first. What followed was a twenty-minute repetition of the phrase, "Sorry, ma'am, it's against our policy, but you can have store credit," while the septuagenarian tried to convince him otherwise under all manners of threats. In the end, Lemat took back the items and paid for them from his own pocket, so the old lady could leave while vowing never to set foot in the pharmacy again.

This was one of those days where Lemat needed to remind himself that things could be a lot worse. He could have left for the United States, where he didn't know anybody and wasted his time studying art, film, philosophy, or some other unprofitable bullshit that would surely leave him in the unemployment line as soon as he received his diploma. Lemat had a steady job with a bright future. One day, when his father passed away, he would inherit his chain of pharmacies. Money would never be a problem. Sure, the job wasn't very sexy. He couldn't pick up women by bragging about selling tampons and cough medicine, but he lived in a swanky penthouse and drove a really nice car. Too bad both things contributed to the general state of paranoia he had to maintain due to his country's epidemic of violent crime. At least he traveled once a year in considerable luxury, regardless of how depressing it always was to return home and face the fruits of corrupt politicians and a failed economy.

Yeah, things could be much worse, thought Lemat, checking the time on his cell phone. The day never ended soon enough.

The sound of keys at the door snapped Lemat from his daydreaming. He turned around from the window and saw Ink walk in.

"Hey! What are you doing?" she said.

"Nothing. I was just thinking."

"Are you packed?"

"Ready to go. You know, I wish you would change your mind about tagging along."

"I told you. The whole publicity thing is not my idea of a good time. Besides, you're going to be busy doing interviews and whatnot. I don't want to be a hanger-on."

"You won't. You'd be my plus-one."

"Not my style either."

"You'd be traveling for free."

"That's not traveling," Ink said. "That's more akin to being driven like cattle."

"Wow, thank you. You just know how to make a guy feel special."

"Don't start. We already talked about this."

Lemat walked to the kitchen counter and produced a cassette tape. He had decorated its case and label with drawings mimicking tattoos. "Here, I made you this." He handed Ink the tape. "You can use my boom box to listen to it while I'm away."

"A mixtape? How retro of you."

"It has Tori Amos, Fiona Apple, Portishead, Dead Can Dance, Blur—all the stuff that you like. I had some space left on the B-side, so I squeezed in some Rodriguez. I think you'll like him. It's like Dylan, but with a street flavor."

"Thanks. That's really cool," she said. "It's going to be weird not having you around for a while."

"Really?"

"Of course, you big dork! You're one of my best friends."

This had been a thorn in Lemat's side since he learned about Ink's musician friend, Grit. They were great friends, benefits and all. But Lemat was confused. Why couldn't this be a serious relationship? Was he a kind of sexual 7-Eleven? Lemat wondered if he was just a step between a vibrator and a boyfriend. There was no romance, that was for sure. No flowers, no dates. But there was unquestionable empathy, support, and care.

"Is that what we are, friends?" Lemat said.

"No, casual acquaintances."

"That's not what I mean."

Lemat had no idea why he had chosen the most inappropriate moment to talk about this. They should have eaten takeout, made stupid comments over a movie, and made love furiously until the crack of dawn. They would sleep for a few hours before T-Rex knocked on the door to take Lemat to the airport. But now that ship had sailed and Lemat headed towards the inevitable storm.

Ink took a deep breath. "I was wondering when this

talk would come up."

"Just answer the question." Lemat could barely contain the anger and frustration that had been building inside him.

"Lemat, I'm not your typical woman."

"No shit."

"I don't do the 'boyfriend and girlfriend' thing. It's just not healthy. I thought you were OK with it."

"You never asked."

"I didn't peg you as the type of guy who cares about those things."

"I don't," he lied. "It's just that we never talked about it."

"There was no reason for us to. I mean, have you ever been a boyfriend?"

"Of course."

"You go from wanting to be with someone to getting used to being around them. Spontaneity gives way to monotony, desire turns into comfort—you even run out of things to say, for Christ's sake. That's why I don't like playing that game anymore. Friends, on the other hand—"

"Friends." Lemat felt just a little smaller, a little less important. He was just a nice guy she enjoyed having around for company and fucked when the mood struck her.

"You have your way of seeing life. You have your plans, your dreams. Well, I have mine. But they aren't about careers or telling stories. Everybody defines happiness their own way, and they go about chasing after it in all sorts of ways. I want to keep my life simple, uncomplicated. I hate drama and I hate being tied down, limited. That's not what makes me happy. If

I get fed up with this place, I take the few things I own and move to another place. If I don't like my job, I just get another one. Something different. I don't care about money, or owning a whole bunch of shit. I just want to be happy, that's all I want. That applies to the people around me. When we're together, there's nothing else that matters in my world."

"Until you go with someone else," Lemat said.

"It's not like that."

"Oh, really?"

"Lemat, I like you. You're one of my best friends. Please don't make me—I want you to be in my life and I want to be part of yours, but you have to accept me for who I am, not who you want me to be. Just like I accept you."

Lemat didn't know what to say. Everything Ink said seemed to be very logical, except for the gut feeling that told him this wasn't right. Later on, Lemat would think about all kinds of things to say, all of them appropriate. He would wish he said that she was full of shit. That he had no idea what had happened in her life to damage her so. Why would she be so afraid of commitment? If there was something Lemat knew, it was that happiness required work, a lot of it. He would wish he had told her that if they really accepted each other for who they were, they would accept all their baggage and shortcomings. Real love wasn't found when you were flying high, but when you crawled into darkness. Yes, Lemat would later regret not being able to have that mental agility. At that moment, all he could see was what was in front of him. The one person he cared to have in his life.

"OK," he said.

"You know, maybe it's good that you're taking this trip by yourself. I think some distance will do us both good. Put things in perspective. Go, do your thing, have fun."

"And when I come back?" Lemat said.

"Hopefully, we'll still be best friends."

CHAPTER TWENTY-TWO

"Next, on *Aria,*" the announcer said during a commercial bump. "The author of the controversial book *Killing Jesus.* The exclusive interview you don't want to miss. Hear what he has to say about the furor surrounding his bestselling novel, and why he's refused to speak to the media, until now!"

The Aria Marx show was the top daytime talk show. She was a half-Caucasian, half-Korean media mogul famous for her insightful exclusives, which was the first stop on Lemat's promotional tour in New York.

"You have to be careful, my boy," said The Don, sporting a bowler hat, a cane hanging from one arm, and silently cursing the federal law stopping him from lighting up his pipe. "It is well known that your hostess likes to get chummy with her guests and then befuddle them with a whopper of a question. Do not be bamboozled by her charms."

"Don't worry, the only way I can be 'bamboozled' is if I suddenly find myself in the 19th century," said

Lemat, feeling quite awkward by all the makeup they had applied on him.

"Now is not the time to get cheeky. Just answer the questions like we practiced. Leave the creativity at the keyboard."

"If I answer like that, people are going to need a dictionary to understand me."

"You can be impossibly vexing when your lady friend is not at your side."

Don had a point. Ink had to stay behind; she had a job and her own life to look after. This made Lemat feel lonely and very vulnerable, like a lost child. T-Rex was always there with him, but he was of little emotional comfort. He was a professional through and through, and he avoided anything that could compromise the performance of his duties; that included getting close to his clients. He was friendly, even charming, but always a pro.

"And why do you always have to wear that dreadful sweater?" said Don.

"Let it go; it's my thing," said Lemat, twirling a plastic straw faster than usual. He had taken to wearing black wristbands to cover his scars, something that Don hoped would become his signature, or even better, a fashion statement that would catch on with readers.

A production assistant rushed into the room. He was a wiry kid, moving at the speed of light, and with enough stress to power a small vehicle. "You're on in five minutes!" he blurted out.

"Hold on," Don said and took away the straw from Lemat. "Chin up, lad."

"Break a leg, L," said T-Rex, walking behind him.

Lemat was so nervous, he was afraid he was going

to throw up. *Why the fuck am I doing this?* he thought. *This is so fucking dumb! That asshole took my fucking straw!*

The PA might as well have been taking him to his own execution. All Lemat could hear was his own heartbeat as it tried to burst from his chest. Sweating profusely, he stood by the side of the stage. And before he knew what was going on, Aria Marx introduced him and the house band blasted a swing rendition of "Sympathy for the Devil."

"Go!" The production assistant pushed him towards center stage.

Lemat made a beeline towards Aria, experiencing tunnel vision. The crowd cheered. When they shook hands, she didn't let on that his was moist. Aria Marx was tiny and thin, with a layered coif and a "jeans and T-shirt" image that was meticulously crafted to appeal to Middle America. They took a seat on a pair of comfortable couches and everything calmed down, except Lemat.

A TV studio looked very different from the other side of the camera. It was smaller than perceived on the TV, flooded with powerful lights, and flanked by thousands of cables.

"So, here you are," Aria said as if they were two good friends shooting the breeze.

Lemat nodded sheepishly.

"What do you have to say for yourself?"

"Hi?"

The audience laughed.

"Hi!" Aria said. "So, your novel, *Killing Jesus*—what a name! This book has taken the world by storm. It just debuted as number one on the *New York Times* bestseller list, there's an incredible Hollywood buzz about a film adaptation, and it's been translated into seven different languages already, is that correct?"

"Hmm, yeah."

"You've been busy."

"Yeah, I guess."

"And he's modest, too."

The audience approved.

"You are hailed as one of the great success stories of the self-publishing world. How do you feel about that?"

Like a sellout? Lemat thought.

"A little overwhelmed," he said. "I mean, it was totally unexpected."

"Remember to smile," said Don, watching from the green room.

"But with a title like that, you must have expected some kind of reaction, didn't you?"

"Well… I just wanted something that was short and catchy."

"Oh, it's catchy all right. What made you write this kind of novel?"

"Well, I like science fiction—"

"What I meant is, the theme. I read your novel and I must confess I was shocked by it. I honestly didn't know if I wanted to read through the end."

"But you did."

"Well, yeah."

"Bully, lad! Well done," Don said.

"The reason I like science fiction," Lemat said, "and the reason I chose the theme for the novel, is because it's the kind of fiction that affords us a way to tackle some interesting questions. It allows the readers to step outside their own experience and gain a different perspective.”

“In this case, a tale about a man who travels back in time to—well, the title says it all, doesn’t it?”

“Exactly.”

“Are you religious?”

“I was raised Catholic, but I’m not a religious person at all.”

“I didn’t think so. Are you an atheist or agnostic?”

“I guess you could say I’m an atheist because I don’t believe in organized religion or the concept of a deity. As far as knowing about what happens when we die or if there’s anything out there that science has not found out about yet, I guess you could call me agnostic.”

“What will happen when you die and you find out you were all wrong. Will God be there, waiting for you at heaven’s door, tapping his foot angrily?”

“She’s a God of love and forgiveness, so I guess she’ll shake her finger at me and let me in.”

The audience loved it and exploded in applause, especially the women in the crowd.

“Wham! Right in the face!” Ink said, watching the show on TV at the tattoo parlor back home.

“Hey, are you going to tattoo me or what?” said her client, a heavily tattooed man about to get the last spot on his butt cheek inked.

“Calm down, OK? It’s not like this is your first

time."

The interviewer continued, "This is your first novel."

"It is."

"And you are, what? Thirty-two, thirty-three?"

"Thirty-eight."

"Wow, you look younger. Must be the Latin blood, right ladies?"

"Uh, thank you." He blushed, in spite of himself.

"So why now? Why write a novel at thirty-eight years old? What drove you to this?"

"Well, I've been writing for a long time and trying to get published, but nothing came of it."

Don was moving his lips along with Lemat's answer. *Atta boy!* the agent thought.

"I had resigned myself to the idea that this wasn't going to happen," Lemat continued. "Then I found myself unemployed and I decided to give it one last shot."

"Amazing," Aria said. "You find yourself without a job, thirty-eight years old, unable to break in as a writer, and now you're living your dream." She looked at her audience for approval and they obliged. "You were born in South America, sí? ¿Es bueno?"

"Sí, en Venezuela," Lemat said, even though the question made no sense in Spanish. Still, the audience ate it up.

"So you come to this country, learn the language, and find this amazing success. Say what you want to say about your work, but that's just the American dream, isn't it?"

"Very much so."

"Now, I'm sure you're aware of the controversy your book has created around the country—around the world, really. There are people picketing outside the studio as we speak. So, why this topic? Is it just a marketing tactic?"

Because it's sensationalist garbage, Lemat thought.

"Religion is a sensitive subject," he said. "What I tried to do was to explore the idea of what would happen if we could go back in time and change a significant event in history. So the novel is really not about religion, but about history."

"But you do take a very peculiar approach in telling the story. It reads at times like an action thriller, a horror story, an erotic romp—"

"I'm a fiction author. My job is to entertain people. I'm not a historian or a theologian. As much as I want to make the reader think, I have to entertain my audience."

"So you see it as harmless fun?"

"Yeah. You know you have a good story when there's a sense of fear and excitement about a subject."

"Your novel has been called everything, from an instant classic to, and I quote, 'the greatest pile of garbage ever committed to the printed page.' How do you feel when you read something like that?"

That they're right, Lemat thought and then said, "I don't know. I guess everybody is entitled to their opinion. If you don't like the book, don't read it."

"Are you concerned at all with the negative

feedback about your novel, the negative reviews, the book burnings, the threats against you?"

"I'm not concerned about it."

"It's definitely helped your sales."

"Sure, but the book is successful because people are intrigued by it. For every person you have burning my book, you have thousands who have enjoyed it. It's definitely started a dialog about the role that religion plays in modern society."

"How so?"

"Because sometimes we tend to take things for granted. Religion plays an important role in a lot of people's lives and in a lot of communities. So, having an honest discourse about our beliefs can lead to a rediscovery of our own faith."

"That's very beautiful. And you definitely don't sound like the Antichrist to me. Lemat, thank you so much for coming to the show. Good luck with your writing career."

Don almost fell to his knees in euphoric praise. Ink was jumping up and down at work, unable to contain her happiness. When the filming ended, Lemat chitchatted amicably with Aria for a few minutes. She confessed she was expecting him to be a dark and belligerent guest, not a charming, eloquent, and insightful person. Lemat shook her hand and walked away from the interview with the ease of a seasoned pro.

"Have you ever considered a career in politics?" said T-Rex, walking beside him.

"Capital, my lad! Capital, indeed!" Don said when they were back in the green room. He held Lemat by the shoulders. Lemat wasn't sure if his agent was going to hug him or not. All he knew was that The Don was not used to this kind of affectionate display.

"I need a drink," Lemat said.

"You might as well have a bottle. They are all on me," the agent said.

Lemat's phone vibrated. It was a text from Ink: *You rocked it! OMG! I thought I was going to have a heart attack! Ahmazing!*

It was the first time they had communicated since Lemat left a couple days ago. He wasn't sure if he wanted to talk to Ink at all. She had made the terms of their relationship perfectly clear, and Lemat wasn't sure if he would ever warm up to them.

Lemat and his entourage walked to the studio's garage, where the black Escalade with a hired driver was waiting. The studio security was also there to make sure things went down smoothly. They drove into the street, right through a crowd of protesters. Lemat tensed up as the mob hit the car and shouted at them.

"Peasants!" Don said. "Pay them no mind. Now, as incandescent as this interview was, I want you to keep your wits about you. I want you to treat each interview as if it were your first."

"Got it," said Lemat, looking out the window as they sped away down the street towards his hotel.

"And you should consider hiring an assistant. You creative types are notoriously a mess, so it behooves you to have someone around you to keep things running on schedule. We have three months of work ahead of us."

"I don't make that kind of money."

"You don't make that kind of money, *yet*. Don't worry. I'll assign an intern. There's this sharp lass at the office."

"I don't know if I'll be comfortable with that."

"You'll be surprised about what you can get used to. You have a radio show in the morning, a book signing, and the taping of another talk show. And that's just tomorrow."

"Wait a minute—did you just say we have three months ahead of us?"

"Didn't you read the schedule? We're going global. Your novel is being rushed into more translations as we speak. We need to work the English-speaking market and lay the ground for the non-English ones. Oh, dear boy, you're definitely getting an assistant."

CHAPTER TWENTY-THREE

A sudden rap on the door woke Lemat up at 6:00 in the morning the next day. *What the fuck?* He counted the hours of sleep he'd had with his fingers as he walked to the door. They weren't enough as far as he was concerned. He was tempted to punch T-Rex in the throat for waking him up at this unholy hour, even though he knew it was the last thing he would ever do.

"What's up?" he said as he opened the door half asleep.

A large mocha was thrust upon him. "Good morning, sir. Here's your coffee just like you like it. No sugar, right? My name is Geraldine Foresi but you can call me Geri." The girl let herself in. "Mr. Maxfield already brought me up to speed regarding your schedule. I'm truly honored to have this opportunity to work for you. Oh, that reminds me." She produced a plastic straw from her handbag and handed it to him. Lemat looked at it, confused. Geri mimicked a twirling motion with her fingers and pointed at the straw.

Lemat scratched his head with the straw, quietly taking in the girl's well-proportioned figure in her slim business suit and high heels. The freckled ball of energy in front of him had to be his new assistant. There was no other explanation as to why an attractive brunette would walk into his room at this hour. Behind her hipster black-framed glasses, her green eyes glimmered with enthusiasm.

"I understand we have a live morning show at nine," she said as she confirmed his schedule on her iPhone. "So why don't you start getting ready. I'll order breakfast downstairs. Would you care for a window view, sir?"

Lemat stopped her with a gesture. "Call me Lemat, please."

"Very well. Window?"

"Why not?"

Half an hour later, he was sitting by a large window overlooking Times Square having breakfast with Geri—her head buried in her phone as she texted with maniacal speed—and T-Rex, who was always keeping an eye out for trouble. Lemat still had the mocha latte Geri brought him. He wasn't used to this much company, especially at breakfast.

Lemat's daily life was quite regimented. He would be wheeled out to some radio or TV studio and milked for answers to the same questions. After a couple of interviews, it became a sort of script he got better at delivering. Every once in a while, someone would ask a different question. Lemat welcomed these rare moments since they broke the monotony and sometimes even challenged him. Some interviewers were affable, a few confrontational, but the majority just wanted to go through the motions. There were interviews by phone, via satellite (the usual signal delay made them quite awkward), written ones for certain blogs, and even live chats. Geri typed for him, since Lemat's dyslexia was a liability. Then there were book signings and readings. Lemat hated the latter. It was one thing to have to write the novel and quite another to have to read that crap out loud, and do so with a slight accent. It was embarrassing, but like everything else, Lemat got used to it.

One city became another, and every show started to look the same. Cities became countries, and with them, jet lag, translators, and time changes. Throughout all of this, Lemat had his three constant companions: Don guided his image, T-Rex kept him safe, and Geri was the only reason Lemat was able to tell what day of the week it was. In fact, he always had so many business people around him that he hadn't had time to consult with his cohorts about the recent whirlwind his life had become. He smiled inwardly as he pictured Dep's forlorn face versus Lisa's angry one; he could almost hear Guy saying "I told you so" and see Talia simply shaking her head.

Life as he knew it before signing with Don seemed like ancient history. One of the great things about keeping busy was that Lemat didn't have time to think much about Ink. They texted each other from time to time. Lemat would send something regarding the tour, and she would reply, but that was the extent of their communication. They were certainly keeping their distance from each other. Lemat just forced those thoughts out of his mind and focused on what he had to do next.

At the end of a long press day in London, Lemat was sitting at the hotel bar and attempting to unwind while the bartender was closing the register for the night. Don had already retired for the night and T-Rex sat nearby. Lemat had just sent Ink a picture of the day's book signing. The line was an impressive five blocks long with only one incidence of potential disaster when a group of picketers started taunting a group of eager autograph hounds. But T-Rex and a handful of store employees quickly squelched those embers before anything erupted.

"The person you're always texting, is she your girlfriend?" said Geri, sitting in the chair next to him. She was having a glass of red, while Lemat was on his second screwdriver.

"No, she's just a friend," said Lemat, putting away his phone and resting his aching feet on the empty chair in front of him.

"Do you like her?"

Lemat took a drink. "I guess... yeah. It's complicated."

"It always seems to be. Is she with someone else?" Geri suddenly realized her faux pas. "I'm so sorry, it's none of my business. I didn't mean to cross a line."

"It's OK. It's nice to talk about something other than the book for a change. Salud," he said as he raised his glass.

"I think I've had enough."

"Nonsense," Lemat poured more wine in her glass. "Here, don't make me drink alone."

"Sure."

"Tell me about you. We've been working together for almost two months and I barely know anything about you," he said.

"Me?"

"Yeah. How old are you? What do you study? What do you want to do after this internship?"

"Well, I'm twenty-two. I just got my B.A. in English Lit from Stanford—"

"Congratulations."

"Thank you." They bumped glasses and chugged. "As for my plans, well, I was just about to finish my internship at MLA. I want to work as an editor for one of the major publishers."

"Why?"

"It's silly."

"Go ahead. You've seen me in my bathrobe."

She chuckled and had a drink. "Well, I want to discover the next great author."

Now it was Lemat's turn to laugh.

"See, I told you it was silly," she said.

"No, it's not. I think that's great."

"I know it's very idealistic, but someone has to try. Look at all those self-published authors. So many stories overlooked by publishers and yet they manage to find their way out to the reader. I mean, look at you."

Yeah, look at me, Lemat thought. "This industry could use more people like you."

"Oh, please." She blushed. "You can't be serious."

"But I am. You said you were done with your internship, so what are you doing here?"

"Mr. Maxfield offered me the chance to be your assistant for this tour during my last week. I think he likes me and knew I kind of needed the money. Plus it was an opportunity to travel and a unique chance to be part of a bestselling international phenomenon. How could I turn this down?"

"This is going to look great on your resume."

"This is nothing like I expected it to be: the security guards, the protesters, the crowds. It's like the closest thing to a rock tour as far as publishing is concerned. I'm glad I have the chance to be part of something quite rare in this industry."

"Your family must be proud."

"Yeah, but my boyfriend is not happy."

"Let me guess—he's intimidated by your success?"

"No. He's paranoid of me running around Europe by myself. He thinks all these European guys are going to be hitting on me."

"That may be true, but what is he afraid of? They can knock at the door all they want—that doesn't mean it's going to open."

"Thank you!"

"You guys haven't been dating long, have you?"

"It will be five months in two days. Well, I've been gone for a while. So I guess we were dating for three months before I took this job."

"What does he do for a living?"

"He's just started as a broker on Wall Street."

"Ah! A deadbeat."

"He also doesn't like the fact that I'm working as an assistant to some writer. He thinks it's demeaning."

"Well, we can't all be financial wizards. Is that why you're always typing away on your phone?"

Geri put it on the table and pushed it away from her deliberately, to make a point. "Not always." She busied her hands with her wine. "I'm doing work stuff and writing a few ideas."

"For?"

She needed a drink before answering that and said, "I do a little writing on the side."

"She's educated, professional, and incredibly efficient. She runs the universe from her phone and writes, too? I think I just started to hate you."

Geri laughed. "It's really nothing."

"Yeah, I'm sure it is. Superwoman Geri just writes silly things. Probably something along the lines of *War and Peace.*"

"Superwoman, huh?"

"I couldn't find my shoes if it wasn't for you. I'm going to miss you when this is all over." There was an awkward silence between them. "What do you write?"

"You're going to laugh."

"You keep saying that. Tell me."

"OK. I write erotica."

"Seriously?" He raised his eyebrows and grinned at her.

"See, you think it's silly."

"Actually, I'd love to read some of your work. If you don't mind, of course."

"Oh no, I couldn't do that."

"Why not? It'd be just two writers talking shop."

"Well, OK. Maybe. We'll see. I think it's pretty terrible."

"All writers think that about their work. You read my novel—did you like it?"

Geri wasn't expecting that question. She sought help from her wineglass. "What can I say? It's the number one novel around the world."

"Commercial success doesn't equate quality. You think its garbage, don't you?"

Geri tensed up.

"Let me let you in on a little secret," Lemat said and he leaned forward. "I know it's crap. That's why I wrote it."

She was taken aback by the bluntness of his revelation and wondered if Lemat had one too many drinks.

"All my life I tried to write things I cared for, things that said something, and at the same time, entertained people. But none of those things ever took off. So I wrote this story to piss people off, hoping it would get some attention. And here we are, flying around the world, plugging away some gigantically successful turd."

Geri couldn't tell if Lemat was being 100% sincere. She didn't know what to say but felt obliged to do so. "You are nothing like I thought you would be," she said. "When I read your book, I thought you were going to be this low-brow, self-centered, hateful creep. I'd never have guessed—this."

"I hear that a lot nowadays."

"God! Look at the time! Mr. Maxfield would kill me if he knew I kept you up so late. We have a busy day tomorrow." She gathered her things quickly.

"Aren't they all?"

"We should call it a night."

"If you say so," Lemat said. "And Geri, thanks for the talk."

"For what it's worth, I don't think there's anything wrong with chasing your dreams. Even if you have to pay your dues first by doing something you don't believe in."

CHAPTER TWENTY-FOUR

Things were always hectic wherever Lemat went. As the crowds got bigger, so did the security surrounding him. Things were not always business as usual. In Brussels, a man tried to break into Lemat's hotel room with a gun. Hotel security found him sneaking around at laundry services and the police promptly made an arrest. In Barcelona, two hecklers were kicked out from a taping of a TV show. In Rome, T-Rex had to wrestle a woman to the ground before she had a chance to splash paint on Lemat's face. The altercation ruined T-Rex's suit, but thankfully nothing else. Wielding a knife, a man jumped the stage in Ireland during a Q&A panel. And once again, T-Rex made the attacker wish he had stayed in bed that morning. Fearing it would inspire more attacks, Don tried to keep all of these events hidden from the press. But things seemed to be getting worse.

While finally enjoying some peace and quiet at a lunch with his team in Lisbon, Lemat got a call from

Ink. They hadn't talked in well over two weeks. Lemat was both eager and scared to hear from her but he did answer the call.

"Hi."

"Hey, can you talk?" Ink said.

"Sure, what's up?"

"Have you heard the news about your place?"

"No, what happened?"

"It's your old place. Here, I'll send you the link."

Lemat didn't bother reading the text; the pictures said it all. His old place had been vandalized. The one window was broken and so was every closet door. The walls were covered with graffiti of crosses and fish, plus insults calling for Lemat's obliteration. He was speechless.

"Are you OK?" Lemat asked Ink.

"I'm fine. Thankfully, it happened one night when I was at work. The police are still looking for suspects, but they think they were some disgruntled religious nuts. No shit! Really? I could have told them that. I'll keep an eye on your new place. You never know."

Lemat took the straw out of Don's gin and tonic and started to twirl. A few drops landed on the agent's clothes, which he didn't appreciate, and he pushed away the drink as if it had been tainted.

"This is the work of a group of cowards who think they're making some sort of stand," said T-Rex, browsing though the pictures on Lemat's phone when he hung up. "I made sure your new place is secure before we left, and I've got a couple folks keeping an eye out, so don't worry."

"That place was a dump anyway," said Lemat. "It doesn't look much different than when I lived there."

He may have been playing it cool, but Lemat was worried. If there was something sacred to him, it was his home.

Australia was the last stop on Lemat's schedule. He had to do four days in Sydney before wrapping up the promotional tour, and Lemat couldn't wait to get back home. Communication with Ink was sporadic. He wanted to call her and tell her the good news, until Don dropped some news on him while having lunch at Harbour Circle, with the iconic opera house as a backdrop.

"We're going to the incongruously called City of Angels," Don said.

"Los Angeles?" Lemat said.

"The one and only. We have about two weeks of meetings with producers. They've been calling my office several times a day."

"Are you kidding me?"

"If I were to kid you, you would be laughing."

"I guess you're going home," Lemat said to T-Rex.

"You're going to love LA," the bodyguard said. "I'll show you around, if we have the time."

Don rolled his eyes. "Oh, please. That boorish town has nothing but film and weather to brag about. I only go there for business, and even then, I pray for an earthquake to make do with their philistine lot."

"I take it you have no love for the West Coast?" T-Rex said.

"I would rather limit my travels to both sides of the Atlantic," Don said.

###

That night, Lemat had a book signing at a large bookstore. The line went around several blocks. Lemat signed copies, answered some quick questions, and smiled for photos. T-Rex kept an eye on the patrons and Geri was on hand to help Lemat with whatever he may need.

A man placed his copy in front of Lemat and said, "Can you sign it for Judas?" The hairs on Lemat's neck stood up straight. T-Rex was already in motion when the man took out a spray can and aimed it at Lemat's face. Geri screamed. Lemat pushed the can away from him, the red paint missing by inches. Wrestling the fanatic to the floor, T-Rex made the man look like a pretzel in the blink of an eye. The crowd was horrified and the people in charge of the bookstore went into overreaction. Don stepped in and told the manager to calm the people down and continue with the signing. "Let the police take care of it on the side," the agent said with aplomb. Unnerved by the attack, the store manager complied.

"I'm signing with pens; no spray cans, please. I'm not that talented," Lemat joked. The crowd laughed nervously and took its cue from the bookstore employees, who by then had calmed down. "Are you OK?" Lemat asked a trembling Geri as he wiped some paint off his fingers with a tissue.

"Yes, I'm fine." She crossed her arms, trying to hide her trembling.

Lemat dealt with his distress by twirling his pen under the table in between signatures. Geri had made sure his pens could always resist such an abuse, after

Lemat had ended up with ink stains on his hands and clothes on a few occasions.

Lemat stayed an hour longer than scheduled to try to accommodate as many readers as possible. But in the end, the bookstore manager informed him that they had to close. Pleasantries were exchanged, and Lemat and his entourage went back to their hotel. T-Rex was hyper-vigilant. Fortunately for him, all four suites were booked next to each other, making his job that much easier. The bodyguard made sure everybody was locked in their rooms before turning in for the night.

Late that night, Lemat took a long hot shower. He was glad that this was his last night of press and that tomorrow he would be flying into LA to hopefully secure a rather lucrative deal for the rights of his book. Then home. His mind wondered about the events of the last three months: the interviews, the readers, and the wackos. He came out of the bathroom feeling a little anxious that everything was going to come to a grinding halt but thrilled to begin this new chapter of his life. Finally, Lemat could just sit down and worry about writing and little else. Regardless, he felt a bit lonely, so he decided to call Ink.

"That's great!" she said when Lemat told her about LA. "I mean, it sucks that I won't see you for another two weeks, but that's awesome news." She sounded a little distant.

"I know. I can't believe it myself."

"And what about this psycho that attacked you?"

"Some religious guy who wanted to brand me. Like a scarlet letter or something."

"Right on your face."

"Yeah. Hey, listen—" Lemat was about to ask her

if she wanted to meet him in Los Angeles, but he suddenly heard a man's voice on the other side of the line. Lemat couldn't make out what he said.

"What's up?" Ink said. "Hello? Did I lose you?"

"Nothing. Never mind. I'm really tired."

"Well, go to sleep. I can't wait to see you in a few weeks."

"Yeah, me too." Lemat hung up.

Why do I keep doing this to myself? he thought.

Lemat opened the minibar and grabbed a handful of bottles. That's when a sound caught his attention. He moved closer to the door that connected his suite with Geri's. The closer he got, the more familiar the sounds became. Lemat was sure Geri was watching porn.

Really? he thought and downed a tiny bottle of tequila. Mustering up the courage, he knocked on her door and could hear her rushing around, trying to make everything presentable.

"Did you knock?" said Geri, wearing tiny pink shorts and a white tank top as she opened the door. She was all flustered and looked particularly hot without her glasses and with her hair down.

"Yeah. Sorry if I woke you up."

"No, I was watching TV. Everything OK?"

"I can't sleep. Here." He handed her a miniature bottle.

"I'm fine."

"Just have one. And come on in. I could use the company." She took the bottle and entered his suite. "It's just that I'm still a little jazzed from tonight's incident," Lemat continued.

"I know, me too. My heart is still beating a little too fast."

"To the crazies, for keeping the tour interesting."
They toasted.

"Have a seat." Geri sat on the corner of the bed, while Lemat leaned against the pillows.

They each recounted the attack. That led inevitably to recalling the other close calls Lemat had during their travels. The conversation was lively. One tiny bottle turned into two, and before everyone knew it, they were starting on the seventh one. By then, Geri was lying stomach down on the foot of the bed. She had become oblivious to the fact that her small pajamas allowed regular peeks of her breasts. They were both laughing and making fun of each other's reactions during the different assaults.

"I wish I had taken a picture of your face," she said.

"We still have LA."

"Yeah, but it's not going to be the same. It's going to be all about meetings and dinners, but nothing is going to compare to this thing. This is probably the most exciting thing I've ever been involved with."

"That makes two of us."

"So," she took another big gulp from her bottle, "what are you going to do after all this is over?"

"Me? Write my next book, I suppose. You?"

"I got an offer at Billhook."

"Nice! Maybe we'll get to see each other after all. Congratulations."

Another toast.

"Thank you. You—you didn't have anything to do with that, did you?"

"Me? Why?"

"They *are* your publishers."

"I may have mentioned something to Don after London." Lemat had used an opportunity to thank Don for employing Geri and to convince him that he should help her get a job at the Billhook Book Company. Lemat had forgotten all about it, but Don seemed to have come through, the old dog.

"I don't care what those crazy people say—you're a pretty decent guy, Lemat. Thank you."

"You're not bad yourself. What did Mr. Wall Street say when you told him?"

"Nothing. We broke up when we landed in Paris. Ironic, isn't it? The most romantic city in the world and that asshole decides to call me to tell me we were through. Then I found out through a friend that he had been seeing this slut while I was away. What a fucking pig!"

"His loss. He'll never find another girl like you."

"Yes, I'm sure the dick really believes that."

"I mean, look at you: you're smart, beautiful, ambitious, interesting. Fuck him. You don't need him."

"You know what?" She sat up in front of him. "You're right—fuck him!" She proposed a toast.

"Fuck him!"

They downed the contents of their bottles in a single drink and threw them away. They looked at each other for a moment. Lemat leaned forward and kissed her. At first, he thought she was going to pull away, but Geri moved forward and increased the passion of the kiss. Then they attacked each other as they clumsily ripped off their clothes, unable to feel their bodies fast enough.

"Is that what you want? You want to fuck your assistant like a dirty little slut?" Geri dared him as he took her from behind. Impressed, surprised, and delighted with this bolder Geri, Lemat tied her hands loosely with his bathrobe's belt to the headboard. He spanked her, which seemed to make her hornier. She was moaning, loudly, and he was afraid T-Rex would burst through the door. She bit his lips, which made him wince, and said, "You wanna fuck me all night, don't you? You want me to remember how your dick feels inside me, even when we're on that plane tomorrow. Oh God, don't stop."

Lemat lost all track of time; he could barely keep up with Geri's cravings. By the time she fell asleep exhausted, sunlight was seeping through the window. The floor was littered with clothes, the empty contents of the minibar, an empty bottle of KY Jelly, and about a half dozen condom wrappers. Passed out on top of him, Geri glistened with oil, with one hand still bound behind her back, and red handprints on her luscious ass. Lemat had scratch marks on his back and chest, bite marks on his neck, and a slight headache coming on. After propping himself up to survey the damage, he collapsed from sheer exhaustion.

When a rapid sequence of knocks awoke him, Lemat was by himself and the room was spotless, as if everything had just been a wonderful wet dream. He stumbled to the door, tying on his bathrobe, which he had found neatly folded on the back of an armchair.

"Good morning," Geri said with her usual smile. Looking refreshed and wide-eyed, she was standing there with his coffee like it was any other day. "Sorry to wake you, but we have to check out and Mr. Maxfield is waiting for you at brunch. You get ready and head down, then I'll pack for you. OK?" she said, a little too enthusiastically.

Unblinking, Lemat stared at her, as he wasn't sure what the protocol here was. "Thank you? Uh, I'll be down in a minute," he said, taking the coffee and shutting the door.

From then on, Geri acted as if nothing had happened. She remained professional and friendly for the rest of the trip. Although, whether by virtue of their sexual encounter or everything else that had happened before, she and Lemat became closer colleagues. They would stay up and chitchat about life and writing. She had even shown him a draft of her novel. But they never ever talked of that one exciting night together. Ever. The only hint of the encounter came three years later, in the pages of Geri's smash debut, *Lust between the Lines.*

CHAPTER TWENTY-FIVE

"Welcome to LA," T-Rex said as they drove away from the airport in a hired SUV.

"Well, bully," Don said with the excitement of a dead plant.

The city was dirtier and looked older than Lemat expected. Its infrastructure had seen better days. The mob waiting for them when they arrived was all media, so not having to deal with religious protesters felt odd. As soon as they got on the freeway, traffic bogged their ride down to a crawl. The congestion wasn't caused by an accident in any of their own lanes, but in the opposite direction. It was ironic that in the capital of entertainment, rubbernecking was one of the main attractions.

"Aren't we going to stay downtown?" said Lemat, looking for a city skyline.

"This isn't that kind of city," T-Rex said. "LA is more like a bunch of interconnected neighborhoods without a real center. There's a downtown, but it's a joke. Nothing really happens there except car commercial shoots."

"A city without a heart. Quite apropos, if you ask me," Don said.

"Where's the Hollywood sign?" Geri said.

"Yeah, that's quite a ways from here," T-Rex said. "If you don't like to drive, this ain't the place for you. You see, to me, LA is a city you live in, not really visit. In order to appreciate this town, you have to experience it up close and personal. There's no other place that you can surf and snowboard all in the same day. There's everything for everyone, but you need to know how to navigate it."

"Yes, preferably in the direction back to the airport," Don said.

The driver dropped them off at the famed Chateau Marmont Hotel on Sunset Boulevard, a Gothic-inspired building sitting atop a small hill, a regular haunt for the Hollywood crowd. Don had arranged for them to stay at the bungalows, which offered guests private gardens and wonderful views of the city. The hotel's history was neck-deep in celebrity lore. John Belushi was found dead in a bungalow. Jim Morrison called the place home for a while. Hunter S. Thompson, F. Scott Fitzgerald, Tim Burton, and Marilyn Monroe were just a few of the hotel's distinguished guests. Lemat thought the choice of accommodations flattering and fitting. The group ate in their rooms that night, as they were exhausted from the fifteen-hour trip from Sydney. The next few days were going to be a storm of activity.

They were ferried back and forth from one studio to the next for a series of meetings with producers and studio heads. Things had gone up a notch in luxury and style since it was the studios that were footing the bill. It was obvious they wanted to make Lemat feel comfortable, but they aimed to dazzle him as well. Lunches, dinners, and brunches ruled the schedule. The places chosen were pretentious and overtly expensive. The food was as ornate as the restaurants, but, sadly, the flavor fell quite short of the price tag. Every time Lemat seemed disappointed, T-Rex would whisper that this wasn't the "real LA." Lemat was curious about this and wished there was time for T-Rex to show him what he meant.

One afternoon, Lemat was sitting in another one of these famed establishments. It was a French-designed, upscale Chinese restaurant in Beverly Hills, which he was told was the new "it" place for Hollywood's elite. The dimmed lights, wood finishes, and a neon-blue lit bar were supposed to create an intimate atmosphere, together with ambient sounds and scents. But to Lemat, it all felt a little claustrophobic. Especially with the intricate Chinese screen surrounding the dining area. It felt like a cage. He sat down with Don, as well as Leon Thomas, a prolific producer of blockbuster fare, Allan Walton, an A-list director, and Timothy Williams, the highest paid actor in Hollywood—a man who bought two small islands last year and, rumor had it, wanted to start his own country.

"We're very excited about this project," the producer said. Leon was in his late fifties, with dyed hair plugs, a fake tan, and an expanding waistline. He donned a suit with no tie, an open shirt, expensive Italian shoes, and an even more expensive watch. "When my personal trainer gave me your book, I read it in one night. Unbelievable! I said to myself, 'This is gonna make an amazing film.' Right?" He turned to the director.

"Absolutely!" Allan said. "I could just see the whole thing in my head." He made a little movie screen with his hands. "The way it was written—it's very cinematic. Right away, I knew how to bring your vision of the story onto the silver screen."

"I only see a few minor hiccups we'd need to iron out," Leon said. The director was of average height, sported a full beard, and wore a blue guayabera shirt under a sports jacket, jeans, and sneakers. A porkpie hat tamed an unruly mat of dark hair.

"Hiccups?" Lemat said.

"Minor things," the producer said. "Take the name, for example. We would need to tweak it just a little to make it more commercial."

"Killing Jesus is not commercial enough?" Lemat said.

"It might offend some people," Allan, the director, said. "Especially in the Bible Belt."

"We don't want to alienate any potential audience," Leon said. "So maybe we can call it something like *The Time Traveler Killer* or whatever."

"Frank Johnson: Time Travel Hitman," offered Timothy excitedly.

"Yeah," Allan said. "Something like that. See, nothing major."

"Minor stuff," Leon said.

Timothy said, "The way I see the character, I don't see him so much as an assassin, but as someone out for justice." He had barely touched his salad.

"I don't follow," Lemat said.

"Nobody will sympathize with an assassin," the

actor said. Timothy was surprisingly shorter and thinner than in the movies, and although undeniably good looking, he showed signs of age moviegoers were probably unaware of thanks to the magic of makeup and excellent lighting. His short-sleeve, button-down shirt, jeans, and leather shoes cost more than some people's cars. He continued as he tried to make a connection with Lemat but focused unwaveringly on his eyes, "But audiences can connect with the idea of a man seeking justice."

"From Jesus?" Lemat said.

"FOR Jesus," Allan said.

"I don't get it," Lemat said.

"I see Frank Johnson as a man that was deeply religious but lost his faith somewhere along the way," Timothy said.

"A crisis of faith," Allan said.

"So when he goes back in time, he reconnects with the very essence of that faith," the actor said.

"From the very man," Allan said. "Right from the beginning."

"Er… But that's not what the book is about," Lemat said.

Leon said, "You have to understand, film and literature are two different languages. You can't just grab a book and turn it into a movie."

"No, you have to adapt it," Allan said.

"Exactly," Leon said. "So certain things have to be changed to make that transition."

"Right," Allan said. "While still maintaining your vision of the story."

"Its heart," Timothy said.

"But the book is just about—"

"Would he be a producer on the film?" Don interrupted Lemat, knowing well what "adapting" meant in Hollywood. He also knew the answer to his question, but he asked it just to keep up with the required back-and-forth of these types of dealings.

"Of course," Allan said.

"Of course," Leon said, just a beat later. "It's always great to have the author close by to make sure everything is kosher."

So the answer was really "no," as Don expected. Lemat would have a "producer" credit in name only. The last thing the filmmakers wanted was interference from the creator of the source material. The story was inconsequential; they just wanted the property.

"It'll also help if I'll write the script," Lemat said.

The actor, the producer, and the director exchanged a quick, silent look.

"That's a possibility," Allan said.

"We would certainly love to see a draft from you," Leon said.

"But again, filmmaking is not like writing a novel," the director said. "It's a completely different animal."

"Totally different," Leon said. "But you shouldn't worry about that now."

"No," Allan said.

"From now on, you should think about kicking back and letting us take care of everything," Leon said. "That is, of course, if you decide to go with us to film your baby."

"We certainly have you on top of our list," Don said. "But we still have a few more meetings to attend before making a decision."

"Of course," Leon said. "But I think—if you don't

mind me saying so—that you can't go wrong with a team like this behind your novel." The producer looked at his companions to emphasize his point.

Lemat couldn't disagree with that statement. Besides, what did he care about how that piece of crap ended up on the big screen? A terrible novel could only be made into a terrible motion picture. The fact that something he wrote might be filmed may have been the sole cause for his hesitation. Lemat always thought that one of his stories would find its way to the movies. He begrudged that it had to be *Killing Jesus,* of all things. The producer might be right after all, so Lemat tried to convince himself that he should relax and enjoy the ride.

CHAPTER TWENTY-SIX

Lemat's busy schedule moved on. The studio meetings, just like the book-related interviews, were essentially the same. Some big-shot producer talked about how great the novel was, and what big star was interested in being in it. They threw every hot name out there. Lemat started to understand why Don disliked the city. These men were without a doubt wealthy and powerful within their business. But it seemed they could buy everything but basic manners, class, and affable personalities.

Then there were the parties. Fashionable, indulgent, and attended by image-conscious extremists engaged in frivolous conversations with vapid looks on their faces. The most memorable of these was on the rooftop of The Standard hotel, at the disappointingly small Downtown. People ordered drinks at the bar and hung around the plastic red waterbed pods scattered about the heated swimming pool. A jazz trio provided the musical ambiance, and *Apocalypse Now* was projected against the building across the way. The city actually looked amazing from that perspective.

Lemat was introduced to a host of people. Without fail, each one claimed to know who he was and raved about his novel. It didn't take much probing for Lemat to see through the thin veneer of their façade. He played along, though. After all, he was there to make a killing by selling the rights to his book. He found himself with a drink in his hand all the time. The more he drank, the easier it was for him to talk to these people. The one undeniable upside about Los Angeles was the seemingly infinite supply of beautiful women. Lemat, a famous author in town to make a movie deal, thought he had his work cut out for him.

"And what do you do?" said a tall blonde with a tiny dress.

"I'm an author."

"That's great. Excuse me, I have to say hi to someone."

T-Rex laughed.

"At least *you're* having fun," Lemat said.

"That's not how you pick up women in this town, at least not that type. Allow me to school you for a moment. The hierarchy goes: producer, director, and casting director. That's the holy trinity in this place if you want to get busy with them honeys."

"I'm a world-famous author."

"And here, that just means you can type."

"I need a drink." Lemat shook the ice in his empty glass, walked to the bar, and ordered a beer.

"Lemat?"

Lemat turned around in time to watch T-Rex intercept a guy before he could get too close to him. He was reaching for Lemat as T-Rex pushed him away. It took Lemat about ten seconds to finally recognize the face.

"Specs?" Lemat said. This Specs was about forty pounds lighter and wired like a wall socket. "It's OK, T-Rex. I know this guy." The bodyguard let him go.

"Give the man some fame and fortune and he forgets all about his friends!" They hugged each other.

"Man, look at you," Lemat said. "You look great. I can get my arms around you."

"You know how it is here in Hollywood—beach bodies."

"I haven't seen you in ages," Lemat said. "Everybody at Fausto's was wondering what happened to you."

"Fighting the good fight out here in Tinseltown. Let me introduce you to my friend Rob." Specs pointed out the short surfer type by his side.

"'S'up? You in the industry, too?" Rob said.

"The industry?" Lemat said.

"Obviously not," Rob said. "I'm going to take a piss. Later."

"What an asshole," Specs said. "Four years ago, he was busting his ass drawing comic books and nobody gave a fuck about him. That is, until a big studio came in, bought one of his creations, and made it into a huge blockbuster. Now you need to stand in line at Comic-Con just to smell his farts."

"What comic book is he working on now?"

"Comic book? He has an office in West LA where he's been trying to develop more properties for film and television."

"How do you know each other?"

"We met back in college when I was in film

school. Now I'm working with him on a new project. Pretty hush-hush stuff."

"What's the project?"

"OK, but you can't tell a soul. We're developing a film based on Monopoly."

"The game?"

"Yeah. It's going to be like *Wall Street* meets *Moneyball* meets *The Firm* meets *Goodfellas,* with the whole housing-market-crash angle worked into it."

"Sounds interesting." Lemat had to take a drink in order to keep a straight face.

"Yeah, but remember—keep it to yourself."

"Sure. Don't worry."

"And you? *Killing Jesus?* You're one crazy motherfucker. I saw you on TV when you were in Europe plugging the book."

"Yeah, we just came back from Australia. This is the last stop before going back home."

"I got two words of advice for you: Ben Affleck. If you're going to get a director, hire that guy. Have you seen *Argo?* Fucking genius! *The Town?* Lame actor, but the dude can direct," the new and improved Specs said.

"I loved *Gone Baby Gone.*"

"Never saw it. Hey, listen—I gotta roll now, bud. I'll be back home in a few days, so let's get together to have lunch or something. There're a few people I want you to meet. I'll call you." He mimicked a cellphone with his hand. Specs disappeared into the throng.

"Friend of yours?" T-Rex said.

"Casual acquaintance," said Lemat, ordering another beer.

"That makes you best buddies in this business."

"OK, you keep talking about all of this 'LA code/Hollywood language' shit. So why don't you give me a hand instead of rubbing it in my face?"

"Oh, it's like that? You think I'm BSing you? All right, let me show you how it's done in my town. You see the Asian hottie with the fuck-me pumps and the blonde with the short hair sitting by the pool?"

"Yep."

"'K, check it out." T-Rex approached them with Lemat in tow. "Good evening, ladies."

"Hi," the Asian woman said coldly.

"I have this small problem and I think you fine ladies can give me a hand. See, my boy here is new in town. He came all the way from Brazil to produce this film and he's been driving me crazy the whole trip just talking about business. Would you two mind taking him off my hands for a few minutes? I just need to get a drink and talk to my buddy over there. You girls want anything?" He waved casually at a famous star across the pool. The actor recognized T-Rex from when he worked as his bodyguard and waved back. "Don't worry, my boy is shy and won't be giving you no trouble. Just don't let him talk your ear off about this new Ryan Gosling project he's casting."

"Sure," said the blonde, beaming.

"No problem," the brunette said as she beckoned Lemat with a finger.

"And that's how it's done," T-Rex whispered to Lemat.

"Brazil?"

"It sounds more exotic. Don't worry; them bitches don't know Mexico from Honduras. Now don't fuck it up. I'm going to say hi to my former client, but I'll be around." He patted Lemat's back and walked away. T-Rex wasn't worried about religious zealots in this city, least of all in this place. Ruse aside, he would stay close to Lemat the whole night without being too noticeable.

"Hi!" the girls said when Lemat approached. They invited him to sit between them on a waterbed, where Lemat's storytelling skills came in handy. Not that he needed incredible persuasive skills to get these two interested; all he had to do was keep up the charade T-Rex started and ask them if they had any acting experience. It turned out that they were models/actresses (what a coincidence). Before long, Lemat was lying on the bed making out with both girls.

"Want to make the party more interesting?" said Sasha, the brunette.

"What do you have in mind?" said Lemat, unable to see how having sex with two models could get any better. Sasha answered by producing a small vial of cocaine. "Er… I don't really do that."

"You're playing with the big boys now," Sasha said.

"Rather, with the big girls," Sienna said, lowering her dress down and allowing her friend to make a line of cocaine between her breasts. "Are you sure you don't want any?"

Sasha licked one of Sienna's nipples and looked at Lemat and said, "It's just one line."

Sienna said, "You're going to need to keep up with both of us."

What the hell? Lemat thought. He was already too drunk to have any decent self-restraint. He had seen this in movies hundreds of times. How hard could it be? Lemat buried his face between Sienna's breasts and snorted the coke as hard as he could through one nostril. It burned and he choked while the girls simply giggled. It was a weird sensation inhaling powder up his nose.

Sasha then put something in his mouth and kissed him before he could do anything about it. Whatever it was, it dissolved while their tongues danced together. Sasha took another pass along her friend's chest and then returned the favor.

Ladies and gentlemen, fasten your seatbelts; we're about to take off.

CHAPTER TWENTY-SEVEN

Lemat was standing naked in an endless desert. There was a red-framed window floating a few feet away from him. It was open and Lemat could see the Milky Way. He moved closer, ever so slowly, and reached inside. He found himself floating in the darkness, contemplating one of his hands. Something was moving inside it and he wanted to see what it was. His body turned to water, clear and translucent. A luminous jellyfish swam inside him with effortless grace. Lemat felt something on his other leg. Another jellyfish swam up his thigh. He watched in awe as the creatures moved inside him, leaving phosphorescent particles in their wake. Soon, Lemat's liquid body was glowing in the dark, as the jellyfish played together like dolphins. He laughed, but no sound came out, only bubbles. A sense of vertigo overtook him and before he knew it, he had crashed back on the desert. His body splashed across the sand. The jellyfish melded together at the center, melting. Lemat's watery form oozed underground like veins that slowly stopped spreading and solidified into roots. As they became thicker and stronger, a tree began to grow from the jellyfish above. The tree creaked painfully as it gained height and girth. It became ancient and twisted, covered with moss, flowers, and a thick canopy spawning from its branches.

The wood crackled once more. A female leg emerged first, daintily touching the sand. Then came an arm, then a head. The other limbs followed. The plant creature tore herself from the tree in the shape of Talia, naked and luscious, her hair a stream of tiny wild flowers. She spread her arms and stood on her toes, enjoying the breeze caressing her body. Her every motion was delicate. Talia got to her knees and kissed the ground. She watched as the small depression she created came to life. It started as a small bump in the sand moving forward. It got bigger and bigger with every foot traveled, until a shape took form.

Lemat was made of sand and he struggled to stand up as he moved along. Each failed step crumbled down like so many grains. It was a terrible struggle to keep his body upright or maintain his form. Lemat was aware he moved towards a valley created by two massive, flat red stones, creating a funnel into a tiny opening. Lemat's frustrating march was painful. He stopped, unable to continue in such a miserable form. He gathered all of his energy and screamed to the sky, his final action. The sound was all around him, muffled and distant. Sand poured out of his mouth like a fountain, until his shape dissolved, revealing a stone.

The stone's shadow elongated, projecting itself farther than the mass of the object could allow. Fingers appeared from inside the shade, pushing it apart to create a wider opening for a man to climb from under the earth. It was Dep, as opaque and ethereal as the penumbra he came from. He picked up the stone and weighed it in his hand before hurling it against one of the massive rock formations flanking him. The stone bounced off, hit the other side, landed on the ground, and rolled to a halt back at Dep's feet once more. A deafening rumble broke the silence. Rocks popped off from both sides of the valley, leaving perfectly scooped holes behind. The boulders tumbled down into alignment behind the tiny stone in order of size. The formation rose up from its wider side, while each rock rearranged itself into an anthropomorphic shape. A chain was hammered into each limb and buried under the sand. Lemat slogged on, now in mineral form.

His steps were laborious and heavy. Each movement threatened the integrity of his new body. The chains made the whole task more difficult, but Lemat kept his body in motion. He could see now what was at the other end of the small opening at the end of the valley—gentle mounds with green fields. Lemat wanted to reach them, but his path felt uphill. The chains started tightening. The friction of his body set his joints aflame. It was all too overwhelming. Lemat froze, a blazing mountain a few feet away from its goal. The fire grew larger and wilder, until an effigy of Lisa materialized, jumping and crackling around Lemat, his face frozen in despair. Lisa caressed his cheek and kissed him, engulfing him in her inferno. The flames sizzled as they extinguished, revealing a glass figure where once there was stone.

A man approached, pulling a small cart impossibly loaded with all sorts of objects belonging to Lemat's life, a fantastic itinerant merchant from old Japan. As odd as the scene was, the man was no stranger. Guy hauled his cart, the lonely sound of its squeaky wheel getting closer to the monument of glass. He paced around it, intrigued. Guy rapped his knuckles on Lemat's chest, as if knocking on a door. That's when the first fracture occurred. One crack followed another, until they covered Lemat's entire body. Guy braced himself for the imminent crash, but it didn't come. He exhaled relief and Lemat shattered into a million pieces. The pieces of Lemat floated down, slowly. Guy was surrounded by hundreds of shards, mirroring his reflection. He held out his hand, so a fragment could land standing up on his palm. This made all the pieces freeze in midair. Guy looked closer at the piece. He could look at Lemat through his reflection. The shards started blinking all at once. Guy was startled and let his piece fall. The rest came crashing down right behind it, breaking into tiny pieces, almost like powder.

Guy looked down at the mess upon him. He hummed a tune and produced an old broom from his cart. Guy observed with curiosity as the bristles disappeared in the glass, as if he were dipping them in liquid. He moved the broom around, trying to sweep, but all he did was stir the melting glass. Guy moved faster; sweeping became mixing, and then it turned into painting. Guy drew lines of glass on the sand like a Japanese calligrapher with feverish crescendo. As soon as he finished, he reached down and pulled the symbols he had written, throwing them into the wind. It wasn't sand and glass anymore, but cloth and ink.

The banner flew out of the valley and into the fields, carried by a strong breeze, and landed by Ink's feet. The snow snuck up one of her legs, crafting a close-fitting toga about her. She just watched the banner, as if she expected something. Lemat emerged from the writing on the banner and stepped forward. Ink reached out to touch him. As soon as she made contact, Ink dissolved like the snow. Lemat was left there, alone. He reached inside his body and pulled something from his heart, his fist dripping with black ink. It was a plastic straw.

Lemat stabbed it in the snow. The ink poured from the straw like thin streams of blood; each created intricate patterns as it flowed away. The patterns became letters, sentences, and paragraphs, quickly drying off. The last feeble line trailed forward another inch. Then it contorted violently, like a dying viper, until it ceased to exist. It resembled Lemat's signature.

"Congratulations, Lemat," the executive producer said once Lemat signed the contract in front of him. "Now let's make a great movie."

CHAPTER TWENTY-EIGHT

Lemat wasn't sure how he made it to the studio meeting that morning. All he knew was that he was sitting there with his eyes shielded by sunglasses and looking like a dirty wet rag in his old sweater and his leather wristbands. He knew he had just signed a very profitable movie deal but he didn't remember what had happened the night before or even a few hours before. T-Rex and Geri must have helped him pull himself together that morning, but honestly, the last thing he recalled was making out with those women on the waterbed at The Standard.

After signing the deal, Lemat and entourage returned to their bungalows. Their LA trip was shortened by four days now that a deal had been sealed. Don couldn't get out of the city fast enough. As for Lemat, he set out to spend the rest of the day ordering room service and sitting in the privacy of his garden, drinking tea, and willing the killer hangover away. He was struggling with the idea of calling Ink to let her know he was coming home earlier. Something told him that he shouldn't.

"How you doing, L?" said T-Rex, walking into the garden.

"Wishing I was dead."

T-Rex laughed and sat on the chair next to him. "That'll show you to pace yourself. Besides, you can't die now. Not after that nice deal you just signed. Congratulations."

"Thanks." Lemat wasn't sure if he wanted to ask, but he did anyway. "What the hell happened last night?"

"What do you remember?"

"... Nothing. I had these images—these, hallucinations? Something about a desert—I'm not sure. I was making out with those girls you set me up with—"

"Oh, you did that all right."

"—And then just fragments of you and Geri helping me up to get to the studio. I think I was still tripping when I signed the contract."

"You're also going to trip after you find out how much they're paying you."

"Tell me what happened."

T-Rex moved in his chair uncomfortably and said, "I'm going to spare you the details, but basically, you took those two girls and somehow broke into one of the suites. Don't ask me how, because I was running around trying to find you. You were in those plastic pods, and suddenly, you were gone. By the time I got there, you were getting busy with those girls. And I mean *be-zaye*. So I stood by the door, hoping you were going to do your thing fast, but you weren't having it.

Somebody finally called hotel security and I had my hands full trying to stall them. By the time they entered the suite, you were gone."

"Where?"

"Gone. I thought that was my ass, as far as my reputation was concerned. I was running around trying to find you, when you called me on FaceTime. There you were, with those two fine females, going down the freeway in a convertible, laughing and screaming your ass off. You mooned me and hung up. So, I made a few phone calls. I still have friends on the force. Lucky for you, I was the training officer of the guy who pulled you over in West Hollywood."

"Oh, man. I'm sorry."

"Don't be sorry yet." T-Rex pulled out his phone and played a video.

The images were from the camera of a patrol car. Lemat was struggling with two cops.

"They had to pepper spray you and taze you three times," T-Rex said. "Then you decided to relieve yourself."

"Shit!"

"Yep, all over. The officers let you go and you took off running like you were looking to break some Olympic record. We lost you when you jumped on the back of a truck of a rubbernecker. We found you in Santa Monica by the pier. I had to fish you out of the water. You were crying and mumbling something about writing."

"What?"

"I don't know. You just kept saying that you wanted some ink or something. So, Don called people, the studio called people, I called people and things were smoothed out. No one charged you with anything. You weren't driving; you didn't hurt anybody or damage anything. The fact that you didn't kill yourself is a miracle. In short, you are one lucky SOB. The officers threw you in the drunk tank for the night, Don paid some fines, and that's it. We picked you up in the morning, brought you here, and got you ready for your meeting."

"You have to be kidding me."

"You know, when I took on this job, I thought it was going to be a cinch. Sure, I knew there was the chance I had to throw down with some religious fanatics, but that didn't worry me at all. 'A writer?' Shit, I thought this was nothing but a well-paid babysitting job. You guys are supposed to live off of cigarettes, coffee, and loneliness. But you? You are one crazy-ass, Led-Zeppelin-rolling cat. Next time, I think I'll take a job protecting someone in the Middle East or some other place where I can chill out. You're a goddamned handful, L." T-Rex playfully punched Lemat on the shoulder and left him to his thoughts.

Lemat was unable to do anything else that day but nap. He was just about to fall into that nice, deep sleep that only seemed to come when one watches late-night TV when the ring of his phone snatched him back from unconsciousness. Lemat reached groggily for the infernal device and read one word: *Dad.* A rush of adrenaline woke him up instantly.

The phone kept ringing and Lemat wrestled with the impulse to let it go to voicemail. He answered the call.

"Hello?" Lemat said in English, as if he were oblivious to the caller's identity.

"How's my artist doing?" his father said in Spanish, in that slow, deliberate way he had of speaking.

"Oh, hi, Dad! How's it going?"

"Well, it seems that if I don't call you, we would never speak."

"Yeah, I know. It's just that I've been incredibly busy lately."

"Too busy to call your own father?"

"Well, you know how it is—"

His father interrupted him. "That's just not right. You think it is? I have to tell you that I'm hurt that I had to find out about your book through someone else."

"Who told you about it?" Lemat hoped his mother had not gone ahead and called his father with the news.

"I saw it on the news. So, you finally made it, after all these years. Congratulations."

"Thank you."

"How much are you making?"

"I'm doing good."

"How much?"

"Enough."

"Tell me."

"Why?"

"Because I want to know."

Lemat wasn't going to play right into his father's game. It was always the same. When Lemat landed his job at the creative boutique after college, the first thing his father asked was how much he was making. When Lemat told him, his old man called it a pittance and his job a waste of time. "You can make much more if you come work for me, and you wouldn't have to listen to some idiot like a fucking peon," his father had said. He was right on both accounts. Lemat had been tempted a couple of times in his life to take his father's offer, when he was on his last thread.

"I'll pay you $250,000 a year (or it's equivalent in Venezuela), I'll give you a fully furnished condo, and whatever car you want." That was the standard offer. Only a moron would turn down such a deal. But Lemat knew his father loved to promise the heavens, and after he got what he wanted, he'd hand you some dirt. The pay would probably be that high, but the condo would most likely be a company apartment with secondhand furniture, and the car, one of his father's hand-me-downs, so Dad could buy a new one.

"So, are you going to tell me?"

"I don't want to talk about money, Dad. How are you? How's everything?"

"It could be better. My blood pleasure is a little high, as usual, but I can't complain.

"When are you going to come visit?"

"Er... I don't know. I've been traveling a lot lately because of the book, and things are still pretty busy. So, I'm not sure. Soon, I hope."

"Maybe you can come down for Christmas."

"Maybe."

"Well, OK. I'm very happy for you, and don't stay out of touch for long, all right?"

"Sure."

"Talk to you later."

Lemat would not be able to go back to sleep until later that evening. That was the effect his father had on him; he always put him on edge. Lemat sat in the living room and turned on the TV to the History channel, which was showing something about Hitler and the occult. He had seen it half a dozen times, but he didn't care. All he wanted was to unplug his mind for a while.

"So, is that it? You become a big shot and you forget about us?" Lisa said to the right of him, putting her feet up on the coffee table. An unlit cigarette hung from her lips and a bottle of Jack rested on her lap.

"I've been busy," Lemat said.

"Oh, I heard you," she said. "By the way, I think you dropped one of your testicles somewhere over there when you were talking to your old man."

"Funny, I thought you always had them in your hands."

"Good one," said Dep, bumping fists with Lemat. Dep was sitting to Lemat's left with his knees against his chest. He was eating a spoonful of peanut butter from a jar.

Lisa sneered. "I don't see why you're so happy, Back in Black. He barely remembers you exist now."

"Wait until he starts writing his next novel," Dep said. "We'll have enough time to catch up then."

"Nonsense!" Talia said, curled up at Lemat's feet while resting her chin on his thigh. "This is a new chapter in his life. Things are going to be different from now on. The book is just the beginning. We should take advantage of being in Los Angeles."

"Agreed," Guy said. He sat in a chair, browsing through an entertainment magazine. "Tell Don to make a few calls to see what he can come up with while you're here. You should strike while the iron is still hot. You're the flavor of the month; you need to take advantage of that."

"That's a great idea," Lemat said.

"That's what I'm here for," Guy said.

"This could be a great chance to spread into other areas," Talia said. "Why limit yourself to being just a novelist? Just imagine the possibilities."

Books, Flash, and Bags Full of Cash

"So what do you say, Lemat? They want six million."

Lemat put his phone down. He wore shades and was dressed in a way that said, *I have money, but I don't give a shit what you think of me.* He was riding in the back of a limousine with his manager sitting in front of him. They were on their way to the airport to fly on a private jet to Tokyo, before heading to Paris for the Victoria's Secret fashion show, where Lemat was sure to pick up a new date before the Cannes Film Festival.

"Six million?" Lemat said.

"For the film rights of your last novel, yes," the manager said.

"Yeah, well, tell them to call you back when they get to ten. Then we can start negotiating."

"I don't think they're going to go for it."

"Then fuck 'em. I don't need the money. They want to play hardball, they can go and rehash another '70s TV show for their next movie. They want to use my shit? I get final cut, back-end points, and I'm the sole writer on the project. Besides, I'd rather take it to HBO and make it into a series."

"All right, whatever you say,"

the manager said.

Lemat had better things to do. He was in the middle of writing his next novel about a man on a motorcycle riding from Morocco to South Africa while trying to cope with his wife's death, all the while learning harsh and heartwarming lessons about life. Lemat had researched the novel by riding across Africa himself. The trip had also produced a wealth of photographs, which became part of an exhibit at the Guggenheim Museum in Bilbao, Spain.

His Hollywood career was an anomaly. At the beginning it was all about getting money up front and forgetting about his books. Studios would take his babies and butcher them to suit their needs, while Lemat washed his hands of the whole affair and simply walked into the bank to make deposit after deposit. But as luck would have it, the films did extremely well, raising Lemat's price tag in Tinseltown. He could then push his weight around and become a producer—in name only at first—then have creative input, followed by getting his hands on the script (no more script doctors or "collaborators") and finally achieving creative control. He did what he wanted and how he wanted it to be done. Film, television, and video games had afforded him the kind of lifestyle of which most people could only dream.

Lemat loved his writing career;

it was exactly as he always imagined it: exciting, edifying, and globetrotting. The only thing he hated was the downtime. That's when all the anxiety, the depression, and the insomnia took hold of him.

The lack of stimulation drove him insane, so he tried to stay busy. Lemat would give lectures, interviews, book readings, and basically anything to avoid staying still for any respectable length of time. So who cared if the only thing he could talk about was about work? And that the models he dated didn't last long enough in a relationship for him to care? Or that his friends were colleagues or business acquaintances he had only met in the last few years? Lemat took a handful of pills, washed them down with a little vodka bottle from the limo's bar, and sighed.

When Lemat came back from daydreaming, a commercial for an expensive rehab facility was playing on the TV. Moving into other creative fields was certainly appealing to someone with his imagination, but he thought it best to focus on his novels. He figured that there would be plenty of opportunities for him to explore other storytelling venues if he succeeded as an author. Things were in a great place at the moment when the phone rang.

"Hello?"

"Good, you're still up. And alive, it seems," Don said.

"Oh, Don. Hey, ah… I was meaning to—"

"No need to apologize. All in a good day's work at the office, wouldn't you agree?"

"Yeah, well—"

"Brilliant! Anywho, I took the liberty of ordering a little bit of supper for both of us in my room. So, if you can make your way here in fifteen minutes or so—that is, if you can still put one foot in front of the other—perhaps we can sit down and have a pleasant chat over dinner."

"I don't know. We're leaving tomorrow and I just want to call it in early. I still feel like a wreck."

"Well, that's too bad. Because we really need to talk about your future."

CHAPTER TWENTY-NINE

The dinner was served at the dining table in Don's bungalow. It was a three-course meal—soup, entre, and something sweet to clean the palate—with tea and coffee to follow. Lemat decided to stick to the soup and some bread, the only things he could probably keep down. Don ran through some pleasantries and a few details about the movie deal, and how the book was doing in the international market.

"So, my dear lad. I must ask you, what's next?"

"We go home," said Lemat, shrugging while breaking a piece of bread.

"I meant book-wise."

"I don't know. I'll take some time off and then I'll start thinking about something."

"Time is everything in this business. We need to be thinking about what your next novel will be. Getting a book from your head and into bookstores—so to speak—takes a considerable amount of time. You should be toiling away on your keyboard."

"It's OK. I have all of these manuscripts I want you to take a look at. I'm sure we can find my next novel among them."

"Are these works related to your current hit?"

"No, they're totally different."

"You can leave them where they are, then."

"What do you mean?"

"You see, when your publisher gave you a three-book deal, it was sort of implied that you would be developing a series."

"Hmm… no. *Killing Jesus* was a one-shot deal. I want to move on to something else."

"My dear lad, that's not how this business works. You see, what you have done is created a brand and a readership. In other words, a following. People know you a certain way now, and they want you to fulfill their expectations. Including your publisher. Genre-hopping does not contribute to furthering your marquee value. The publishing house gave you three books, and so, they expect a trilogy."

"But I killed off the protagonist, the time machine blew up, and the scientist that created it was murdered. How can there be a sequel?"

"How about if there was a second time machine? A spare. Or someone else replicated the experiment? You're the writer, not me. Figure it out."

"Oh, 'cause that's going to be a classic. Why not wedge in a fight with ninjas while I'm at it?"

"Whatever works."

Lemat couldn't believe his ears. "You can't be serious. If the publishers wanted a series, they should have said something about that to begin with."

"Well, nobody in their right mind expects an author

who just found astounding international success to sabotage his own career by not making the obvious choice. Take my advice and start working on a sequel."

"And who am I going to kill now? I already killed Jesus. It's doesn't get bigger than that."

"Hitler seems to be a popular choice. Whatever you do, stay away from the Middle East. You'll go broke on security fees alone."

"Great, thank you. And what about my other stuff? I have six novels ready to be published."

"You can hold onto those. If we manage to pull off a successful series of *Killing Something-or-Other,* then you could risk indulging in some vanity project somewhere down the line."

Vanity project? Lemat thought. *Somewhere down the line?* "But… these are the stories I really want to get out there. *Killing Jesus,* was just—Don, you're my agent. I thought you were supposed to be on my side."

"Am I not? My duty to you, first and foremost, is to make sure you have a career, a prosperous one. I know authors always want to pander to their more artistic leanings, but this is a business after all. You have to do something to pay the bills so you can keep on writing. If you wanted to be an author just for the sake of expressing your thoughts, you could have done that by staying self-published, am I correct? But that's not what you wanted. That's not why you penned *Killing Jesus.* You wanted to get out there and swim in a bigger pond, didn't you? Well, here you are. Welcome to the blooming ocean."

Don paused for dramatic effect and then continued, "Now, it's up to you how you want this story to continue, but I don't think you want it to end. The way I see it, you have two options: number one is to do what your artistic voice tells you. I'll take it to the publisher and see if they want to print it. But I know how this works. They are going to sit on it and demand you come up with a sequel to your novel. You'd probably refuse; cue the lawyers, breach of contract, and whatnot. Then your career would be in peril. Or, number two, you can play it smart, do what they expect you to do, and hope it sells as well, if not better, than your first book. Because otherwise, you'll be living the rest of your life by the graces of the money you already made. And may I remind you that you artist types are creative about everything but your finances. Either way, I'll represent you. But it's up to you how we proceed."

Lemat was speechless. This was not how things were supposed to turn out. It wasn't what he had planned. Lemat was gripped by a sense of dread and regret. It slowly dawned on him that he had become the architect of his own creative cage.

"If you're going to regurgitate, please have the decency of excusing yourself to the loo?" Don said.

"… I… I'll start working on something right away."

"That's my boy. Let me know when you do. I can help you steer it in the right direction."

"Sure… OK."

Lemat spent the rest of the meal in silence with his eyes cast down on his plate. After all those years struggling, trying to break in, he had finally made it, only to become a peddler of meaningless, soulless garbage.

The next morning, the driver dropped off Lemat and his companions at the airport. Don had Geri book the earliest flights she could find. T-Rex and Lemat had to wait an extra hour at the first class lounge before their flight back home.

"Lemat, my lad. It has been exhilarating. I would be lying to you if I said I would not miss you. Watching you go from a crude, self-published writer, into a sophisticated, media-savvy author has been truly a pleasure. We'll be in touch, of course. Safe travels."

"Until the next novel." Lemat shook his hand. Then he turned to Geri. She was trying not to cry. "Well? Come here." He hugged her.

"I'm going to miss you." She was sobbing. "Thank you. Thank you for everything."

"No, thank you. It was great to meet you. You're going to do great things, you'll see. Go on and follow your dreams."

"Please take care of yourself."

"I will," T-Rex said, winking at her.

She produced a plastic straw, gave it to Lemat, and faced the bodyguard. "Take care, T-Rex."

"Knock 'em dead, Little G. Mr. Maxfield."

Lemat and T-Rex sat alone at the VIP lounge, waiting for their flight. They were both quiet most of the time. Lemat's mind was back at home, wondering what he would find upon his return.

It's going to be nice to go back to the old routine, he thought. Lemat was tired of sleeping in hotels and running around airports. All he wanted now was to be alone for a while. Otherwise, he would take advantage of his newfound free time and generous funds to go on a vacation somewhere. Preferably a place where nobody knew about *Killing Jesus.*

Lemat slept for most of the flight. A driver was

waiting for him at the airport back home. Everything felt weird. The signs were familiar, but Lemat felt like a tourist. It would take him a couple of days to get acclimated. T-Rex checked out Lemat's apartment for the last time. It was his last act as his personal security specialist.

"Everything looks fine," T-Rex said. "But I advise you to consider hiring permanent security. At least until the heat around you cools off, you know?"

"It's OK. I don't see any more controversial novels in my future."

"Just giving you my expert's opinion." He offered his hand. "L."

"Thank you for everything. I wouldn't be standing here if it wasn't for you."

"That's my job."

"Sorry about LA."

"Now *that's* a different story. Be safe."

CHAPTER THIRTY

"You'd be amazed at the things you get used to," Don had once said. Lemat felt strangely lost at home. There was no knock at the door, waking him up. The bags were still packed. His breakfast wouldn't be served. Nobody was waiting for him, looking over his shoulder, or telling him what to do. Everything was eerily quiet. He turned the TV on to make some noise. A show about CIA secrets was playing. His apartment felt twice as large as he remembered. He decided that he needed to do something trivial to get himself going.

The refrigerator was empty, except for a couple of takeout containers, the remnants of his last night with Ink before he left for New York the second time around. He dumped them in the trash and went to the grocery store. He made a mental note to call his mother when he came back.

Even after his success, Lemat rode the bus. He didn't want to own a car; it seemed like nothing but a big hassle. He wore a beanie and shades, walked down the aisles, and tried to think what he should bring home. He couldn't live on takeout for the rest of his life.

"Excuse me, do I know you?" a woman said.

Lemat was squeezing fruit. He saw a guy doing it when making his selections, and now he tried to decipher his method. "Sorry, what?"

"You look familiar," the woman said (early forties, dark-rooted blonde, yoga outfit). "Do you go to the Prana Center on Tuesdays by any chance?"

Lemat shook his head. It just dawned on him that T-Rex was no longer around. "Sorry, no."

"Really? God, you look very familiar. I'm sure I know you from somewhere."

"I get that all the time. I have one of those faces." He put the pear back, knocking some to the floor. Lemat wasn't sure if he should pick them up or just go away. He decided he had enough groceries and headed to the cashier.

"Are you the guy?" the young girl at the register said.

"Huh?"

"It's you, isn't it?"

"I don't think so."

"You are. You wrote that novel, *Killing Jesus.* I loved it! I read it in a single sitting. I overslept and got to work here late. My manager was, like, all agro. And I'm like, 'whatever.' Just between you and me, he's a humongous a-hole. Anyway, so it's you, isn't it? Man, I wish I had brought my copy so you can sign it. Are you coming back next week? I don't work Mondays and Thursdays—"

"That's great; maybe next time. I'm in a bit of a hurry, though. Sorry."

"Yeah, no; for real. Don't worry. See, I knew it was you—"

"OK, take care." Lemat couldn't leave the store fast enough.

The supermarket encounter left him paranoid. He pulled his hat further down, pulled up the collar of his jacket, and looked away through the bus window to avoid eye contact with anyone else. He didn't think things over very well. Perhaps his days of mundane chores could wait until the storm of publicity blew over. It wasn't as much the wackos Lemat feared, but all the unwanted attention. He had gone from the guy sitting at the fringes of a gathering to being on center stage. "Everything has a price," Guy's words echoed in his head.

Once back home, Lemat tried to keep busy. He put the groceries away and did some laundry. *OK, what now?* he thought, looking around for something else to do. That's when he saw his old boom box in his office. Lemat sat down with pen and paper and started drafting a playlist for a new tape. Lemat would write a couple of song titles and then cross them out. He finally decided on a whole punk-rock set: The Clash, The Ramones, The Stooges, Black Flag, Death, The Sex Pistols, and so on. Something with energy and attitude. That kept him busy for a few hours. He looked at the time and it was too late to call his mother. *Tomorrow morning*, he promised himself.

The apartment felt as if it grew even bigger during his errand. Lemat sat in the living room, facing the balcony. It was already dark and it started to rain. He took a straw and twirled away. Thoughts of his next novel were spammed by ones of Ink (a little hypocritical of him, to be sure). While on the road, he had no problem having sex with other women. He had even precipitated his dalliance with Geri, not to mention his run-in with Clover. They were all great fun, but there was something lacking. He could understand why Ink loved to live such a free life. She fucked when she was horny, she only hung out with people when it was fun for her, she only worked when she was inspired—it was life with all the crummy parts taken off, like bread without crusts. There was no doubt in Lemat's mind that someone was keeping her warm every night in his absence. But something was lacking in this seemingly logically cohesive argument.

Lemat missed the companionship, the conversations, the way they commented on films to make each other laugh while sharing takeout. He had this image of them in that very home: he writing on his laptop while she sketched on her notepad. The idea made Lemat feel warm inside.

"You have better things to worry about now," said Talia, lying down and resting her legs on Lemat's lap. "There will be other women, better looking, and less complicated. Why waste your time with this girl?"

"I like her," Lemat said.

"Oh, for fuck's sake," said Lisa, sitting on the floor. "She sure seemed special when you had those two skanks on top of you in Los Angeles."

"And Geri," Talia said. "Nicely done, by the way. That was so hot!" She stretched out sensually.

"And the busty bartender," Guy said from his chair as he checked his phone. "But I get you. What happens on the road stays on the road."

"I don't think Ink will be happy with that," Dep

said. He was sitting on the side of Lemat carefully painting Talia's toes.

"What, The People's Vagina?" Lisa said. "Probably the only thing that would bug her is that she wasn't part of the fun."

"That's a little hard," Dep said.

"Like the dick she had inside her while this idiot was gone," Lisa said.

"OK, you need to back off, sweetheart," Talia said.

"Or what, you're going to inspire him to write a nasty letter?" Lisa said.

"You people are just wasting his time," Guy said. "Look, kid. You want to go after her? Go ahead. What do you have to lose? If it doesn't work out, have a one-night stand with a groupie or something."

"Yeah, you can have the bartender again at the very least," Lisa said.

"You won't be hurting for company any time soon," Talia said.

"I say, stay home, watch a film, and let things be," Dep said. "Maybe Ink wanted some time apart to think about your relationship, to make sure she wasn't making a mistake."

Lemat thought maybe he was the one making the mistake. Two people sleeping around did not make a "relationship." But Dep could be right—this time apart could be the thing they needed to put things in perspective. His life had moved into a different place and he would love nothing more than to have Ink come along with him in this new adventure. Of course, Lemat could only wonder what she would have to say about it.

CHAPTER THIRTY-ONE

"Fuck! Fuck! Oh, fuck me!" said Ink with her head tilted back as she grinded her hips on top of Lemat, her nails gripping his chest. Lemat held onto Ink's hip as he reached his own climax. Ink collapsed on top of him afterwards.

"I guess you *did* miss me," said Lemat, out of breath. He reached down to cup her butt.

Ink lifted up her head. She moved a lock of sweaty hair away from her flushed face. "You're such an idiot. I can't believe you waited this long to call me."

"I told you, I had things to do."

"Yeah, namely, me."

She rolled over to the side, revealing her glistening body. There was something wholly erotic about her. Ink lit up a joint, took a drag, and passed it to Lemat. He had called her when he woke up mid-morning. Ink was still asleep, as expected, but she was happy to hear from him, and even more so that his trip was cut short. Two hours later, Ink showed up at his door with a bag of

Indian food, half a dozen films, and a few joints. Lemat was already playing a tape he had mixed for Ink a while ago with the likes of Tori Amos, Ani DiFranco, Regina Spektor, Fiona Apple, and Björk.

There wasn't much talking on her arrival; Ink placed the things on the kitchen counter and walked to the bedroom as she stripped of her clothes. They made love, desperately, quietly—just whispers and moans— like two lovers ravishing each other in a public place afraid of getting caught. Then they had some food, talked about Lemat's trip, laughed, and had sex again. This time, loudly and without restraint.

"Are you going to do it?" said Ink, taking a hit. "Are you really going to write a sequel to *Killing Jesus?*"

"I don't see how I have any other option," Lemat said.

"Yeah, you do. You can just *not* write it."

"It's not as simple as that. What about the publisher?"

"Fuck them. They can go on and exploit someone else."

"And then do what? Throw my career away?"

"It's just one novel. You can barely call that a career. And, anyway, that's not the point. You should care about your work first."

"I do, but in order to do that, I need to keep myself afloat."

"Well, it looks like you have a pretty good lifeboat as far as I can tell. Money is not really an issue anymore, so do what you want to do."

"It's that simple."

"It is."

"I have a contract."

"For three books."

"The publisher expects sequels."

"Too bad for them," said Ink as she turned away from him to lounge and take another toke.

She handed it over to Lemat but the argument was spoiling his buzz. He began, "It's just…"

"What?"

"I just don't want to go back to where I was before all of this. The websites, the living paycheck to paycheck—I'm finally in a position where I can exercise my creativity and not worry about money. How many people can say that?"

"Not you. Listen, this is all great and I'm happy for you, but there's nothing artistic about fulfilling some company's demand. What's the difference between you churning out graphics in your old job and writing what your publisher wants?"

Lemat had no answer. Or, rather, he did, but it wasn't the answer he wanted to hear. He took one last smoke before passing it back to Ink and got up to go to the bathroom.

"Lemat?"

He didn't answer. He used the toilet, washed his hands, splashed water on his face, and stared at his reflection in the mirror. There was a feeling of disquiet squirming about inside him.

Assassination, Inc.

"Our guest tonight is renowned science-fiction author Lemat, whose best-selling series about time-traveling hitman Frank Johnson has grossed millions of dollars and has been successfully adapted numerous times for the big screen. His latest book, *Killing Jack the Ripper,* marks the twentieth entry in the saga. It's great to have him on the show. Welcome, Lemat!"

"Thank you," a sixty-something Lemat said. He was balding, with a scruffy beard and glasses. His heavy figure was barley contained in a turtleneck sweater, tweed jacket with elbow patches, and dark chinos.

His host, Oliver Ivy, was a respected journalist with a tall, thin frame and the craggy face of an aging leading man. His eponymous talk show was a series of intimate interviews with political figures, artists, celebrities, and athletes in the stark setting of a bar's booth.

"This is book twenty of the *Killing* series," Oliver said.

"Twentieth, yes."

"And to what do you attribute the outstanding success of your novels?"

"Well, if I have to pick one element, it would be the themes. Each story deals with the death of a historical figure and the consequences afterwards."

"And you started big. In your first, you did away with Jesus."

Lemat nodded, grinning. "That's what started it all."

"Maybe not today, but some people considered that quite a bold move back then."

"Yep, I got all kinds of flack because of it. I even had some uncomfortable brushes with a few... overzealous fans. Well, readers, I guess."

"Religious fanatics, it seemed, who objected mightily to your first work. Any close calls?"

"No, nothing like that. I always had good security."

"And it certainly didn't hurt your sales."

"Not at all."

"Now, as successful as the series has become, you're also no stranger to some rather harsh criticism. Your work has been called 'The new lowest common denominator,' 'Everything that's wrong with the publishing industry today,' 'Compost for the semiliterate'—"

"Occupational hazard," said Lemat, waving his hand dismissively. "It comes with the territory."

"But those are some pretty strong comments, if you don't mind me saying."

"They are, but that's OK. Not everybody has to like what I do, but for those who do enjoy my novels, they are a lot of fun."

"But why such a polarizing point of view? You have in one hand, a whole group of people that can't get enough of your books; on the other, people are essentially saying you are the literary equivalent of a 'hemorrhoid,' I quote."

"Jealousy? Elitism? I don't know, and I really don't care.

Numbers don't lie."

"And they are definitely in your favor."

"Precisely."

"And you truly don't care?"

"I mean, nobody likes to be judged. What I do is provide entertainment and hopefully entice readers with the idea of what our world would be like if any of these relevant figures never existed. Is it historically accurate? I'm not a historian. Are they in any way realistic? Who cares? I'm a fiction writer, not a journalist or a scientist, or whatever. Every time you have something as popular as the *Killing* series, you're bound to have people who attack it for whatever reason. It's just the way these things go."

"Your work has been adapted into five blockbuster films. A sixth is already underway. And there's a TV series in the works if I'm not mistaken."

"No, the TV thing is based on my other book series."

"The counterpart to your *Killing* novels, *Loving*. Which is basically—"

"Which is basically an offshoot of the original series, only this time, the protagonist is Sarah Silverhart, a member of the time-traveling team who goes back in history and falls in love with prominent men."

"And even women, as in the very controversial fourth installment, where Sarah has a relationship with Cleopatra."

"Very true."

"And once again, this is a series that has become as successful as the original one, but it has also attracted an incredible amount of negative criticism, especially from women. The work has been called 'sexist,' 'chauvinistic,' 'juvenile,' 'asinine,' 'shameful,'" the host read from his notes.

"Those are people who are missing the point, once again. After so many years of the *Killing* series, I was looking to tell another story, and the obvious choice was to counterbalance the original novels."

"Death and love."

"Exactly. Those are strongest driving motivations in the world. In the *Loving* books, you have a woman who gets to see these influential men as that, men. So the idea was to demystify a lot of these legends."

"You're killing the myth, so to speak."

"Yes. So all that stuff coming from feminist groups, and what have you, is complete nonsense."

"You mentioned moments ago the need to tell other stories."

"Yes."

"And you did try to steer away from your usual science-fiction fare with three other books: one was a crime story, the other one was a drama, and there was also a paranormal story. And they didn't come from your usual publishing house."

"Yeah, my publisher didn't think a drama fit in with their overall catalogue, so I had to find someone who'd actually publish it. The same thing happened when I wrote the crime novel."

"And then the paranormal story you had to self-publish."

"That's correct."

"None of these books were particularly successful. Especially when compared to the behemoth sales your two famous series have managed to accomplish."

"Yup." Lemat sighed.

"Why?"

Lemat took a few seconds to answer. "If I knew the answer to that, then you wouldn't be asking me that question, would you? I'd be touting yet another franchise."

Both men laughed. Then Oliver's silence made it obvious that he expected a more thorough reply.

"I don't know. I mean, I guess people expect certain things from me."

"You're the sci-fi guy."

"Exactly. Every time you walk away from that which you are known for, you run the risk of alienating your core readership and you might not be able to connect with a new one."

"But you said this about the drama, *The Oddman,* and I quote: 'This is the most personal work I have ever written, what I consider my greatest writing achievement... This is the one I'd love to be remembered by.' We're talking about a very special story. Something of great significance to you."

Lemat squirmed uncomfortably in his chair. "Very much so."

"And what happened? The man who has sold millions of copies around the world suddenly fails at what he considers his best work. How can that be?"

Lemat took a sip of his water and cleared his throat. "I guess it just didn't connect with an audience," he said after taking a deep breath.

"Well, for what it's worth, I read it and thought it was terrific. It shows such an intelligent, touching, eloquent side of you that most readers familiar with your more popular works are completely not used to."

"Thank you. Thank you very much. That means a lot to me. Sadly, only you and my mother thought so."

Oliver laughed. "So, what's next for you?"

"Your phone is ringing!" Ink said from the bed.

Lemat's eyes focused again on his reflection. They were red because of the weed. Water ran down his face and dripped into the sink.

"Your phone!"

He dried off and walked out of the bathroom with a single thought running through his head: *What are you going to do next?*

CHAPTER THIRTY-TWO

"Kill someone!" said Guy, typing something on his smartphone. He sat in the living room with his feet up on the coffee table. His jacket was neatly folded on the armrest of the sofa and his tie was undone. "Anyone. Just pick somebody famous and important and off him… or her. That could be a nice twist for a sequel."

It had been raining hard since the night before. A mixed tape with jazz acts played in the background: Béla Fleck and the Flecktones, Weather Report, Herbie Hancock, Screaming Headless Torsos, Me'Shell, Charles Mingus, Mongo Santamaría, Django Reinhardt, and any other band that Lemat thought could help get his creative juices flowing.

He had started to brainstorm the follow-up to *Killing Jesus* the next morning after Ink went back to her place. She had agreed to tag along tonight to meet up with Specs. To be honest,

Lemat never thought he would ever hear from his bar buddy after their LA run-in, but there he was, on the phone last evening, inviting him to a club downtown to hang out with some friends.

"Mohamed," said Lisa from her perch on the long couch, sitting cross-legged with her hands behind her head.

"No!" said Dep, lying on the floor writing on a heavily scribbled notebook with a great number of entries crossed out.

"Come on! Have some balls," Lisa said. "You know that's the obvious choice."

"He's writing a sequel, not his obituary," Dep said.

"The controversy alone would be priceless, promotionally speaking," Guy said. "Maybe even greater than the first book. I think you have something there, sugar lips."

"I told you not to call me that, you business ball sack," Lisa said.

"No! Forget it! You're all out of your minds," Dep said. "How about, *Killing Gandhi?*"

"Gandhi was killed," said Lemat, sitting on the couch between Lisa and Talia, working on his laptop. He twirled a straw in one hand while he watched the blinking cursor on the screen.

"Killing the Guy Who Killed Gandhi?" Dep said.

"Next," Lemat said.

"Mohamed!" Lisa said. "I'm fucking telling you!"

"No!" said Dep and Lemat at the same

time.

"If you ask me, this is just a big waste of time," said Talia, filing her nails while resting her head against Lemat.

"What a surprise!" Lisa said. "Change the tune already for fuck's sake."

"Then it's a good thing nobody asked you, toots," Guy said.

"Because it's obvious," Talia said. "Ink is right—you should forget about what those corporate drones say and do what you want. You already gave the pigs enough manure to keep them content. Why defile your brilliance again?"

Dep said, "Hello? Because we have a nice home, a full fridge, and money in the bank. You would throw all that away out of ca…capriciness… capuchiness—"

"Capriciousness," said Guy, tapping a cigarette against his silver case.

"That!" Dep said.

"Hardly," Talia said. "Anything Lemat writes can blow that sorry excuse for a novel out of the water, any day."

"Not to mention that he actually wrote that sorry excuse for a novel himself," Guy said just before lighting a match against its box with one hand. He leered at Talia through the dim, eerie glow.

Talia lifted her head up. "You really don't care whether he wastes away in office drudgery or prostitutes his soul, do you? You only care about a paycheck."

Guy puffed his cigarette vigorously. "I care about results."

"Even if it ends up killing him?" said Talia, sitting up.

"I'm a facilitator, gorgeous. Not a decision-maker. He asks, I provide. And I delivered."

"He didn't ask for this," Talia said.

"That's a crock and you know it."

"Killing Einstein!" Dep said.

"Be quiet, sweaty," said Talia, still staring at Guy.

Lisa sprung open her switchblade and offered it to Talia. "Here you go, princess, go at it. Just make sure you wipe the blade clean when you're done."

Guy spoke without breaking Talia's stare. "No Einstein means no time machine, sport. Keep at it."

"All right, I think we all need to settle down. How about a break?" Lemat said.

"No, let her say her peace," said Guy, calmly smoking. "Go ahead, sugar pie. Tell me how I screwed things up, how I destroyed Lemat's life by helping him get the break he so desperately wanted."

"Stick and twist, love. Stick and twist," said Lisa, mimicking a stabbing motion.

Guy continued, "Why don't you regale us with the tale of how you planned to achieve success before I came along to spoil everything? I'm sure that after Lemat tried to kill himself you had everything under control, am I right? Go ahead, lay it on me." He opened his arms, welcoming the criticism.

Talia got to her feet very slowly and, in a fit of rage, threw the knife at the talent manager. The blade struck right next to Guy's head. Talia stormed off into the office and slammed the door behind her. Guy pried the knife loose and studied it, while exhaling a gust of smoke. Lemat closed his laptop and went to his room to get ready to meet Specs.

CHAPTER THIRTY-THREE

The rain raged on that evening. Specs had chosen "Pandemonium," a trendy club downtown built from a former 1920s movie theater. The place's original Neo-Renaissance style was maintained with its stained glass murals, marble lobby, and gilded hand-carved moldings. The theater seats had been removed to give way to bars, tables, and a dance floor. The stage, majestically draped with a red curtain, still served as a screening area—a collection of old anime was being projected at the moment—and bandstand. The six large balconies were converted into VIP rooms.

"What a shame," said Ink, looking at a speaker that hung from one of the frescoes.

"What?" Lemat said. The industrial-rock song playing in the background drowned out Ink's voice. He saw her frowning at the candelabra, which had become part of the red, gold, and blue lighting scheme of the place, so he knew it had something to do with the décor. "What did you say?" Lemat moved closer.

"This place!" she screamed.

"Cool, huh?"

"Not really. How much cooler would it have been to watch a movie in this place back in its heyday? Like a little place for film worship."

"Warship?" Lemat attempted.

"Worship!" She put her hands together as if praying.

"Oh!"

"And now look at it… It's sad."

"What? I can barely hear you."

"Nothing. Forget it."

A sultry hostess, seemingly wearing nothing but a buttoned-down men's shirt, guided Ink and Lemat to one of the balconies. The handsome staff was meant to look as if caught "the morning after."

Specs was holding court among an interesting group of people, the kind of crowd that spent a lot of money to look like they were broke.

"Hey! I'm glad you could make it," said Specs, getting up and giving Lemat a big hug. Specs' apparent jitteriness revealed he had started the party early.

"This is my friend, Ink," Lemat said.

"'Ink?' I love it! Nice to meet you! I'm Harry Chaser, but you can call me Specs." He came in for a hug but was stopped by Ink's outstretched hand.

"Hi. Lemat told me a lot about you."

"Really? All lies, I'm sure. Nothing but lies. What are you two drinking?"

"Cranberry and Absolut," Ink said.

"Er… a screwdriver," said Lemat, feeling somewhat ashamed of his dated choice of drink.

Specs turned to the waitress and said, "You got that, sweetie? And make sure my buddy's drink is made with Scourged, OK?" He pointed at the green vodka bottle on the table and then turned back to Lemat. "Here, let me introduce you to a few friends." He put his hand around Lemat's shoulders to guide him around the room. "I'm sure you recognize this guy. Scourge, this is Lemat. He's the author of *Killing Jesus.* He lives here, too."

"What's up?" said Scourge, thrusting his chin forward as a greeting. The guitarist looked like the byproduct of a car mechanic and a Cenobite. Melvin "Scourge" Castro was the lead guitarist of Sorrow for Psychos. A cross between Black Sabbath and Tool with a dash of Megadeth thrown into the mix, the band stomped the touring circuit in relative obscurity until their fourth album, *Unresolved Defenestration,* hit the mainstream like a sledgehammer. The bottle Specs had mentioned before, "Scourged Earth Vodka," was the musician's own brand.

"I'm a big fan," Lemat said.

"Thanks," Scourge said. He was accompanied by a young woman with too much makeup and not enough clothes to cover her generous attributes.

"You may also know this guy," said Specs, turning to a slim guy with his signature train-conductor cap, soul-patch beard, red scarf, and leather vest.

"Eugene Finn, or course. I love your movies," said Lemat, shaking his hand.

"A man of good taste," said the director, winking at him. He was there with a pretty Hindi woman in a bohemian getup.

"I caught Gene in town while he was doing location scouting," Specs said.

Everybody knew Eugene Finn's story: the half-black, half-Jewish Australian learned about film while working as a teenage usher at a multiplex. He moved to the States and hitchhiked to Los Angeles, where he worked as a production assistant on a Ridley Scott movie, until one of the producers found out nobody had hired him in the first place and he was subsequently kicked out. Finn then worked as an Alaskan crab fisherman for six months to finance his first movie, *Nicotine's Fix.* The darling of that year's independent film festivals and the sleeper hit at Cannes, it soon propelled him to prominence.

"And last, but not least, this is Cinco," said Specs, pointing to an unassuming guy with Asian features dressed like a skater. "He's—"

"One of the best street artists in the world," said Ink, beaming. "That dragon you painted on the side of the London Underground was amazing."

"Thanks. You an artist?" Cinco said with a French accent.

"I am," she said. "I've been doing tattoos lately."

"Cool. Scourge hired me to decorate his new tattoo shop just around the corner."

"Maybe you can drop by one of these days to check it out," Scourge said. "We're always looking for talented artists, especially when they're hot chicks."

"Yeah, definitely. I'll check it out," said Ink unenthusiastically, already turned off by the remark.

Cinco—nobody knew his real name—was the son of a Chinese immigrant and a Belgian mother, who first came to the public's attention during the Spanish protests of the Movimiento 15-M in 2011 that helped spark the whole "occupy" movement around the world. Cinco sprayed stencils on banks and financial institutions across Madrid of fat rats with bandanas covering their faces and holding puppet strings. He signed his work with a number five for some reason, and the legend was born.

Specs also introduced Ink and Lemat to his companion, a woman who could only be categorized unequivocally as an escort. She didn't say much but smiled a lot and nodded along with the conversation.

"So you're the guy who killed Jesus?" Scourge said as Ink and Lemat got comfortable on the wraparound couch.

"The one and only," Specs said.

"Congratulations on the movie deal, by the way," said Gene. "How does it feel to be part of Hollywood?"

"Thanks. Great, I guess," Lemat said. "I really didn't do much. Just sign the deal. They said they might contact me to work on the script, and work on some details about the story."

Gene chuckled. "Better not hold your breath. The first thing the studio does is put as much distance between them and the original author as possible."

"Really?" Lemat said.

"Oh, yeah," Gene said. "The best thing you can do now is to separate yourself from the project. If it sucks, you can always wash your hands of the whole thing. If it's a hit, more power to you."

Lemat didn't know what to say. He just grinned and nodded.

"But wait a minute, wait a minute. We were talking about Cinco's shoes," Scourge said. "Go ahead, man. Show us those suckers."

The street artist put one foot on top of the coffee table. The sneakers were meant to look as if stitched together from other shoes, and the sole looked like it was made of used car tires.

"'The Phantom Footprint,'" Cinco said proudly.

"Are they made from recycled materials?" Ink said.

"No. But they're meant to give off that

vibe. Cool, huh?"

"So much for running around in the night with a backpack full of spray cans," Gene said.

"Whatever. The only cops he sees now are guarding his art when he has a gallery opening," Scourge said.

"You're giving me heat? The guy who just recorded an album of country standards?" Cinco said.

"*Metal* versions of country standards," Scourge said.

"Kiss my ass," Cinco said. "What's next? Line dancing in the mosh pit at your concerts?"

"Stepping on their Phantom Footprints, I'm sure," the musician countered.

"So why are you scouting locations here?" said Lemat to Gene, trying to blend into the group.

"Oh, I just signed a three-picture deal to adapt *Madman* into film."

"Really?" Lemat said. "Were you a big fan of the comic book?"

"No, never read it. Have you?"

"I—"

"Dibs on the script!" said Specs, cackling, almost spilling his drink.

"I would love to see another film like *The Edge of Her Skin* or *Shadow of the Night*. I love those movies."

"Thanks. Me, too," Gene said. "Sadly, studios don't want to finance those kinds of projects anymore, and getting anyone to distribute them is a nightmare. But I'm glad I managed to make those flicks early on. The film industry is a very different animal now."

"It's all 3D, remakes, and sequels," Ink said.

"Yeah," the director said. "And reboots, and series, and adaptations, and all that crap. I hope this trilogy does well. I want to use some of that money to finance this project I've been aching to do for a long time. We'll see."

"Hey, like I said, let me know if you need help with the music," Scourge said. "If the band doesn't want to get involved, maybe I can do something on scale or something."

"Thanks, man. I'll keep that in mind," Gene said.

"Likewise if you need a writer," said Lemat, not wanting to let an opportunity go to waste.

The director laughed. "Sure."

"And call Cinco if you need shoes," Scourge said to everyone's amusement.

"Why don't you just score it for free, like among friends?" Ink said.

"It's not that easy," Gene said.

"Yeah, when agents get involved, things get all messed up," Scourge said.

"Why? You don't need them. You can just talk among yourselves and get it done, right?" Ink said.

"No, not really," Cinco said. "That would screw up your value."

Confused, Ink looked at him expectantly.

"You know, the price that you can

command when negotiating a contract," Gene said.

"Yeah, you don't want to fuck with that," Cinco said.

"If you sell yourself too cheap, then everybody will take advantage of you," Scourge said. "It's one of those business things."

"Oh, I get it," Ink said with an exaggerated expression. "Of course, business. Can't fuck with that."

Lemat shot daggers at her, but Ink just looked at him sardonically and said, "That makes me wonder, what's your asking price these days, Lemat?"

The question blindsided him. Lemat grasped for some witty retort or anything that could dispel the awkward moment. But sadly, his mind didn't work at that speed. "Er... I don't know." He shrugged. "Not much, I guess—I...I really don't know. Seriously—"

"Ah! She's just fucking with you," said Specs, punching Lemat playfully on the shoulder, "You know what? We need some Cristal in this mother, right? Hey, sweetheart! A bottle of Cristal for the table. We have a lot to celebrate tonight."

"I pass; I don't drink champagne," said Lemat, still staring at Ink, befuddled. There was something strange about the way she was looking at him; almost as if she didn't know who he was.

"Good, because it's actually sparkling wine," Gene said.

"What about you, man. What are you working on now?" Scourge said.

"Oh… I'm—I just started to work on the sequel to my novel," Lemat said.

"Killing Mary?" said Cinco, making everybody laugh. Specs' was particularly loud.

"No, dude. You should kill Lee Harvey Oswald and then explore what the history of this country would be if Kennedy never died," Scourge said.

"I'd read that," said Gene, drawing the approval of the group. "I'd read that in a second."

"There you have it! Problem solved!" Specs said. "You have your next bestseller. Here, cheers!"

Cristal flutes were passed around. Lemat exchanged a sheepish look with Ink before forcing himself to drink. She smiled back at him sarcastically and just wet her lips.

The rest of the evening was spent talking and drinking. Lemat and Ink tried to engage some of the women, but they quickly found out the ladies were little more than accessories. Lemat really wanted to seem part of the group, seeing as he was among fellow artists, after all. But he soon discovered that these guys were in a very different stage in their careers. So Lemat switched strategies and became more interested in learning from them, all the while trying to puzzle out why he was now getting daggers from Ink.

"Hey! Let's go to Scourge's and continue

the party," Specs said.

It was just after two in the morning. Lemat, Ink, and Cinco were the only ones that didn't have cocaine fueling their party drive. Cinco was fine, though. He was used to being up all night.

Ink leaned over Lemat and whispered, "It's time for us to get scarce."

"We're going to take off," Lemat said.

"No way! Come on, the night is young," Specs said. "Let me buy another round and then we'll get going." He got closer and lowered his voice. "And if you need a little…" Specs touched his nose. "You know what I'm saying?"

"Yeah, but I need to work in the morning," Lemat said.

"Whatever! You're a fucking writer!" Specs said.

"I'm not that far up the ladder to make my own schedule," Lemat improvised. "It was really great meeting you all."

Specs protested some more, but Ink and Lemat got up, said their goodbyes, and took off.

"God, I thought that was never going to end," she said.

"It wasn't that bad."

"You couldn't fit another ego in that room with a shoehorn. What a bunch of phonies!"

"I thought you were having fun."

"Did you really?"

Lemat groped for the right words.

"Thank you!" said Ink, finally flagging down a taxi. "Come on, let's go get something to eat."

"I can't."

"What? Why?"

"I have a phone meeting with Don in the morning, and they're sending me the artwork for the book cover for the Netherlands and Russia."

"You can do that later," Ink said halfway inside the cab.

"No, I can't. Plus, I have to keep working on the new novel."

"A second ago, you were going to party with those assholes, and suddenly you have all of this shit you have to do?"

"I wasn't going to go. The club was about to close and I was going to head home. I just didn't want to be rude."

"You mean you wanted to fit in with the cool kids."

"Don't be ridiculous."

"Then what is it?"

"Are you getting in or not?" the cab driver said.

Ink let the taxi go and waited for Lemat's answer. Lemat felt stupid having to explain himself. He didn't know what made Ink react this way.

"They're good people to know," Lemat said. "It's good networking."

"You can't be serious."

"A famous artist, a member of a huge band, and an A-list director? Yeah, I'm serious."

"They're a bunch of sellouts, talking about franchises, selling shoes and vodka, and using their names to open stores that they'll probably never set foot in."

"So?"

"'So?'" Ink couldn't believe her ears. "What the hell happened to you on that trip? You come back and it's all sequels, meetings, schedules, and 'networking.'"

"That's not true."

"Aw, come on. You barely talk to me when you were away, you don't call me until a few days after you arrive, you blow me off because you have all of these important things to do, and you'd rather hang out with those idiots—" She let her words linger in the air.

That's bullshit, Lemat thought. Yet, he couldn't just put things in perspective. Was he supposed to tell her that he didn't call her right away because he knew she was sleeping around? That he, too, slept with someone else? And besides, they weren't a couple. Ink had made that perfectly clear. Would she understand that he needed a day to himself when he returned, just to try to come to grips with his new life? And how about the fear and frustration he was experiencing about his career?

"Things are different now," he said.

"They are," said Ink, looking disappointed as she walked away.

CHAPTER THIRTY-FOUR

Death was the only thing Lemat could think of. He sat cross-legged, facing a bare wall in his home office, and wrote the name of a historical figure on an index card. Lemat taped it on the wall and stared at it, thinking about possible story ideas, which he'd write on another card tethered to the name. Unconvinced by the plot, he would write another name and try to craft a viable story. A mixed tape of progressive rock played in the background: Rush, Dream Theater, Blue Öyster Cult, early Genesis, Marillion, and others provided an ambiance conducive to inspiration. Lemat would write in longhand little synopses to each story in a notebook. As days went by, the wall disappeared in a chaos of index cards and tethers, and the floor was littered with crumpled notes. He had most of his meals in the office, and his only breaks came in the form of phone interviews, or calls from Don, or a few attempts to contact Ink.

"Hey, it's me. I got VIP passes for the Sorrow for

Psychos concert this Friday. I'd love for you to come. Call me."

But the calls went largely unanswered. His text messages were ignored for hours and the eventual replies were indecipherable rain checks. Lemat agonized over this while he sat in darkness on the floor in the middle of the room among his garden of disposed ideas. Lemat stared at the modernist mess that had become his wall, twirling a straw in his hand. Four piles of cassette tapes surrounded him. The days he spent cooped up with only Guy, Lisa, Dep, and Talia for company were getting to him. His lack of motivation and progress on his new novel dragged him down into mental quicksand.

He talked to Specs twice more after meeting him at the club, but now Specs was back in Los Angeles. The other people he had met that night seemed to have gone on with their lives and their careers. They were busy, and even though they reiterated that they should get together, it never happened.

Lemat lay down; his neck and back were sore. He closed his tired eyes, not minding if he actually fell asleep. In that moment, between wakefulness and slumber, he thought about his future.

Winters Gone, Summers Gained

It took the flashlight ten seconds to hit the shallow water. The young man leaned over the bridge. *Ten seconds. That's quick enough*, he thought. It certainly seemed high enough. The road was deserted. From time to time, the lights of a car would pierce the sheltering veil of the night. He feared he would be spotted, his intentions deduced, and his actions thwarted. But no living soul showed up.

"Pretty high, huh?"

The young man straightened up, quite startled. It took him a few seconds to focus on the stranger, pale in complexion, a mat of unruly black hair, and dressed in a dingy gray sweater.

"Pretty cold night, huh?" the stranger said. The kid noticed the man had on wristbands as he blew air into his hands to try to warm them up.

"Yeah, freezing," he said with some apprehension.

"Out for a walk in the middle of nowhere?"

"Look, man, I don't want to be rude. I just— I just want to be alone with my thoughts," said the young man, whose name happened to be Dave.

"I get you," said the stranger, leaning on the side railing next to Dave. "I used to do that a lot, be by myself inside my head... sometimes it feels like that's the only thing I did in those days."

Dave took a closer look at his unwanted companion. They looked about the same age, but perhaps the man was one of those guys who looked younger than he actually was; he struck him as older somehow.

"Listen, I want be alone, OK?" Dave said.

"It's a free bridge."

Getting heated, Dave exploded,

"Are you deaf? Just leave me alone! Fuck off!"

Unfazed, the stranger replied, "You seem pretty alone to me. Although, that ring on your finger tells me somebody is waiting for you at home. That's nice. Having someone that cares when you're gone."

"That's none of your fucking business," Dave said. "Just let me be."

"Is she the reason you went for a stroll?"

Dave took a hand to his hair and slicked it back, trying his best not to pull at it. He looked around, desperately searching for a way to deal with this intruder, or some sort of solution he just couldn't fathom. He took a deep breath and rubbed his face, trying to calm himself down.

"I... ah... we..." Dave sighed. "We had a big fight. My wife and I. We just... things are not that great at home."

"I'm sorry to hear that. I guess the silver lining is that once the dust settles, you still have someone to make up with."

Dave sneered at the idea, shaking his head. "Yeah... well. It just doesn't look like that right now."

"Of course, you're still in the middle of it. You'll look at it differently once it's behind you."

"You married?"

"Nope."

"Girlfriend?"

"Not in a long time."

"And you're giving me marriage advice on a bridge on a rural back road?"

"I don't know anything about marriage advice. I'm talking about having someone in your life that cares about you. You said a minute ago that you wanted to be alone? You have no idea what you're talking about. Trust me. *That* I know lots about."

Dave was going to repeat that he just wanted to be left alone; that is, he wanted to be left alone to gather enough courage to jump off the bridge, but of course, he wasn't going to cop to that. Something intrigued him about this stranger; something told him to listen.

"Is it about money?" the stranger continued.

"Yeah, kind of. My job."

"That's an easy fix."

"Really?"

"Just go back and make some changes. No job is worth dying over."

"How would you know anything about it?"

"Look, once upon a time, I was all gung ho, take no prisoners about my own career."

"What do you do?"

"Now? Nothing. Back then? I was an author of some note."

"How long ago was that?"

"Not nearly long enough. Anyway, it was all very cliché. My writing and all these other side projects consumed me. You know how it goes: all work, no play, nobody to play with."

"But you did achieve something, no? I mean, you were a professional writer."

"Oh, yeah. It was great while it

lasted. But then life took its course, things happened; the career went down the toilet and I had nothing saved up for Act Two. By then, the only thing I had for company was an apartment full of dusty books and some cherished memories. The money was nice, though. It made things a little easier when I hit hard times."

"And let me guess—the only thing that was missing in your otherwise blessed existence was a woman?"

"No."

"No?

"That's not the point I'm trying to make."

"Then what is it?"

"It's not about having someone to share your life with, but having a life worthy of being shared."

Dave took in this wacko for all he was and really just looked at him, this strange man, who right now seemed to be twirling something feverishly in his left hand. And for once, he truly listened.

The stranger kept talking. "So before you spend the longest ten seconds of your life, only to find out that the bridge is *not* high enough to kill you, but only enough to shatter your bones, and then suffer the agony of a slow, cold death in a dark river, I suggest you take a good look at yourself, find out what you really want, and then sit down with your wife to figure things out."

The stranger put his hands in his pockets and walked away. Dave was stunned, not only by what the guy had told him, but also by the realization of the huge mistake he almost made. He searched for something appropriate to say, but his mind was reeling.

"Hey," he called out to the retreating figure, "how do you know the bridge isn't high enough?"

Because of the plaque behind you," the stranger managed before the darkness engulfed him.

Dave turned around and looked at the sign he hadn't noticed was attached to the metal beams. He made out the words by moonlight:

This bridge is dedicated to the loving memory of author Lemat. May he rest in peace...

The PLAY button on the boom box popped up with a loud click when the tape reached its end, forcing Lemat to open his eyes.

Why are you postponing it? Lemat thought and got to his feet.

CHAPTER THIRTY-FIVE

Lemat had no patience to wait for a bus, so he hailed a cab. The taxi left him a block away from Ink's work. He wanted some time to organize his thoughts, and the short walk was perfect for this. Gathering courage, Lemat stood at the foot of the stairs and looked up at the tattoo parlor. He took a deep breath and went up. The sound of a foghorn alerted the artists that a client was at the door.

"Can I help you?" said Ruz.

Lemat stood by the door, waiting for them to recognize him, but of course they didn't. And if they did, nobody gave a hint. He didn't see Ink anywhere. "I'm looking for Ink."

"And you are?" Ruz said.

"A friend."

"Well, friend. She's not here tonight."

"I thought she worked on Wednesdays."

"Not tonight."

"She took the night off," said Vinci.

"Do you know where she is?"

"No, but I can call her if you want me to," Vinci said. "Is it an emergency?"

Yes, Lemat thought. "No," he said. "It's not important. I'll come back another day. Thanks."

"Nice ink. Hers?" Ruz said.

Lemat looked at the ouroboros on his wrist and said, "Yeah." He had completely forgotten to cover up his scars with his wristbands.

"Cool."

When Lemat left the parlor, it started to pour harder. He put on his black wristbands and rushed down the street while fast-dialing Ink's phone number.

"Hey! Back from the dead, how are you? We haven't talked in, like, ages."

"You've been hard to reach yourself."

"Yeah, I know. I was in Coachella with some friends. How about you, what have you been up to?"

"Same old, work."

"Ah."

"Are you home?"

"No, why?"

"Where are you?" A car sped by, splashing Lemat. "Shit!"

"What happened?"

"Nothing. Where are you?"

"I'm in this awesome café slash bar where they play old movies every Wednesday. We should check it out one of these days. Your timing is excellent, by the way. I'm in line to use the restroom and it's long."

"Cool. What's it called?"

"That Place."

"Yeah."

"No, that's the name. That Place."

"Oh," Lemat hailed a cab he saw coming down the street.

"Yeah. It's pretty cool. You'll love it."

"We'll have to check it out. Hey, listen, somebody's here. I have to go. I'll call you later." Lemat got in the taxi and then said to the driver, "Take me to a café called That Place. I'll find the address for you."

Once on his way, Lemat went over in his mind what he wanted to tell Ink: *I know what you said about wanting to keep your life simple. I know you're afraid of commitment, and I know I should have said something to you, that day we talked about this. I regret not doing so. I was scared. I was afraid of losing you, because your friendship means more to me than my own feelings. A lot of things have changed in my life lately. I had all of these experiences in such a short period of time. I have finally started to live the life I always dreamed about. But none of it matters. None of it matters, because there's always something missing— you. I love you, Ink. And I want to share my life with you.*

"Here you go, buddy," said the cabbie, dropping him off in front of That Place.

The café was a brick building that used to be an old warehouse. There was a long line outside. Lemat walked to the doorman, who told him to go to the back of the line as the place was hopping tonight.

"Please, I need to get in," Lemat said.

"So does everybody else," the doorman said.

Lemat took all the money form his wallet and said. "Here, that's $152. It's all I've got. Please, it's really important. You have to let me in."

"Have you lost your mind?" The doorman said. "Get out of here. Hey, Mario! Get this guy out of my face."

Mario, a muscular guy with a face like a catcher's mitt, came out of the club and grabbed him by his jacket. He pulled Lemat around the corner and into a back alley. Lemat protested and tried to break free, but Mario wasn't having it. Now in the alley, Mario let go of Lemat. He banged on the back door with his fist and another bouncer opened it from inside.

"Give me the money," Mario said.

Lemat was confused.

"The cash!"

Lemat finally caught on and gave the money to Mario, who counted the bills and said, "And next time, try to be a little bit more discreet, buddy."

The pub was spacious and packed with patrons. The main attraction was *Apocalypse Now* being projected on the back wall.

Why is it always Apocalypse Now? Lemat thought.

He started to search for Ink. Only the sizable back room was used to show films. Movies could be seen from both the first and the second floors. Lemat guessed Ink would want to be on the upper floor.

"Sorry, sir. There aren't any more tables available for the movie," whispered a waitress who suddenly appeared before him.

"I'm looking for my friend," Lemat said and then he spotted her.

At first, he hoped he was mistaken, but there she was. Ink sat on a plush, leather sofa with her head resting on some guy's chest. He wasn't the musician

Lemat had seen before, but some artsy guy draped in black with a striped scarf and crazy black hair. Time slowed down and Lemat felt as if his insides had evaporated. It wasn't the fact that Ink was with another man, but how perfectly at ease she lay on his chest. She then looked at the guy; he had said something. Their eyes met with an intimacy all too familiar to Lemat. And then she smiled; no, she laughed. Ink touched the guy's torso playfully and then they closed in for a quick kiss. Her eyes semiclosed; she wanted it. Lemat couldn't breathe. Images of possible scenarios and a torrent of feelings flooded him in rapid succession.

"Sir, I'm going to have to ask you to sit down, please," the voice of the waitress came though as if he was underwater. "Sir?"

Lemat had no idea how he managed to walk away. He stumbled outside, using a fire exit. Lemat paced back and forth in an alley. He wanted to tear off his flesh as a way to exorcise the pain within.

"Fuck! Fuck! Fuck!" Lemat said. He slammed his phone on the ground and stomped on it, until his foot hurt.

"SHUT UP!" an angry neighbor said in the distance.

"FUCK YOU!" Lemat said and disappeared down the alley.

He needed to walk. Like a shark, Lemat felt that if he stood still, he would drown. He had never felt so stupid, so angry, so… betrayed. Was it really treachery? Ink had always been upfront with him about how she lived her life. It was Lemat who agreed to continue their relationship regardless of this.

Stupid fucking me! he thought. Ink had always

managed to keep her life masterfully compartmentalized for the most part. *You knew it, you idiot! You knew it and now you can't handle it! What the fuck were you expecting to see?* Lemat started to walk in no direction in particular. All he wanted was to get away from that place as fast as he could.

CHAPTER THIRTY-SIX

Lemat jumped up startled, clawing at his face to rip out whatever was on it. He fell down, sweating and gasping for air.

"Whoa! Settle down, chief. No need to freak out."

Lemat looked around confusedly, until he recognized Big Mick sitting on his makeshift couch. Lemat had no idea how he ended up in Mick's apartment, but it was obvious now that he had been sitting on the hand-shaped chair wearing the gas mask, just like the guy he saw the last time he was there.

"You OK?" Big Mick said.

Lemat was about to answer. Instead, he pushed himself to his feet and fumbled his way to the bathroom. He barely made it to the toilet with the Domo seat cover. Lemat puked his guts out until all he had left were painful dry heaves. He was feeling that particular kind of sickness and pain that only death could relieve.

"Here, drink this," said Big Mick, handing him a

Gatorade.

Lemat drank half the bottle in one swig, wiped his mouth with the back of his hand, and said, "What happened?"

"From a purely professional standpoint: you needed to get fucked up last night. And based on the results, I can safely say, 'Mission accomplished.'" The drug dealer took a peek inside the toilet bowl.

"How did I get here?"

"Well, let's see. You knocked on my door at an unholy hour. Lucky for you, that's when we purveyors of escapism make a lot of our living. You were drunk—not surprising for a man in your current profession—and soaking wet. I asked you, 'Taking off or landing?' You said, 'Taking off.' So I got to work. I gave you a little cocktail of my own making: a little bit of this, a little bit of that, and I sent you down the rabbit hole to chase after Alice."

"A fucking nightmare, that's what it was; I dreamt I was a fucking pharmacist," said Lemat.

"Do you blame pilots when they hit turbulence? I don't think so. You wanted to fly and I gave you wings. The destination is entirely up to your subconscious. Here," Big Mick said as he cut a cocaine line on a small mirror by the bathtub. "Snort this and you'll feel copacetic. I don't want you to wander off in the state you're in and get gang-raped by some guys in an alley. You're the only celebrity client I have." He left the bathroom.

Lemat wasn't keen on doing blow, but the agony that gripped his bones was such that he was willing to do just about anything to get some relief. He did the line a little too hard, feeling as if he had inhaled a nail up his nose and into his brain. Big Mick was right, though; a few moments later, Lemat felt a lot better.

"Er… listen, I have no cash with me right now," said Lemat, searching inside his empty wallet.

"No worries, I know you're good for it. You want to take something for later?"

"I think I've had enough."

When Lemat left Big Mick's apartment, it was still raining. The storm beating down on him was nothing compared to the one inside his head. All Lemat could think of was the image of Ink cuddling up with another man.

His old neighborhood felt more decrepit than ever before. It had been raining lately and the building complex never took to water well. It was like a badly bleeding animal about to burst from the severity of its wounds.

Lemat took the path to his old apartment. The building somehow looked worse without the drying laundry overhead. Leaks spouted everywhere. Mr. Freeman played something apropos for the weather. Lemat took the old shoe, put a dollar inside and threw it into the cellist's window. There was a long silence. Lemat waited until the cello belted out a mournful tune.

Lemat gazed upon his old place for a moment. It was the only place in his life he ever considered home. The fact that it was no longer so made him sad, even lost. But there was no point on entertaining such thoughts. He didn't need the extra grief. And with that thought in mind, he went up the stairs towards Ink's placc.

Lemat knocked on the door and waited for an answer. A seminaked man opened the door; it was the same guy from the café the night before.

"What's up?"

"I'm looking for Ink."

"Babe, some dude's looking for ya!" The guy walked back into the apartment while scratching his ass.

Ink came out of her bedroom wearing a sweater and socks. She looked at Lemat with a mixture of surprise and trepidation. Her widened eyes screamed the obvious question: *Lemat, what are you doing here?*

"I need to talk to you."

"Now is not a good time."

"It will never be."

Ink was upset and confused. "I'll be back," she said to the guy and walked with Lemat downstairs. It started to rain again.

"When did you get back?" she said. "I've been calling your phone like an idiot, and you never returned my calls. And now this? You know I don't—"

"Just listen to me for a second. Please." Lemat walked out to the patio, while Ink stayed under the cover of the stairs. "I don't want to do this anymore. I know what you said about your own happiness and freedom, and I was an idiot for not saying anything before. It's just that the fear of losing you was greater than my need to have you. But I can't take this anymore."

"Lemat, don't do this."

"Do what? Tell you how I feel? Tell you that I've been traveling the world, making my dreams come true and getting all this fucking money, and all I can think about is you? That all of those fucking things are meaningless because you're not with me? Because that's what I've been doing. That's what you don't want to hear? Why? Because of that idiot upstairs? Or the musician? Or whoever else you spend time with? Are you so fucking afraid of getting hurt that you'd rather run away from the one man who's willing to be with you even when it's not fun anymore? I thought happiness was doing what you loved for a living, but it's really living for what you love. Life is not just the great parts—it's the shitty ones as well."

"Not for me," Ink said.

"And what are you going to do, run from person to person like some sort of happiness junkie? Who's going to be by your side when *you're* the one that becomes a drag? Shouldn't they pack up and move on, too?"

Ink had no answer. She just averted her eyes and clenched her jaw.

Lemat choked up. "I love you, all right? Is that what you *don't* want to hear? Is that what you're so fucking afraid of? I love you!"

The sound of rain took over. Tears of hurt ran down her face. She said nothing. Not a word. Ink turned around and she was gone, like a whisper in the darkness; like the void inside his soul.

CHAPTER THIRTY-SEVEN

Lemat sat on the bench waiting for the bus in the rain. He rubbed his arms, trying to keep warm while seeking refuge in his jacket, but he couldn't stop shaking. His lips were turning purple with the cold and the raindrops stinging his face hid his tears. Yet the chill couldn't numb the pain he felt inside. Still, Lemat didn't want to move. He didn't want the bus to arrive either.

What's the point? Lemat thought.

His thoughts were not comforting, but they seemed to stave off the rain. At least until Lemat realized there was something above him. He looked up at the black umbrella before seeing Mr. Freeman standing behind him and shielding him from the downpour.

"Come along, son," Mr. Freeman said. "Let's get you out of this rain and into some dry clothes."

Lemat nodded, a little confused by the cellist's sudden presence, but followed the older man anyway. Mr. Freeman put his arm around him and took him back to his apartment. They took the front route to the building, a sight foreign to Lemat since he had always used the back alleys. The building looked bigger somehow, and there was far more activity than what Lemat was used to when coming home. Lemat was distracted by the seemingly endless rows of mailboxes, while Mr. Freeman unlocked the security gate. It made him realize how many people lived in this building and how many more in this vast urban complex.

Mr. Freeman's apartment was bigger than Lemat's old one. The few items and furniture inside seemed ancient but were pristinely preserved and neatly arranged. Pictures of the cellist with family hung on the walls. Only one of them—a black and white one—showed a young Mr. Freeman in a tuxedo among the members of an orchestra. The only other group picture was of an even younger Mr. Freeman with some fellow soldiers.

The old man handed Lemat a towel and guided him to the bathroom. He came back with some clothes that were ironed and folded to perfection. So much so that Lemat hesitated before disturbing their neatness. The plain white shirt, chinos, and sweater fit a little big, but they were warm and comfortable, especially the thick argyle socks.

When Lemat came out of the bathroom, a bowl of steaming chicken soup was waiting for him in the living room. A semblance of life seemed to enter Lemat's body with each spoonful of broth.

Lemat sat by the same balcony upon which he tossed old shoes with a dollar inside. The well-worn cello rested on a stand close by. He had forgotten how the whole thing started but wondered aloud what became of the money.

"It went to the cello fund," said Mr. Freeman, sitting on the couch across from Lemat. The musician pointed at a jar on a mantlepiece. "Every time the old gal needed new strings or a visit to the luthier, I took a little from the tip jar."

The awareness of this unwitting symbiotic nurturing that had been taking place for years made Lemat felt warmer inside.

"I don't want to sound ungrateful, but how did you—" Lemat didn't have a chance to finish his question.

"Sound travels," said Mr. Freeman, casting a glance at the balcony. "It's been a rough transition, has it?"

"Unexpected," Lemat said, speculating on the meaning of the question.

"Success always is," Mr. Freeman said. "Everyone prepares for failure. We make plans for rainy days, but nobody worries about the sunny ones."

"I thought things were going to be different."

"What we think and what it turns out to be is never exactly the same thing, is it?"

"Is that why you never became a musician?"

"Oh, and who says I'm not one?"

"Well, you know what I mean."

"No, I don't," the old man said. "Let me ask you this: if Picasso worked as an office clerk and painted in his free time, would that make him less of a painter?"

"I guess not."

"If Mozart was a shoemaker who played music on the side, would that make him less talented?"

"Well… no."

"I am a musician. That's what I am and what I

always will be. The fact that I have to sell insurance to provide for my passion doesn't change that. Not one bit. Art—whether playing an instrument, being on stage, or writing—is about self-expression, not fame or cold cash. You do it because you have to, not because you want to. Am I right?"

Lemat nodded, trying not to choke up. This was the first time in his life he felt somebody understood him.

"Now look at you. You're young, obviously talented, and you've managed to achieve the dream of any artist: you have the luxury of dedicating your life to your passion."

"I guess," Lemat said.

"You guess?" Mr. Freeman let the question hang in the air for a while. "You aren't happy with it. Why?"

"I didn't want the attention… and I hate that stupid novel. I just wrote it to—"

"To get attention."

Lemat didn't know if he felt more like a hypocrite or an idiot. He wanted to be heard, all right—to be read and appreciated. Lemat wanted his *work* to be noticed, not him per se. But in the end, wasn't that one and the same? Could people really separate the work from the artist?

"And what about your girl?" Mr. Freeman said as he pointed towards Ink's apartment.

Lemat chuckled bitterly. The possessive seemed woefully out of place. "She had her own definition of our relationship."

"That's a shame, but you can't really blame her for that. Women are . . . complicated. I've been divorced for over thirty years myself. We have two daughters. They're grown women now, but I never remarried. We were married for more than twenty years—war newlyweds."

"World War II?"

"Korea. I was a marine. Anyway, after being married to someone for such a long time, and living through so many things together, it's easy to think it'll last forever. But people change. They grow— sometimes in different directions—and that's that. I guess what I'm trying to say is, life is not perfect. When we're young, we tend to project all of these expectations on life, but the fact is, it doesn't care about what we hope. Life is life, and nobody can change that. So we have to make do with what we're given, and what we can manage to work out of it."

"They should start with that lecture on the first day of preschool," said Lemat, setting the empty bowl of soup aside.

Mr. Freeman grinned and said, "How about some tea?"

"Please."

The old man took the bowl to the kitchen and put a kettle on the stove. "If you don't mind me asking," Mr. Freeman said from the sink, "do you have any family?"

"Not in this country."

"That has to be tough. What does Dad do?"

"He's a businessman; he owns a number of pharmacies back home."

"Smart man, well-to-do." Mr. Freeman was impressed. "Didn't drag junior to work in the family business?"

"He tried… many times. Even to this day, he's still pushing for me to go back and take over."

"And yet, here you are, blazing your own path.

Like they say, the apple doesn't fall far from the tree."

"Yeah, well, I turned out to be a watermelon."

Mr. Freeman's jovial laughter roared from the kitchen before he walked out holding a tea tray. "And Mom, what does she do?"

"Nothing. She stays home. My parents have been separated for many years, but he still takes care of her."

"I see. She's on retirement." Mr. Freeman began to serve tea. "That's a heck of a job, rearing children. Tough, thankless—there isn't a college course that can prepare a person for something like that. No sir. Sugar?"

"Please."

"Seems to me, Mom did a good job. So why not let the blessed lady enjoy her golden years, wouldn't you agree?"

Lemat nodded. Mr. Freeman sat tiredly on a sofa.

"They must be proud of what you have managed to achieve."

"I think so."

"How come? You didn't ask?"

"We rarely talk. And now, with the book thing... well, you know how it is."

"Nobody can be so busy that they can't pick up the phone and call their folks," said Mr. Freeman, sipping on his tea. "Then again, they might worry if they heard their son was suffering by himself out in the rain, and coming down from Lord-knows-what."

"It's not like that—"

The musician stopped him with a gesture. "I don't care how it's like. What matters is how it's going to end. I get it. I've been there before, believe or not. You get a little recognition, some cash, a good-looking girl or two." He flashed a knowing smile. "Soon—if you're not careful—you get a little too big for your britches, and temptation is waiting just around the corner. That's when your mind starts to become twisted. Your vision stops being clear. Sounds familiar?"

Lemat felt Mr. Freeman was a little far off from the target, but he understood the point the old man was trying to make. "I just," he took a deep breath, "I don't know what to do. Things were always so clear to me, in my mind. I always knew what I wanted and worked hard to make it happen."

"And now that you have it?"

Lemat thought for a moment. "That's the thing—I don't think I do. I guess I took a wrong turn on my way there, and now everything is all messed up."

"You're lost."

Lemat scoffed at the obvious. "You could say that."

"That doesn't mean you can't find your way again."

"I wish it were that easy."

"But it's really not that hard. All you have to do is remember who you are."

Lemat drank his tea, but he was really taking in Mr. Freeman's words. He placed the empty cup back on the tray and looked out the window. The rain had subsided.

"I should get going," Lemat said. "Thank you again, sir. If there's anything I can do for you—"

"There's no need for that. It was my pleasure. I meant what I said before—my door is always open if you need someone to talk to. Take care of yourself, son. And God bless you."

CHAPTER THIRTY-EIGHT

By now, getting on an airplane had become second nature to Lemat, even though he still hated flying. He took the first flight back to Caracas. It was long, but he didn't care; he had plenty to think about, and traveling first class didn't hurt either. Since his talk with Mr. Freeman, he had hunkered down at home, totally incommunicado. It rained the whole time, so that definitely helped with the mood. Takeout containers littered the place. Lemat listened to nothing but Pink Floyd's *The Wall* and watched *Fight Club* on a loop. He was fed up with the outside world. How could he possibly face the world when his inner one was in shambles? But after a week of wallowing in the crapulence of his misery, Lemat finally worked up the nerve to buy a plane ticket and end his self-imposed exile.

Lemat watched through his window as the approaching ocean turned into land, and a few seconds later, he felt the bump of the undercarriage touching the runway. He felt strange. It had been seven years since his last visit. There was nothing there for him as far as he was concerned. All his life he had known his future lay somewhere else.

The country had not changed much since his last visit: the inefficiency, the traffic, the crime, the poverty, the corruption, the daily chaos its inhabitants called life. It was a land blessed by nature and cursed by man. To make things worse, the country had descended into revolutionary madness, pitting the poor against the rich, the worker against the educated, the apathetic against the fanatic, and an imperfect past against a dysfunctional present, which could only result in an abysmal future. Even the president, the architect of the aforementioned revolution, had been assassinated four years earlier under allegations of a shadowy conspiracy backed by the CIA.

Lemat didn't understand why he felt any affinity for this place. His parents had migrated from Spain, looking for a better life. "You're not really from here, you know?" Lemat heard that as early as his brain could process speech. His parents did their best to root him in their culture. Those he met growing up reminded him of this by saying things like, "You were born here by accident," because in their eyes, he was really from his parents' country. Ironically, by the time Lemat visited "the homeland," some twenty years later, he quickly learned he was an outsider there as well. After all, he was born and raised somewhere else. As for America, the land he actually chose to make his home, he was just another foreigner from the Third World, a culturally indistinguishable member of a place called Latin America.

Lemat didn't make any phone calls. He told no one where he was going, or rather, nobody knew that he was gone. It was better that way, he thought. The whole purpose of this trip was to get away from everything. The taxi took two hours to drop him off in front of his old home. It should have taken forty-five minutes, but this was a country of hard facts, not hypotheticals. Traffic and other disruptive elements always had to be taken into account.

Lemat stood there with his backpack and luggage bag swung over his shoulders, hesitant about ringing the intercom. He pressed the button, hearing the familiar buzz. The maid answered and she could hardly believe it was Lemat. It took a while for the cleaning lady to let him in. Lemat's childhood friends used to called his building "Alcatraz," because of all the keys and metal bars used to keep criminals away. This was the rule, not the exception, of housing in the city, but somehow Lemat's condo ended up with a moniker. When the doors to the elevator opened, Lemat saw his mother waiting on the other side, speechless by the surprise.

"¡Hijo mio! ¡Que sorpresa!" she said with tears of joy, unable to believe her own eyes.

"Ma!" Lemat dropped his bag and hugged her. He was a male mirror of his mother. She was short and plump, the descendant of Iberic Celtic stock. A childhood full of harshness had made her incredibly strong.

"Why didn't you call me? I would have picked you up at the airport, prepared something special for dinner, or at the very least, cleaned the house. It's a mess." It was nonsense—her home would make a drill sergeant cry with pride.

"I wanted it to be a surprise. Plus, I didn't want to attract the media's attention."

"Who's going to bother you here?"

"You'd be surprised."

His mother ushered him into the apartment, touching his face regularly as if to verify she wasn't dreaming. They sat in the kitchen and she offered him coffee, like they had done so many times when he was young. Her next reaction after the first bout of happiness was one of concern. She told him he looked too skinny, too pale. His hair was too long, he needed to shave, the circles under his eyes were too dark, and what was the deal with those wristbands? Lemat deflected her inquiries with wit and charm, as usual. He drank his coffee. Nobody made it like Mom. They talked about everything, but especially his writing career.

"You were always a very bright boy," she said. "Incredibly lazy when it came to school, but nonetheless brilliant. So artistic and creative." But, his mother was more interested in his everyday life. "Have you met someone?" was one of her habitual questions.

"Nah, and now I'm too busy for that," Lemat said.

"You're not telling me the truth."

She's like the freaking CIA! Lemat thought. "I met someone."

"And?"

"She's… otherwise engaged."

"She's married?!"

"No! She's not interested in a committed relationship."

"Bah! She's an idiot! You don't need her. There

are plenty of pretty girls out there that would trample over each other to date you. And now, with your book? Ha! You'll have to keep them away with a fire hose. You'll see; don't you worry." She pinched his cheek. "How long are you staying?"

"I'm not sure. A couple of weeks maybe? Maybe less. I don't really have a plan."

"Two weeks? No! You should stay longer. I haven't seen you in ages. Why don't you stay for a month at least?"

"I don't know if can do that, now, with the novel and everything."

"Of course. Then, stay as long as you can."

"OK, Mom."

She was beaming. "Are you going to see your father?"

The mere thought gave Lemat a stabbing sensation in the stomach. "That's the plan."

"And as well you should. He's your father. And I'm sure he's going to be bursting with pride because of your book. Did you talk to him like you promised the last time we spoke?"

"I did."

"And?"

"He was good. Same old story: 'My blood pressure is too high, things could be better,'" Lemat imitated his dad down to his mannerisms, with that irritating way he had of rapping his knuckles against a table to accentuate his words. His mother always found that amusing.

Lemat changed the topic to his brief time in Hollywood. His mother loved celebrity gossip, and he knew that would steer the conversation in a lighter direction. When dinnertime arrived, Lemat said he was too tired to go out, so they ate serrano ham, manchego cheese, bread and canned sardines, squid, and mussels, accompanied by a bottle of red. Afterwards, they adjourned for more coffee in the living room. Even though they were talking nonstop, Lemat's mom had the TV on in the background.

"It's what they call white noise, plus it keeps me company," she reasoned.

Their chat ended when the current Brazilian soap came on. They never cared for the uncouth scream-fests produced locally. But the Brazilian ones were a different story. They were superiorly produced, better written, and covered more interesting plots. There he was, coffee in hand, sitting with his mom watching telenovelas, and commenting on them during commercial breaks, just like they did twenty years ago.

When the news came on, Lemat said, "Ma?"

"What?" She woke up startled. She had been dozing off since the end of the program.

"Go to bed."

"I'm watching the news."

"No, you aren't. You've been sleeping for the last fifteen minutes."

"I'm just resting my eyes. Let me hear what they're saying."

It was useless. Lemat knew he would have to come back after taking a shower to take his mother to bed. She would protest, denying she was sleeping, only to begrudge calling it a night. Nothing had changed, really. Finally, Lemat was alone in his room. Well, what used to be his room. His mother had turned it into a den. Just another place where she could display more of her collections: spoons, elephants, Buddhas, Chinese vases, you name it. He had to set a futon cushion on the floor, but Lemat refused to sleep anywhere else. This place was his sanctuary when he was a kid. Here he spent countless hours with his face glued to blank notebooks, writing and drawing his own comic books (the literary bug would bite him later), and dreaming of success, while his loyal boom box blasted tunes from *Surfing with the Alien, Appetite for Destruction,* Metallica's black album, or anything by Iron Maiden. He did so until the wee hours of the morning, even on a school night.

Gone were the posters by Jim Lee and photos of Cindy Crawford and life-sized bikini models. No boxes of comic books, no role-playing things, no CDs or VHS tapes, no novels, and no Playboy or Penthouse under the bed. Lemat's old TV was still there, though. And so were a few other remnants of his past, like a gold medal from a karate tournament that nobody attended. At least his mother had been straight-up with him: "If you want to take karate, fine. But I'm not going to watch my son get hurt."

There was also that one-page story he wrote in the seventh grade. It was written in longhand, when Lemat still had good penmanship, and his mother had it framed. It was one out of three works selected from the whole school to be displayed on the main board for everyone to see.

"I don't want to read anymore about space, robots, or war," his Spanish teacher had warned him before the assignment. She was tired of Lemat's usual fare. So, under the threat of an automatic "Fail," Lemat composed a tale inspired by his mother's childhood stories of growing up in her rural village. She used them as bedtime stories on Lemat's request. Lemat had forgotten all about it, until his teacher called him to her office and accused him of plagiarism. Lemat never knew why his teacher still put his story up on the board, since she never believed him.

The last memento was a tiny figurine of Drizzt Do'Urden, a badass dark elf ranger from the Forgotten Realms campaign setting, who wielded dual scimitars and had a pet panther. Lemat was surprised to see it still on the bookshelf. He had won it as a third-place prize in a role-playing tournament held at a university. It was the same figure his friends had leered at with jealousy and spite when the winners were announced at a small hobby store.

Small trophies, to be sure, even pathetic, as most would say. But they represented some of the few victories Lemat had achieved as a kid—tiny fractions in time that told him he wasn't a complete waste of life. Minor triumphs nobody celebrated, except in a remote corner of his heart. And yet his mother had saved them. Maybe she really knew what they meant to him, or perhaps they were the only things she could brag about him.

Lemat woke up late. This time, it wasn't because of a creative all-nighter, but the product of jet lag and fatigue. He put the futon away and jumped in the shower. His mother had left him a note, telling him she went to the supermarket to run some errands. That was fine with Lemat. He had enough things planned to do today to keep him entertained. First, he wanted to visit his school. Lemat had gone to five of them during his formative years, but he had only one in mind—the place where everything really began.

He took the bus. Lemat actually enjoyed walking in this city, as dangerous as it was. He would stroll about, dreaming up stories and getting inspired by the most menial of things. Public transportation always ran late and it was always packed. Lemat had no choice but to hang from the bus' door with half his body sticking out to the street. It had been a while for him, but he still remembered how to dodge the passing traffic. Three buses later, he arrived at one of his old schools.

The place looked like a regular one-story house. Only a small sign by the main door announced the building's true purpose. Lemat had attended this place from seventh to ninth grade. He wasn't a bad kid, nor did he act up, seeking attention. In fact, most of the time, nobody knew he was there. Lemat was one of those kids for whom the system just didn't work. The assembly-line system of education could not accommodate a single student that didn't fit the mold. To their credit, Lemat's frustrated parents once explored the possibility of sending Lemat to a Montessori school, a place where a child was treated like an individual, and he would have the freedom and independence to develop according to his personality. But his father, an old-fashioned man, thought the school was for "retarded kids," and rather than besmirching the family name, opted out, and thus evaporated Lemat's one chance for positive and enriching development. Instead, he was condemned to struggle within a structure where he was met with nothing but failure and mediocrity, from which his departure was heralded by one of his teachers unceremoniously as "I don't want to see you here next year." And thus spoke the prophet.

Lemat was left to find a new school, and thanks to his scholastic shortcomings, his choices were to work or to scrape the bottom of the academic barrel. Lemat opted for the figurative spatula and managed to graduate from high school by the skin of his teeth. *How I hated this place!* Lemat thought as he stood in front of it. The old fantasies of taking a flamethrower to the joint came back in Technicolor. The place would be empty, of course. He was an angry and frustrated kid, not a raving psychopath. Lemat had spent the three saddest years of his life within those walls. He and Dcp would become lifelong friends in these halls. The day he left was one of his happiest. Another victory he kept to himself, due to his parents' ire.

"May I help you?" said the groundskeeper, who was watering the plants in front. He wasn't the same man Lemat remembered.

"I used to study here." Lemat took off his shades, lest he was suspected of being some shady character with less-than-noble purposes, the default choice in this city. "I'm in the country visiting my family for a few days, and I wanted to see my old alma mater."

"The school is closed for the day. Nobody is here."

"That's why I wanted to know if it would be possible to see the classrooms. Mine was at the very end of the patio, by the boy's restroom. My name is Lemat, by the way."

The groundskeeper shook his hand, still suspicious. "Where did you say you come from?"

"I live in the United States now, but I was born here. Do you think you can let me in? I promise I'll be quick."

"You just want to see the classrooms?"

"Just mine. In and out, I swear."

"OK, I guess."

The old jailbird walked inside his former prison. The place, like all good nightmarish sites, hadn't change much. Lemat made his way all the way back to the large, Spanish-style patio flanked by classrooms. It held about 275 students or so, from seventh grade to high school. *Small town, big hell,* Lemat thought. There were only two isolated classrooms in the back. One of them was Lemat's. It was virtually as he remembered it, bare and cold. Lemat made it all the way to the last desk on the left row. That was his spot. He sat on the desk; it was for a right-handed student, just like his always was. God forbid that a lefty gets some comfort. "It's all the same," the teachers would say. That was, until a righty sat on a southpaw's desk and started whining like a victim of the inquisition.

The place didn't feel ominous at all, but rather pathetic. How could such an insignificant place inspire so much resentment? But there was a light in all the darkness.

This was ground zero. This was where a fifteen-year-old Lemat decided he would pursue a creative life. It was more an epiphany than a conscious choice. It came to him while drawing one of his own characters in his daily planner. How many lessons did he ignore while drawing on that thing? Were Lemat in school today in the developed world, he would have been diagnosed with attention deficit disorder, depression, and dyslexia, not to mention a total lack of parental involvemcnt.

But these were the good, old days. If you didn't make the grade, you were simply stupid. Because to memorize and regurgitate facts to pass a test has always been a sign of brilliance. If you happened to be one of those "out of the box" kids, you were on your own. Get in the box or drop dead. Lemat understood deep inside that his future lay nowhere in particular, but far away. And there he was now, a massively successful author. He had gone further than anyone would have ever imagined or expected of him.

Lemat wasn't there to gloat or to look for some kind of vindication. He didn't care who knew of his achievements. The reason he was sitting in the place where he had found his calling was simple—he wanted to meet with the memory of his younger self to fulfill a promise he made on that very day, more than twenty years ago. All Lemat wanted to do was to give that poor misunderstood kid a simple message: *You were right all along.*

CHAPTER THIRTY-NINE

The next three days passed in great spirits. Lemat had lost contact with his small group of childhood friends when he moved overseas, so he had nothing better to do than dote on his mother. Lemat took her shopping, to the movies, to the theater, and to her favorite restaurants. They talked, laughed, and reminisced about old times. When news of his novel's success and the upcoming film came up, his mother would cry with joy and lavish him with praise. When the news pointed at controversy, his mom would turn to him with shock and concern. She would repeatedly ask him why he chose to write something so polarizing.

Mom leveled with him by saying she didn't like the plot of his novel. She wasn't particularly religious, a nonpracticing Catholic, really. But Mom didn't like the idea of being offensive or unkind to others, despite Lemat's eloquent oratory debunking faith. "It's just not right," she would say. Lemat told his mother the truth: that the shocking plot line was meant to anger people into promoting his work. He told her that he didn't like what he had done either, not because of some newfound respect for religion, but because his heart wasn't in it.

"It's just a gimmick," he said. "And it worked."

"You are smarter than that. All of those *Star Wars* things you created, the robots, the monsters. You don't need to lower yourself by resorting to deception and slurs."

His mom always referred to the things Lemat created as *"Star Wars."* It was her own unique way to make sense of her son's imagination. Lemat tried to put her mind at ease, promising her it was a one-time thing only to get his career started. As for the news about him being attacked by religious zealots during the promotional tour or the defacing of his old apartment, Lemat downplayed them all.

"Mom, you know how they are. They take something and blow it out of proportion to sell newspapers. Somebody yells something at me at a book reading and they claim I was attacked. It makes for good television."

"Don't lie to me—I've seen the videos on the news."

"They are not as bad as they look. Besides, I had this big black guy who was an ex-cop protecting me. If anyone as much as looked at me funny, he would throw them out like a sack of potatoes."

"Still, I don't want anything to happen to you. You should be careful."

"Well, if anything happens to me, you should know I'm leaving you everything. So, you might want to reconsider."

"Jesus, don't say that! And why would you leave

me everything? I'm fine."

"And you'll be better than that. No more asking Dad for anything. Besides, who else am I going to leave all my stuff to?"

The sole implication of the conversation was enough for Lemat's mom to change the subject. "Anyway, all I'm saying is that you should take precautions."

"Says the woman who lives *here*. Maybe you should start thinking about going back to Spain, now that I can help you find a place there." Lemat knew that making the conversation about her would get him off the hook.

"And what am I supposed to do over there? I've been living in this country for fifty years. This is my home now."

"That's funny coming from you, Mom. And your 'home'? It's just one breath away from been condemned. Go back to Europe, where you can be safer and you don't have to deal with any of this crap."

"Yeah, well. We'll see. You should visit your father. You've been here for four days now and you haven't even called him. He's not going to be happy when he finds out." His mom could play the changing-the-topic game as well as Lemat did.

"I'll visit him before the week is over, I promise."

Once again, he would never understand why his mother kept the memory of his father ever present. It wasn't as if their marriage was a fairy tale. Lemat's father was a devoted disciple of the Latin Macho Paradigm and its archaic tenets:

(1) Men work; woman spawn children, raise them, and take care of the house.

(2) Men have a right—nay, a genetic obligation—to keep a mistress/mistresses on the side.

(3) Men are always right.

(4) Good fatherhood equals being a good provider; also known to Lemat as "The Absence Equation." It went something like: Father – Presence x Money = you have no right to complain.

(5) Money is everything, and it allows anything.

(6) As does the father, so shall do the son.

(7) When everything else fails, deny, deny, deny.

This did wonders for Lemat's mom. She was blamed for their marriage: "The biggest mistake I ever made," as Lemat's father liked to say. She was kept at home taking care of her son with a tight budget and a bunch of empty promises, while the lord of the manor traveled the world in the company of twenty-something bimbos who massaged his ego. Their time together wasn't that great either. Lemat's father forced his mom to stop working, berated her in public, threatened her with physical violence (to his credit, he never acted on it), and left her with his son to live the life of a playboy. To be fair, he did offer to take Lemat with him, but Lemat chose to stay with his mother. A life of nannies and "stepmoms" that would eventually equal his age was not appealing to him. It was one of the few good choices he would make growing up.

Lemat managed to put off his meeting with his father for two more days, but his mother wouldn't allow him to forget it. He finally called his dad, hoping that he could postpone seeing him for a few more days. He wasn't that lucky. His father wanted to meet the very next day for dinner. He invited Lemat to come to his house and voiced his disappointment at his son's negligence in calling him sooner. Lemat's mother was happy. She was very optimistic about the reunion, even though she noticeably wasn't invited.

The next day, Lemat took his mother's car to meet his father at his large home on one of the hills overlooking the city. The place was cold and ostentatious. It gave him a sense of not being lived in; it wasn't a place anyone would call "home." There were at least three servants working for his father, as far as he could tell, but Lemat's father was there to greet him at the door. He was a man etched by sacrifice and harshness. The strength of his character projected well beyond the limits of his physical being. Dinner was of his father's choosing. He never made a habit of asking people for their opinion.

"Where's my genius?" the father said with outstretched arms and added in terrible English, "Hawaii you?"

"Hi, Dad." Lemat embraced him as was customary.

His dad bragged to the attentive servants about his son. His business ambition didn't allow for friends, only yes-men. Lemat's father had come to the country without two cents to rub against each other. He had held a number of odd jobs; he worked construction, coal mining, upholstering, driving a truck, door-to-door sales, and anything else that could make him money. He was always looking out for a business opportunity. Lemat's father would find it in a pharmacy, working as a cashier. The pharmacist was a simple man, content with owning his little store. One day, Lemat's father made him a proposition: he would put down all the cash he had saved so they could open a second drugstore with him as a partner. Intrigued by the prospect of increasing his earnings, the apothecary accepted. In time, and with guile, sacrifice, and effort, Lemat's father turned the two into one hundred fifty-two, the largest pharmacy chain in the country.

"I always knew my son would do something great," Lemat's father said. "Even when it appeared that you were too old to make something out of yourself. I knew you could still surprise me." That was true—his father had always expected great things of Lemat, even if their definition of greatness differed immensely.

"I never knew what possessed you to think that about me. Everything I've done in my life proved the contrary." Lemat kept his eyes on the plate in front of him. He was grateful they were having wine with the meal, so it could help ease his discomfort. His father's girlfriend du jour was in attendance, a barely twenty floozy, decked out in loud designer clothes and enough jewelry to open her own store.

"And yet, here you are, an international bestselling author. See, parents know their children better than they know themselves. You were always wired differently than the other kids."

"How so?"

"I don't know. The way you think, the ideas you had. You were… different. You know what I'm talking about. You were a disaster in school, but I knew that grades are not a measurement of intelligence. Look at me—I barely have a secondary education. I had to finish it by attending night school."

"Mom is fine, by the way. She says hi."

"That's good that you visit her. Next time, though, you should stay here. Maybe we can find you a little friend." He winked at his barely legal mistress. "I'm sure now you don't have a problem in that department."

Lovely, Lemat thought. This coming from the man who thought his son was gay because he was too shy around girls.

"So what are your plans now? I'm sure you're going to invest your money wisely. If you want to, you can give it to me and I'll put it together with my stock portfolio. Depending on how the market goes, I can probably duplicate your earnings."

"No, it's OK. I'm fine. I'll probably just put it in a bank and live off the interest."

"That's not very wise. Look at what happened to the banks during the financial meltdown. They can't be trusted, even the big ones."

"And you can trust the stock exchange?"

"Listen, a bank is going to give you some pitiful interest rate for your money. Don't argue with me, I know what I'm talking about. You finally did something right; now don't blow it all away."

"I'm not throwing anything away. I just don't want to go into the stock market. As far as money goes, I still have a deal for two more books, and I have some percentage on the back end of the movie based on my novel. Don't worry, I'm going to be fine."

"Fine? And what happens if the next book is not successful or the movie tanks? What then? What's going to happen when you run out of money? Maybe it's better that you put all that money in a business, something more tangible. Just in case. I was reading about the funeral business the other day. Do you know how much an average funeral costs? It's a gold mine."

Once again, his father managed to surprise him. "I don't know and I don't care, Dad. I'm not opening a funeral parlor or investing in a business. I'm finally doing what I love and getting well paid for it. If all of that goes to hell, at least I could live in relative comfort for the rest of my life off of interest. Are you listening to me?"

"Well, you're wrong. And as your father—"

"I'm almost forty."

"And you're still acting like a child. Listen to yourself. Living off interest? A real man wakes up early in the morning and goes to work, every day. And he does so doing something serious, not some bohemian bullshit. You've basically just won the lottery. If you were smart, you would listen to your father, who has nothing but your best interest at heart."

"Well, Dad, I guess I'm not smart. And a real man? You really think this," Lemat looked all around the Rococo living room and then finally at the awestruck mistress, "is what you call being a real man? Please!" He got up.

"Where are you going?" His father was flabbergasted by his son's outburst.

"According to you, nowhere. I love you. I really do. But you're never satisfied with anything. I could be the president of the world, and you'd still look down at what I do."

"You know that's not true! All I want for you is to have ambition! To do something useful with your life! You know how I got to where I am today? Because I have never settled for less!"

"No, you never settle for *anything!* It's always more and more and more. When does it stop, Dad? When are you going to be happy?"

"Never! I'm successful because I refuse to be

mediocre! I work hard, and thanks to me, you and your mother had a comfortable life. Even as an adult, how many times did I have to help you when you found yourself in a bind, huh? How many?"

"Too many." Lemat lowered his voice. "And I'm grateful for it. We all are. But I'm not you. I have my own dreams, my own ambitions, and my own life. Even if you don't understand it, at least respect it."

"I can't respect something I know to be wrong."

"Then we have nothing else to talk about, Dad."

CHAPTER FORTY

"I love that you visited your father," Lemat's mom said the following day. When his mother had asked him about the dinner, Lemat told her it had gone well— another white lie, like the reason for always wearing wristbands, even when he went to bed. Lemat hated lying to his mother, but if there was something he hated more, it was seeing her suffer. He knew his mother just wanted him to have his father's presence in his life. She had been doing it since day one. Still, part of Lemat wanted to grab her and shake her, in a last-ditch attempt to make her see the reality about his father. But Lemat knew it would be useless; it would never work. So he had to swallow his anger and frustration and accept things for what they were.

His mother wanted to cook him something special, pulpo a feira (Gallician-style octopus), which was Lemat's favorite. So she left for the supermarket and to run some more errands. Lemat sat on the balcony, checking his emails. There were quite a few. Most of them were work-related. Nothing from Ink. He decided he needed some air, so Lemat took a stroll up the hill where his mother lived. On the way, he saw his reflection on one of the windows of a car parked on the street and immediately his mind wandered.

The Trial of Error

Lemat was in an airport taking a flight to London to promote his latest novel. Traffic and long lines to check in and during the security checkpoint had made him run late for his plane. He rushed through the crowds as best he could, fearing he wasn't going to make it. Lemat bumped into a gentleman, a businessman of sorts, and immediately apologized. The man did the same and reached for his dropped briefcase. When he looked up, Lemat couldn't believe his eyes. He found himself in front of a mirror image. The businessman had the same realization, but his reaction wasn't the same. Instead of awe, the man looked very tense. He hurried through the multitude, trying to get away.

Lemat was stunned, but he felt a need to follow him. He could hardly make out the shape of his double as he dashed off.

The man handed over his boarding pass at a gate and disappeared into the ramp while Lemat was stopped at the door by an attendant who said, "Sorry, sir. You have no boarding pass." Lemat looked at the flight information and hurried to the airline's desk.

He bought a ticket, first class. Money was no issue; getting on that plane was. He made it through the gate when they announced the final call.

Lemat had to wait until the "fasten seatbelts" sign was turned off to move about the plane. He walked all the way to the back of the craft looking for his double. The man sat by the window in business class. He looked nervous. The double saw Lemat as soon as his lifted his head to take a sip of his beer. They locked eyes, but Lemat just kept on walking and locked himself in an economy class lavatory. He didn't know what to do or say. Lemat wasn't even sure what the hell he was doing on that flight. The whole thing was just insane. Was it all a coincidence, just a man with a remarkable likeness? He felt that there was something more.

Lemat returned to his seat, avoiding eye contact with the man who shared his face. It wasn't hard; the man was using the airplane's phone. Lemat spent the rest of the flight coming up with ways to approach the man and what to say. Every scenario was more absurd than the next. But what was he going to do? He was already there. Lemat was committed to getting to the bottom of the strange encounter.

They finally landed at their destination, after a seemingly eternal flight. First class passengers deplaned first. Lemat's plan was to wait for his double by the gate, but to his surprise, someone was already waiting for him.

The two hulking men dressed in black wore shades and were nondescript. They showed him a badge and escorted him to a waiting car outside the terminal. No explanation was given. "Please follow us," the only response. Lemat was taken to an old, industrial building, and he was guided to the center of an empty factory floor. He was left alone for a few seconds, until a light went off in the walkway above him.

"We thought we had lost you forever," a man enveloped in shadows said.

The walkways flanking Lemat were dimly lit right on cue. Anonymous men and women watched him from the darkness.

"What's going on?" Lemat said.

"An aberration of careful planning," the man said. Lemat's double took his place right next to him.

"Who are you?"

"He's you," the man said. "The real you."

"That's nonsense!"

"Very much so, but not in the way you think," the man said. "You see, we worked very hard to produce him." He rested a hand on the double's shoulder. "A perfect expression of your true self."

"This is crazy! How can that

be?"

"With a lot of effort," the man said. "Copy after copy was made, until we found the ultimate balance. And then we gave him all the tools to succeed. He made us all proud; exceeding all expectations. You yourself would be amazed at *our* Lemat's achievements. He's one for the books."

"That's bullshit! So what does that make me, a copy?" Lemat found the concept laughable.

"One of the early ones. The only one unaccounted for." The man exposed his wrist, as if to make reference to something. Lemat checked his own and realized there was a 3 etched where his tattoo should be. "The first two died in the lab," the man continued. "That's how flawed they were."

"And the others?"

"Destroyed. Why keep substandard copies?"

"Except me."

"A clerical error from the warehouse manager. You were mislabeled 'Scrap' instead of 'Dispose' and ended up in a dumpster. We lost track of you for a long time."

"So now you're going to kill me?"

"We can't have two of you running around the world. That's not how this experiment works."

With a single step, an army of the husky guards stepped from out the darkness, curtailing any escape fantasies.

"Why do this now? Why not before, when you found out I still existed?" said.

"We were going to, but scientific curiosity got the best of us. You see, everything about you is defective. Your life wasn't conducive to success. We even made sure of that once we learned of your existence."

"You sick motherfuckers! What were you trying to prove?"

"The exact opposite of your better self."

"Well, I hope you choke on your fucking findings!"

"I couldn't have said it better. Despite our best efforts and your own shortcomings, you managed to beat the odds again and again to our astonishment. It didn't matter what all the data said; somehow, you found your way on top. Remarkable!"

"Yeah, fucking great! Congratulations! Now let's celebrate with a good old-fashioned execution."

"Like I said, there's only room for one of you in this experiment," the man said and, with one simple motion, pulled a lever.

With a violent snap, Lemat's double ended up hanging from the trap door that opened underneath his feet. Lemat watched his lifeless, perfect self swing limply. The looming guards melted back into the shadows. The lights on the walkways turned off. A massive double door opened, letting in a blinding shaft of light.

"Why?" Lemat said,

overwhelmed by what had
transpired.
    The voice of his host echoed all
around Lemat, "Why, indeed."
    And Lemat walked into the light.

"I thought I'd find you here," Lemat said, arriving at his destination.

Guy was sitting by the edge of the vantage point contemplating the view of the city. His jacket rested beside him and his tie was undone. Lemat sat next to him on a cement bench.

"Beautiful, isn't it?" Guy said. "Millions of people going about their business; every life a unique experience, a world within themselves. Out there, there could be the cure for cancer, the next great invention, or the most beautiful piece of music. So much potential, and yet, how many could really live up to it? Who would have the courage, the strength, to follow their dreams?"

"You're just saying that because you know I fucked up. So don't get all philosophical on me now."

"My promise to you was to help you break in, to get you the chance to become a successful writer. It seems to me you're well on your way, or am I missing something?"

"No, you certainly delivered."

"Remember the rules?"

"Everything has a price that should be named at the beginning."

Guy tapped one of his filterless cigarettes against his silver case. "You paid the price, all right, but you never told me what your limit was."

"I was all in."

"You did always have more balls than brains, kid," Guy said while lighting up his cig. "That's the only reason you've made it this far. Call it perseverance, willpower, stubbornness, or just blind stupidity. But you have more drive in you than the entire population of a small city. I always liked that about you. Even before we met."

"Thanks."

"So, what now? Are you going to keep playing or fold?"

"I was thinking about upping the ante."

Guy's laughter produced puffs of smoke. "See? Chutzpa! And how do you plan to do that?"

"By publishing the work I want to."

"Face it, slick—you're a victim of your own success. Nobody wants you to do that. Not in the wake of *Killing Jesus.*"

It was Lemat who laughed now. "You know what I realized by coming back here? That if I ruled my life by what others wanted or expected of me, I'd be nothing. Nobody ever believed in me. Nobody gave me anything. Whatever I've achieved, I fought for, inch by inch. This whole *Killing Jesus* thing is just a chapter in the same story. And I'm going to do what I've always done—carve my own way. I sacrificed my artistic integrity to get to this point. So why not make a sacrifice to finally get my voice heard?"

Guy stood up and swung his jacket over his shoulder, still watching the city below them. "Sounds like a plan. Insane, but a plan, nonetheless. Then again, that has never stopped you before. At least you're seeing things clearly now."

"You bet."

"Well, for what it's worth, it was nice working with you, sport."

"So that's it? You're leaving me?"

"You don't need me anymore, and if you ever do, you know where to find me."

"You can help me sort out this mess."

"Not really. You seem to have a good hold on things now. Maybe you should work some of that magic inside you. Take care, kid. I hope whatever you're planning to do works out. God knows you've earned it.'" Guy flicked the dying cigarette away and walked away whistling "When You Wish upon a Star."

CHAPTER FORTY-ONE

Lemat spent a week longer than planned in Caracas. He had fallen into a lazy, comfortable routine with his mother. Lemat relished spoiling her and laughing together until the wee hours of the night. His mother noticed that her son seemed more relaxed and cheerful than when he had first arrived. Still, when Lemat announced that he was going back home, his mother was deeply saddened. She was just beginning to enjoy her son's company. But as disappointed as she was, she understood. Lemat was a busy man now and had important things that required his attention. She was so proud of him.

On the day of his departure, Lemat's mother insisted on taking him to the airport. Lemat acquiesced and promised he would return for Christmas. It was a promise he wouldn't be able to keep.

On his trip back, Lemat felt a strange sense of stillness. He had left the proverbial wreck, but now, even his mind was empty, like in a state of Zen meditation. Perhaps it was because he knew what he had to do, and he was determined to do it.

Another airport, another cab ride, and Lemat found himself in front of his home. Lemat gathered his mail and rode the elevator to the third floor. When the door opened, there was a woman coming out of the only other apartment on his floor. Lemat had yet to meet his neighbors.

The woman caught Lemat's fancy right away. She had no makeup on and was dressed in a very flattering exercise getup that made him take immediate notice. She was Asian—a Pacific Islander, most likely—with long, black hair, and she had a spunky aura about her. She wasn't expecting anyone inside the elevator.

"Sorry," said the woman, trying to pass by him. Lemat tried to accommodate her by moving aside when he dropped his bag by accident, blocking her path. She dropped her purse and some of its contents fell out. They tried to help one another, and in the confusion, someone called the elevator away. Lemat apologized and picked up her bag. That was when he noticed the novel she was reading: *Killing Jesus.* The bookmark showed she was in the last quarter of the story. There was also a hefty glass ashtray inside the bag and Lemat checked it for cracks.

"I'm so sorry," he said. The ashtray seemed fine.

The woman laughed, somewhat embarrassed. "It's OK," she said as she gathered her things.

"Serious smoker?" said Lemat, trying to make light of the situation.

"Safety measure." Her answer obviously left Lemat befuddled, so she explained, "I walk around a lot by myself, sometimes late at night."

"So you invite potential stalkers for a cigarette?"

She laughed. "No, but I can smash it on their heads to change their minds."

"Not a big fan of pepper spray?"

"Not a big fan of taking chances. I got the idea from my mother. She was a secretary and used public transportation all the time. Sometimes some creep would get ideas when she climbed on the bus wearing a skirt."

"Nice."

"Yep. She did the same thing once with a can of paint. My mama didn't mess around."

"I'm your neighbor, by the way," said Lemat, offering her his hand.

"Oh, I don't live here. I'm just checking on my friend's place while she's out of town. I'm Mia."

"Lemat."

"Funny. Like the guy whose book I'm reading."

"Is it any good?"

"It's pretty awful. I just wanted to know what everybody else was talking about. Have you read it yet?"

"It's not my kind of book."

"You're probably the only one. Back from a trip?"

"Yeah. I went to visit my parents in Venezuela."

"Really? I always wanted to visit. I want to do that hike into Machu Picchu."

"The Inca Trail. It's not in my neck of the woods, but I'd like to do it someday, too."

"Yeah. Well, I have to run, sorry. It was nice meeting you."

"Are you staying at your friend's place?"

"No, I'm just popping in twice a week or so to take

care of her plants and pick up mail."

"That's funny. I just moved here and I haven't met her yet. What's her name?

"Dana, but you won't be seeing her for a while. She only spends six months here and then six months in Canada. She's a TV producer. So, you have the floor pretty much to yourself." She looked at her watch. "I have to run, sorry." She hurried off when the elevator arrived and Lemat purposely made eye contact, smiled, and waved as the door closed.

The next morning, the sun shone through the window, forcing Lemat to open his eyes. He had forgotten to draw the curtains closed, but it didn't matter, because he felt rested. Lemat slept better than he could remember. It was only 7:03 A.M., but there was something odd about this day; it felt peaceful. He got up, stretched, and went to the bathroom.

Lemat heard the sound of the television in the living room while he was peeing. Lemat half-smiled as he went through the morning motions. He knew what the sound meant all too well.

The trip to the kitchen over the hardwood floor was cool on his feet; it comforted him. Lemat ignored Dep, sitting on the couch in front of the TV set, absorbed by whatever he was watching. He wanted to avoid breaking the soothing morning spell he was experiencing. He ground up some coffee and let it brew, enjoying the aroma. It made sense to him that his coffee intake needed to be upgraded, along with his living standards. No more canned stuff. A few minutes later, Lemat sat next to Dep with coffee in hand. They watched the TV quietly for a while.

Lemat finally broke the silence. "What are you

watching?"

"It's a show about the Nazis underground city."

"What about it?"

"Did you know there's this whole network of tunnels under Berlin?"

"No, I had no idea."

"It's pretty interesting. Cookie?" Dep offered one from his large bag, without looking away from the screen.

"I'm cool. Thanks," said Lemat, also watching the TV.

"Pretty bad stuff, huh? The trip, your dad, the whole sequel thing."

"Terrible."

"Pretty brutal."

"Yep."

"Just when everything seemed to be working out for you."

"It happens." Lemat took a drink. "I went back to our school."

Dep exhaled, obviously upset by the mere thought of the place. "Did you bring the flamethrower?"

Lemat appreciated Dep's wit. "No. It felt sad, you know? Small, insignificant... It's hard for me now to understand how such an irrelevant place could carry so much weight in my head... all those years. Such a waste."

"Had you met Lisa back then, you'd be one of those kids on the evening news—manifesto and everything."

"That's what I thought when I was there. But I don't think so. I was angry, not crazy. In the end, I knew those years would come to pass. Like some kind of prison sentence."

"Well, you did try to kill yourself."

"I did."

"You didn't tell your parents."

"Why? You know how my mom is. And why give my father another example of something I failed at?" Lemat looked at his reflection in the coffee. "That was a mistake, that day. I lost track of something that has always kept me going all these years."

"Courage?"

"Hope. The thought that nothing can be bad forever."

"Or good," Dep said with his mouth full.

"That's life." Lemat sipped some java. "I think in the end, when we look back from our deathbed, it's not about where we got in life, but how we arrived there."

"That reminds me of something I saw on TV once," said Dep, facing Lemat. "The show was about samurai. It said something about living as if they were dead. Like when they went to battle, they didn't care if they died, as long as they gave it their all. It was seen as an honorable death. Pretty gnarly stuff, huh?"

"To live without fear," Lemat concluded. His words hung in the air.

Lemat finished his coffee and turned to Dep. There was an odd silence between them. Lemat patted Dep's leg affectionately, got up, and went back to the kitchen. Dep, the image of melancholy, watched him walked away. Even though Lemat knew Dep would always be a part of him, their deep-rooted bond was shattered. With a long, dejected sigh, Dep faded away.

"What the hell is going on?" Lisa said, sitting at the counter by the kitchen, holding her lighter under her switchblade.

"I want to thank you," Lemat said.

"What the fuck are you talking about? Don't you dare fucking lump me with Chicken Little over there."

"You were always there when I felt down on my luck. You protected me from everything and everyone… I would have never gotten this far if it wasn't for you. You kept pushing me when nobody believed in me."

"No! Don't you fucking dare!" Lisa jumped to her feet. "Go ahead, get rid of Dep. I never knew why the fuck you let that asshole in. He did this to you!" She grabbed Lemat's hands and showed him his own wrists. "This is what you got for listening to that dickhead, but me? Give me a break! You want me watching your back! You need me to protect you!"

"I think it's time for me to fight my own battles." Lemat peeled her hands from his wrists. "I don't want to hold onto my anger. It's not worth it. It might have made me strong, but it's also chained me. All the grudges, the bitterness, the hate… that's not how I want to live. Not anymore."

"Oh, yeah? So you're a tough guy now?" Lisa pushed him. "You think you're strong?" Another shove. "You finally get some attention and all of the sudden you think you're some big shot?" She slammed him against the wall. "Wake up! There are people out there right now waiting to hurt you: critics, pundits, journalists, religious assholes, and all sorts of vile fuckers just waiting to take a stab at you." She thrust her blade on the wall next to his face. "Do you really think you can handle it? You think they won't hurt you when I'm not around? Who's going to help you get up the next time you fall?"

"I guess I have to stand up on my own two feet."

The strength of her punch blinded Lemat for a second. Lisa's eyes were filled with anger and tears of hurt. She gripped his face and showed him the scar on one of his wrists again. "DON'T—DO—THIS! DON'T!"

Lemat wiped her tears with his free hand, his eyes welling up, too. "You'll always be with me, just like the others. And I'd be lying if I said to you I'm not afraid. But I need to move on with my life now… I have to let you go."

Lisa's hold of him crumbled and she hugged him so tight that it hurt. She sobbed inconsolably, quivering, with her head buried against his chest. Lemat just held her in his arms until she became quiet, and just like a feeling attached to a memory, the presence of Lisa was gone.

Talia was waiting in Lemat's office, sitting by his computer with a lustful gaze and itching to consume him. She was wearing his sweater like a small dress. Talia stood up and greeted him with a needy embrace. Lemat liked this. He missed the warmth of her touch, but Lemat had to be careful, like handling a flame.

"Are you going to cast me away, too?" said Talia, sitting Lemat down and straddling him. "You know you want me."

Lemat grabbed her hands. It took all his will to do so. "Not like this," he said.

Talia was puzzled. Her eyes were pools of fear. The thought of being sent away like the others terrified her.

"You know I could never do that," said Lemat,

kissing her hand. "I might as well stop breathing. You're my life."

Talia laughed her tension away and said, "Then why do you stop me?"

"Things have changed. We have to do things differently now."

"What do you mean? Are you going to squander everything that makes you special, your gift? Please tell me you're not going to waste your time creating another worthless story. It's beneath you, and it hurts you." She caressed him tenderly. "Let me help you show the world what you're really capable of. Let us astound them with your talent."

"We're going to do it together, but we need some ground rules first."

She was confused. There had never been rules between them. Their encounters were spontaneous bouts of passion wholly unrestrained. The results were magical, even if they were both wrecked in the end. It didn't matter. Once Lemat was ready, they would start all over again. Yet, Talia had to admit that this sudden change of heart intrigued her. Lemat pulled up a chair for her and kneeled down in front of Talia, holding her hands.

"OK. This is how we're going to do things from now on," Lemat said. "You're going to sit right here next to me, and we're going to work every day for at least eight hours. We're going to start early and take a few breaks. If an idea comes up at night, we'll make a note and deal with it the next day. I want to get a good night's sleep every night. We're also going to organize our ideas in a database and tackle them in a structured way, OK?"

"OK…" said Talia, a bit stunned by Lemat's proposal. "What are we going to work on?"

"We're going to a write a new story."

"No more garbage."

"Nope. At least not this one."

Talia beamed. "What about all the stories you already have?"

"They'll have to wait. I want to write a brand new one. I want it to be my best story yet."

"You know how to get a girl interested, honey," Talia said. "So you're not afraid about what Don and your publisher will say?"

"Oh, they're going to hate it, I'm sure."

Talia gave him a knowing glance. "I know that look. What are you planning to do?"

"I'm going to give them no choice."

"How?"

"By giving them exactly what they want."

"OK. I'm confused. I thought you said no more garbage."

Lemat grinned and told her his plan.

Talia cackled delightedly and kissed him on the cheek.

From that day on, Lemat would wake up, have breakfast, and sit at his computer at 9:00 A.M. sharp everyday with Talia right beside him. He would work no less than eight hours and no more than twelve. He would usually produce a chapter a day. Lemat would start jogging at night, too. He found the exercise was not only a stress reliever, but it helped to clear his mind. No more takeout, or at least, not as often as he used to. Lemat would go grocery shopping once a week. His insomnia wasn't a problem any more either.

When he was recognized on the street—he did try to keep a low profile—he would stop and sign an autograph. Lemat found out that those who approached him were usually fans of his work and would let him be after exchanging a few pleasantries or their favorite part of the novel. He would also have dinners with Mr. Freedman every so often, enjoying the older man's stories and humor.

A couple of weeks passed when Lemat received a check-up call from Don.

"Man alive, lad. I was beginning to fear you went on another one of your nights about town. I haven't heard from you in a while."

"I know, I'm sorry," Lemat said. "Something came up and I had to take care of it."

"Somewhere underwater perhaps? A place with no phones?"

"Just some housecleaning. No big deal."

"I trust you've been working on your next folio."

"Way ahead of you," said Lemat, sitting on his terrace smoking a joint.

"Bravo, my boy. You're truly evolving into a proper model of a prosperous novelist. And may I inquire about the nature of the plot? Who are we doing away with this time?"

"You may not. I don't like talking about my projects so early in the creative process."

"I'm your agent, dear lad. A career such as yours should not be left to the whims of capricious minds, or the recklessness of chance. It should be molded and trimmed like the proverbial bonsai tree. I doubt I have to tell you that the publisher expects the sequel to your book sooner rather than later."

"I know. Don't worry. You'll be the first one to read it. I'll probably be done with the first draft in the next four weeks or so."

"But I trust—"

"In my talent and that I'm doing something special."

"Don't get cheeky with me, lad. I'll have you know that I have shown the backside of my door to two Pulitzer Prize winners and a Nobel laureate. Best-selling authors, I eat like crumpets with my tea."

"*International* best-selling author, and save the tea for when I send you the novel. I think everybody is going to be pleased."

"Let us hope so. If there's something true about the publishing business, it's that they don't like to take chances."

CHAPTER FORTY-TWO

A month later, Lemat was working on the last few chapters of his new novel. He was pretty satisfied with how this first draft had turned out. *The Serpent's Circle* was a tale about a man who killed himself but who had to come back to fix everything that was wrong with his life before he could move into the hereafter. Lemat knew there would be rewrites; there always were. That wasn't a problem at all; Lemat actually enjoyed them. It was the way story started to come together, like a sculptor chipping away imperfections and polishing his work. Then there would be notes from his agent, his editor, and so forth. That was just par for the course. What mattered right then was that he was extremely satisfied with what he had done. Whatever changes came later, he had a strong foundation.

Lemat also began to browse his external hard drive to look for old stories he wanted to publish. After careful consideration, Lemat chose three other manuscripts he had written. Those would be the novels he would like to get published as his career progressed. Hopefully, his continued success would allow him to push for these stories to finally see the light of day. The idea excited him, but Lemat had to be patient.

He stretched out on his chair tiredly. Lemat saved his work for the last time and turned his computer off. It was a quarter to seven. Time to have some dinner and relax. Lemat covered Talia with a blanket and kissed her forehead. She was exhausted after a long day of work. He went to the kitchen and stood in front of his open fridge, deciding on what to eat, when he heard a noise. Lemat chalked it up to some random sound. Then he heard it again. It came from somewhere close.

Lemat closed the refrigerator and wandered about trying to pinpoint its source. There it was again. It came from outside. Lemat looked through the peephole. It was just a finite portion of the hallway it allowed him to see, nothing more. The sound came again, louder. Lemat thought he could hear some mumbling as well. He unlocked the door and kept his hand on the doorknob, while still looking through the peephole. Lemat opened the door slowly. The cool breeze of the hallway came into his apartment. There was no one outside. The next sound he heard quite startled him. It was the crashing of glass, along with the thumping of wood, followed by a litany of cursing. It was coming from the apartment next door. Lemat put his ear to the door. A woman was very angry on the other side. He knocked and the swearing continued, when the door finally opened.

"Oh, hi," said Mia, the woman Lemat had met the other day. She was dressed in sweats with her hair pulled back. Her clothes were wet and her pants rolled up to her knees.

"Are you OK?" Lemat said. "I heard noises."

"Shit! You heard that? I'm sorry. I'm having some trouble with the kitchen sink. Say, you wouldn't happen to know anything about plumbing?"

"I can give it a shot."

Lemat walked in and immediately saw the problem. Water was sprouting from somewhere under the sink, making a mess of everything. Mia had placed towels all over the place trying to stem the flooding, but she must have knocked the dish rack down at some point, as there was broken glass being swept away by the water. Lemat squatted and used the light of his phone's camera to pinpoint the problem. He tried to shut the water off by using the valve, but Mia had already done it.

"I think it's coming from that joint," said Mia, squatting next to him. "That seal seems to have broken off."

Lemat tried to tighten it, but he only managed to squirt a jet of water on himself. "Hold on a second," he said and ran back to his apartment. When he came back, Lemat proceeded to wrap the pipe with duct tape. He did so until the water stopped flowing, leaving a fist-sized ball of gray adhesive behind. "There."

"OK… that's a solution. It's definitely better than anything I came up with."

"I'm not done." Lemat looked for something in his phone.

"You got an app for this?"

"No, I'm trying to find the number of a 24-hour plumber." Lemat found one, called, and was assured by the plumber that he would arrive within the hour.

"Thank you," Mia said. "I'm sorry that I dragged you into this mess."

"No problem. Listen, would you like to have dinner while we wait for the plumber?"

"Oh, no. You really don't have to wait here for him. I can manage."

"I know, but I'd feel better knowing you're not here alone with some stranger. You never know. You don't live here, it's late—"

"OK, but dinner is on me, then. You can ask for anything, as long as it's in this pile of takeout menus." She placed her hand on top of a bunch of flyers on top of the kitchen counter. They decided on Indian food and she offered him something to drink. They settled on wine and opened a bottle of red, while they sat in the living room and waited.

"By the way," she said. "Thank you for making me look like a complete putz."

"Excuse me?"

"*Killing Jesus.* My friend Dana—the one who owns this place—told me the other day that she had heard her new neighbor was a writer. You're the guy who wrote it."

"I am." He smiled impishly.

"Why didn't you say so?"

"I thought it would be tacky, 'By the way, that book you're reading? Well, guess what genius came up with that…'"

Mia laughed.

"Besides, I had just finished doing the press tour for the novel, and I was a little fed up with the cameras and the attention."

"You're breaking my heart."

"Seriously, I just wanted to come home, relax, and be alone for a while."

"So I guess fame isn't everything it's cracked up to be?"

"Fame is just loneliness while surrounded by strangers."

The comment brought a small twinkle to her eye. Lemat found it very attractive. They kept talking until the food arrived but the conversation was nothing special—hobbies, travels, books, movies, and music they loved. Eventually, they touched on each other's lives.

Mia had an impressive education; she had a doctorate but hated using the title. She worked as a biochemist for a large biotech company, but her passion was jazz and Broadway singing. She loved her sports, too—things like softball, surfing, and snowboarding. She was divorced with no kids and still "a hopeless optimist when it comes to romance," she had said. That's when the plumber decided to show up.

The plumber did his thing in twenty minutes and left unceremoniously, not without laughing at Lemat's duct-tape solution first. By that time, however, the evening had lost momentum. There was only the familiar awkwardness of having lost something precious, and the helplessness of not being able to find it again. Lemat helped Mia clean up the table and pick up the disaster in the kitchen.

"Thank you so much for coming to the rescue," Mia said as she walked him to the door.

"No problem. You scared the crap out of me. I thought it was one of those crazies coming after me because of my book."

"Seriously?"

"I ran into a few on the tour. But don't worry, I'll be fine."

"Oh, I'm not worried about you. I'm worried that one of them will blow up the building while I'm watering Dana's stupid plants."

They laughed and then everything went quiet. They were both reaching for the right words to end the night.

Lemat talked first. "Listen, I'm about to finish some work in a couple of weeks." He didn't really know where he was going with this. "I'd like to have coffee or something with you then if you're free. That is, if you promise not to flood your friend's apartment again."

"You know, you're nothing like I expected you would be. Judging from your book," Mia said.

"I hope that's a good thing."

"Sure, I'd love to have coffee or something with you." She smiled then and he instantly felt at ease.

"Great. I'll give you a call.

Mia gave him her number and Lemat floated back to his apartment.

Exactly two weeks later, Lemat finished the first draft of *The Serpent's Circle.* He called Mia and they had coffee at a nearby Arabic café. The meeting was supposed to last an hour or so. Mia had made plans to have dinner with a colleague that evening, but—much to his delight—she canceled and instead talked to

357

Lemat for hours, unaware of the passing of time.

"I've got to ask you, what's with the wristbands?" Mia said. "I always see you wearing them, and that dingy gray sweater."

Lemat felt a little bit tongue-tied. "It's terrible, huh? Well, the sweater is an old friend. It's kind of like an armor."

"OK, now I'm afraid to ask about the wristbands."

Lemat smirked self-consciously. He pulled the right one back—he didn't want to get into the tattoo on his left—and showed Mia the scar.

It took Mia a few seconds to understand what she was looking at. Her expression changed from tickled to concerned. The scars looked fairly fresh. Mia immediately regretted asking the question for fear of what this revelation meant to Lemat. "I... I'm so sorry. I didn't—"

"It's OK," Lemat said, covering the scar again. He feared that his chances with Mia had become equally eclipsed. "I went through a very rough spot a while ago. I got very depressed... It was a very stupid thing to do. Needless to say, this was the one thing in my life I was glad I failed at."

"That makes two of us." Mia reached over the table and put her hand on one of his wrists. The gesture was one of genuine empathy. "When I was in college, I once took a whole bunch of pills because of all the pressure I was under. My roommate found me passed out on my bed and called 911. They took me to the hospital to pump my stomach. The whole thing was pretty crazy, especially when my parents got wind of it. It's nothing to be ashamed of; it could happen to anyone."

Lemat was touched by her candor. "Thank you."

After that, the conversation turned much lighter. Sharing their intimate tribulations had made them a little closer and more comfortable with each other. Lemat felt as if a big weight had been lifted from his shoulders. A few laughs later, the dark turn of their conversation was all but forgotten. When the night was over, Lemat walked Mia to her car.

"By the way, I hope you've noticed that Dana's apartment has remained intact," she said when he closed the door for her.

"So far."

"So, are you going to ask me out again, or do I have to break something?" said Mia, resting her arms on the car's window.

Lemat was smitten. He said, "How about dinner?"

"Perfect," she said and smiled that iridescent smile of hers. "But I'm away next week, so perhaps the week after?"

"Wait, where are you off to?"

"Singapore. I'm attending a five-day seminar."

"Tell them you already have plans."

"Yeah, I'm sure they can find someone else to give my award to."

"Are you serious? You're getting an award?"

"'For excellence in the field of research,' no less. So as you can see, I can't disappoint my hordes of loving fans. Not that you can relate."

"I have no idea what you're talking about."

They laughed.

"How about the Thursday when I come back? I'll have a four-day weekend all to myself."

"That works for me," Lemat said, sounding genuinely delighted for the first time in a long time.

CHAPTER FORTY-THREE

"Have you lost your mind?" said Don over the phone a few days later. He had read *The Serpent's Circle* overnight and called him first thing in the morning. The agent puffed on his pipe, sending out gusts of smoke like a speeding steam train. "This is not what we talked about. Correct me if I'm wrong, but didn't we agree that the best step forward for your burgeoning career was to write a sequel to *Killing Jesus?*"

"We did," said Lemat, pacing around his apartment. The straw twirling in his hand was a blur. "And you also said that it was my choice on what to do next. So, please, hear me out. I want you to take that manuscript to the publisher as my next novel."

"They might simply decline to publish this for any number of reasons, or they'll just shelve it and demand a sequel."

"And they're going to get it, after they publish this as my second book. I'm already working on it, but I don't want you to tell them that."

"My dear boy, your fiction has gone straight to your head. There's no way we can force a publishing house to print something they have absolutely no interest in."

"How do you know that if they haven't even seen it?"

"Call it a professional hunch."

"You read it. Do you think it's bad?"

Don's response took a moment. "You're missing the point," he finally said.

"No, that *is* the whole point."

"Not in this business. By God, lad. I'm your agent. Trust me."

"I do, but you have to trust me. So what if they don't want *The Serpent's Circle?* We'll take the *Killing* sequel to another publisher, then. Or we'll do it ourselves. At this point, that would just create more press in my favor: 'International best-selling author ditches publishing house to self-publish.'"

Don paused to consider what Lemat had just proposed, then said, "We can hold the third novel in the series for ransom as leverage when we negotiate your next book deal with them." The agent started to like his client's idea. "The problem is that if they lose a lot of money on this book you sent me, it might muddle the negotiations."

"That's why, to quote another great Don, 'You're going to make them an offer they can't refuse.' If they agree to get fully behind my new novel, I'll give them *three* sequels to *Killing Jesus.* Starting with the next one, *Killing Washington.*"

"My dear boy, that's genius! Why didn't you send me that first? They're going to go bonkers for it just by the marketing potential alone."

"I can even give you a tagline: 'He knew the British were coming, but not the assassin from the future.'"

"Brilliant!"

"But I need the publisher to get behind *The Serpent's Circle* one hundred percent. If they don't like the terms, I'll fulfill my three-book contract with them with unrelated works and take the *Killing* sequels somewhere else. I'm sure any publisher would be happy to give the series a new home."

"Well, look at you—a lamb among wolves who suddenly grew teeth," Don said. "And I thought you authors could write everything but a good contract for yourselves."

"What do you think?"

"I think I can definitely make this happen without much effort. The publishing house would be thrilled to get a *Killing* series, not to mention the good people in Hollywood who are forever obsessed with a good franchise. There's a caveat to your stroke of brilliance, though. If these apocryphal writings to the series don't pass muster, as it were, it could damage your brand and endanger your career."

"That's a chance I'm willing to take."

"Ah! The old 'bleeding for one's art.' How romantic and utterly impractical! I don't tend to bequeath my clients with genuine accolades, but you, my boy, are the only one I would be tempted to represent even if it was just to publish leaflets."

"Thank you, Don. That means a lot to me."

"I said 'tempted.' Don't get any ideas in that crazy head of yours. Very well, I shall bring this and your persuasive offer to the publishers and start with the negotiations. We'll be in touch."

When the agent hung up, Lemat stood by his balcony, looking though the window with the phone against his chest. He wanted to burst out in pure joy. If the publisher accepted his offer, his works—the ones that he truly cared about—would finally be out for the world to see and, hopefully, enjoy. Lemat would have to keep producing a few more entries of his schlocky novel and deal with the fallout each one would generate. That was fine as far as Lemat was concerned. It was his way to carve his own path once again. He felt the tender arms wrapping around him from the back. Talia put her face next to his, contemplating the same view and elated by the news. She planted a kiss on his cheek.

The next day, Lemat put his celebrity to good use, by doing one of the few worthwhile things such status conveys: he got a reservation at an ultra-exclusive, invitation-only sushi restaurant. The place was distinctly omakase, no prices were posted, and it catered to only a handful of patrons a night.

When Mia returned from her trip, Lemat hired a driver to take them to their date. They were eager to see each other despite the fact that they had been texting during her absence. The driver dropped them off at an inconspicuous building in the middle of a predominantly Japanese neighborhood. The place may have been exclusive, but not ostentatious. It was almost like eating at somebody's cozy home—wooden furniture, with a few tastefully selected mementos from Japan. Mia loved the place. She couldn't believe such a restaurant existed and was excited by the culinary delicacies to come.

She was draped in a fetching white dress that contrasted nicely with her naturally tanned skin, framed her gracious neck and shoulders, and accented her toned legs. She carried a small purse and a mysterious bag she claimed held a surprise for Lemat. For his part, Lemat wore a black sports coat, matching buttoned-down shirt, and jeans—he couldn't be bothered with slacks. The perennial wristbands were conspicuously missing.

"OK, I want to give you this before we start," Mia said, handing the bag to Lemat. "It's not a big deal, but I thought of you when I saw it."

Lemat looked inside the bag and laughed. He pulled out a brand-new gray sweater. "I guess now I have no excuse but to throw away my old one," he said.

"Do you like it? I hope I got the right size."

"I love it. Thank you so much," said Lemat while pouring her some sake. "So tell me about your trip."

For the rest of the night, Lemat listened to Mia's stories from her Singapore trip, only interrupting her a few times with questions about the city, the culture, and her work. The night seemed to have passed in the blink of an eye. They drank, they laughed, and the food was simply amazing. They were locked in each other's gaze, oblivious to the rest of the world, and looking for subtle chances to touch one another.

"And what about you? Anything new or exciting?"

Mia said.

"There's something, but it can wait."

"No, I want to know."

"I'm saving it as an excuse to go out with you again."

"Come on, tell me."

But Lemat just dodged the question and focused the conversation back on something more interesting to him: Mia. Like all good things, though, the evening had to come to an end. The driver took them back to Mia's apartment. It was raining and Lemat walked her all the way up to her doorstep on the fifth floor.

"I had an amazing time. Thank you," Mia said at her threshold.

"Thank you. And thank you for the sweater. I can't wait for a chance to wear it."

"How about next time? I know this great place for brunch."

"Sunday?"

"Sure."

"That reminds me, I have something for you," said Lemat, trying to keep his cool.

"What is it?"

Lemat leaned forward and kissed her. It was brief, almost innocent. Mia looked at him a little dizzy. They fumbled into the apartment, more focused on undressing each other on their way to her bedroom than on watching where they were going. They collapsed onto the bed, enraptured by the sensation of their bodies.

It would be a while before they cuddled as their bodies cooled off in comfortable silence in the dark, with only the moon to light them and the sound of rain for company.

"That's an interesting tattoo," said Mia, caressing Lemat's wrist. "It looks recent."

The mark brought Lemat bittersweet memories. "It is," he said.

"Where did you get it?"

"New York. I had just signed up with my agent. Right before everything changed."

"So what's the meaning of the snake eating itself? I've seen it before, somewhere."

"Life, death, rebirth. Nature's cycle."

Mia thought about that for a moment. "You know, the human body replaces most of its cells throughout a person's life. It was first believed that we did so every seven or ten years, but new research has shown that the replacement occurs at different rates throughout the body."

"So we are a whole new person after enough time has passed?"

"Not really. For example, two of the things that are never replenished are our neurons and most of the cardiomyocyte tissue. So, essentially, your mind and your heart remain the same, no matter how much you change."

"That's pretty profound. Especially for pillow talk."

"I think that's very fitting. You are who you are, no matter what," she said as she kissed his nose.

Lemat held Mia close while meditating on her words and watching the rain fall outside. Maybe people were projections of an unknown center, echoes spread out through an infinite multi-universe. It occurred to Lemat that what he wanted to be was not as important as *who* he was. And with that profound thought and a settling sense of peace, he fell asleep with Mia in his arms.

CHAPTER FORTY-FOUR

For the next year, *Killing Jesus* continued to top bestseller lists with no hint of slowing down as the international market gobbled up the novel and its surrounding controversy. It had been translated into forty-four different languages and the movie adaptation was one of the most awaited blockbusters that following summer. The A-list cast made expectations even higher. Lemat was happy but happier still because he and Mia were officially a couple.

Don had managed to sell Lemat's deal to the publishers. They were hesitant about publishing *The Serpent's Circle,* but the prospect of securing three sequels to *Killing Jesus* was too tempting for them to pass up. The publishing house would take the calculated risk and throw their resolute support behind the new novel. They reasoned that with enough marketing behind it—whether it was successful or not—they could sell enough copies on the strength of his debut hit alone. It would take the release slot next summer, to coincide with the opening of the film.

Lemat had also finished *Killing Washington* but was holding onto it until his newest novel was published. His path as an author was clear. He would sign another contract—more restrictive—but if everything turned out well, Lemat would have the recognition and financial security to pursue his own projects, even if he had to do so independently. Who knows? Maybe he could actually segue into other creative arenas.

With so much work to be done, Lemat had to call his mother and break his promise of visiting on Christmas. His mother was saddened by the news, but the reasons for Lemat's change of mind were the best gift she could ever have. Her son's career was soaring and he had a woman in his life, with whom he seemed to be madly in love. "Maybe you can bring her next Christmas," his mom said. And no, Lemat did not talk to his father, no matter how much his mother insisted.

Lemat never went back to Fausto's after his post-NY party. Not for any particular reason or even a conscious choice, it just happened. It was as if Lemat had outgrown the place and its cast of peculiar customers. Each of them would eventually go their separate ways.

Clover would hold a number of odd jobs in the service industry, before moving back to her parents' house after they passed away. She would get married, have a daughter, and ultimately divorce, but she would never be lonely again.

Harry "Specs" Chaser would get another chance to return to Hollywood, after penning a script for the live-action film version of the '70s cartoon "Jabberjaw."

The brainchild of a marketing department, it would see Specs riding high again. Later, under the spell of vodka and cocaine, he would be arrested after crashing his Porsche on Sunset Boulevard while accompanied by a high-priced escort. The last everyone heard from him, he was in some trouble with the IRS.

Fausto would end up selling the bar a few years later and moving to Costa Rica, where he would work for a tourist company as a driver. The bar would go to the Coin brothers, who tried to turn it into a strip joint—"Heads n' Tails"—against Heads' numerous objections. The place would linger on for a year and close for good. The lot would remain vacant for over a decade, before it was torn down and made into a tanning salon.

Mr. Freeman would retire and move in with his daughter. With the help of his granddaughter, he'd connect with a few fellow retirees though the Internet and form a small jazz band, "The Old Tunez." They would have a blast playing local gigs, family celebrations, and retirement homes. Five years later, George Simon Freeman, Jr. would die quietly while napping in his living room as he listened to classical radio.

Lemat never heard from Ink again after that rainy night. She had moved, of that much he was sure. One day, driving by in the back of a cab, he saw that her tattoo parlor had closed and become a psychic's office. He also learned in the news that his old apartment complex was demolished and turned into a parking structure for a new shopping mall.

Everything had a beginning and an end.

"If the novel flops, we'll go to Italy on your dime," Mia said. "That way we can eat a lot, surround ourselves with gorgeous artwork, and get all romantic while I nurse your ego back to health."

They were having breakfast right on the ocean in a boathouse-turned-café one beautiful Sunday.

"Not a bad way to fail," Lemat said.

"And if it becomes a hit?"

"Then we'll go to an island, say… Bali. We'll go to Bali on *your* dime. We can relax, shut the world away, and get freaky."

Mia cackled and said, "Sir, you have a deal." They shook on it.

"What do you think about having children?" Mia suddenly blurted.

Lemat looked at her, stunned. He almost choked on his Eggs Florentine.

"Don't freak out," she said. "I'm not implying anything. All I want to know is where you stand in regards to children."

Lemat cleared his throat by drinking some coffee. "Well… I don't want any. I mean, it's not like I hate children or anything. I actually like them, just as long as they're not my own. Kind of like the rent-a-kid program, you know? Have fun and then give them back to their parents. I think I could be a kick-ass uncle."

"Ok, calm down. I didn't know this was such a touchy subject for you."

"It's not touchy," Lemat said, wiping his mouth

with a napkin. "It's just that… well, you know. Women can be—"

"What?"

"Well, children are a sensitive subject to women."

"Yet you are the one mumbling nervously about this."

"OK, sorry. My bad." He took a deep breath in a mocking gesture to regain self-control. Then he changed his tone to a cool and collected one and said, "So, what are your thoughts regarding children?"

"I want the golden standard, a boy and a girl. Not necessarily in that order, of course."

Lemat was stupefied. This was the answer he feared.

"I'm just playing with you," Mia said, bursting out laughing. "Oh my God! You should have seen your face! It was priceless!"

"Ha-ha, very funny. You almost gave me a heart attack. But seriously, what's your opinion on children?"

"Are you kidding me? I don't want any either. I'm too busy with work, I haven't traveled enough, I love my lazy mornings on the weekends, and most of all, I'm not interested in the job. Plus, pushing something the size of a watermelon out from between my legs has absolutely no appeal to me."

With that settled, they proceeded to finish their breakfast, when a fan looking for an autograph approached Lemat. He obliged, even though he never got used to autographs; he didn't see the point of getting another person's signature if it wasn't to sign a contract or pay a bill. As far as he was concerned, he was giving his readers the one thing in his life anyone would be remotely interested in—his work. Everything else was rather trivial. But Lemat was resigned to the fact that this was just another aspect of his new career. One he had to make peace with. Mia also had to get used to the attention. As long as Lemat fans were courteous, she didn't have much of a problem with the casual run-in with his readers. The fan was elated by the encounter, and the couple were left alone for the rest of their meal.

When the fan left, the subject reverted back to travel plans. Lemat had told Don that he wanted to keep a low profile regarding promotion. Don disagreed but in the end decided he could play the reclusive author angle to great marketing effect. Lemat had placed his life in danger on the last tour and now he wished to be a writing hermit, or some dramatic news fodder of that sort.

They had also toyed with the idea of moving to Europe at one point. Perhaps even dividing the year between America and the Old World. These were dreams, perhaps, and whether these plans ever took form was irrelevant. They were having too much fun fantasizing together.

They moved on to Mia's research on bioprocess engineering and the latest advances in her field.

"That's amazing," Lemat said. "Even though I can barely understand what you're talking about."

"I've been dumbing it down for you."

"You have to go dumber, then. You know, I think I want to use your work as the topic for my next novel."

"Killing Science?"

"You know what I mean. I think it could make a great sci-fi story."

"Yeah. Sounds like a great idea. I'd love to help

you with the research."

"Oh, you know me. I like to explore my subjects thoroughly. Get in deep."

"Is that so?"

They finished their meal and walked hand in hand along the dock towards the parking lot to Mia's car. When Lemat heard his name being called, he turned around and saw a clean-cut man dressed in an expensive suit. The man was holding a large cup of steaming coffee in one hand and a copy of *Killing Jesus* in the other.

"Excuse me. I'm sorry, are you Lemat? The author of *Killing Jesus?"* the man said. "It *is* you, isn't it?"

"I am," said Lemat, hoping one day people would ask him if he was the author of *The Serpent's Circle.*

The man handed him the book and asked if he could sign it. Lemat was happy to do so and never saw the snub-nosed revolver the man withdrew from his jacket. Three shots rang out.

"He died for your sins, you ungrateful bastard!" the man said before Lemat hit the ground while Mia screamed. Impulsively, she hit the gunman with her ashtray-loaded purse. The impact flattened the assailant in a single blow, fracturing his cheekbone and breaking a few teeth.

Lemat lay on the cold ground, struggling to breathe. The sky above him was so blue and tranquil, it helped him relax. His novel was near him; a bullet had struck it. A few bloodied pages were carried away by the wind. Mia appeared in his field of vision; she was crying and screaming something into her phone.

"Please hurry!" he heard her say. She sounded as if she was so far away. Lemat felt cold. "It's OK. You'll be OK, baby. Help is coming!" Mia said as she applied pressure on his wound.

Lemat thought of his mother. He felt sad that she was going to be upset about this, and he hated that.

"Come on, baby. Stay with me!" Mia said.

Lemat clumsily touched his torso and then looked at his hand. More blood. A drop ran from his palm and over his tattoo. Lemat chuckled. Mia held his hand against her chest. He tried to say something to her. His lips were dry, but he managed to move them. Nothing came out, and then everything went dark.

EPILOGUE

Everything was blurry, peaceful, quiet. Movement was weightless and slow. He needed to breathe, so he surfaced. The sun was gentle and made the white shore glow. Lemat came out of the water. The ocean was calm, the sky was clear, and the sand felt soft. The island seemed empty, but Lemat knew that wasn't so. He smiled at the familiar figure on the horizon. After all, this was where he belonged. It seemed like a fitting ending to a dream, or perhaps it had just begun.

ALSO FROM HENRY MOSQUERA

- **Winner of the 2014 Los Angeles Book Festival for Best Genre-Based Fiction**
- **Winner of the 2012 IndieReader Discovery Awards for Best Thriller**
- **Winner of the 2011 Reader Views Reviewers Choice Awards for Best South American Novel**

War on Terror veteran, Eric Caine, is found wandering the streets of Miami with no memory of the car accident that left him there. Alone and suffering from PTSD, Eric is on a one-way road to self-destruction. Then a chance meeting at a bar begins a series of events that helps Eric start anew. When his new job relocates him to Venezuela-the land of his childhood-things, however, take an ominous turn as a catastrophic event threatens the stability of the country. Now Eric must escape an elite team of CIA assassins as he tries to uncover an international conspiracy in which nothing is what it seems.

ABOUT THE AUTHOR

Henry Mosquera is a writer and artist born in Caracas, Venezuela. He is the author of the critically-acclaimed, award-winning political thriller, "Sleeper's Run." He attended the University of Miami, Florida, where he obtained a double major in Graphic Design and Film. Henry currently resides in Los Angeles with his wife and dog.

Made in the USA
San Bernardino, CA
30 April 2014